TWENTY EIGHTY-FOUR

Innes Hamilton

The Book Guild Ltd.
Sussex, England

The Book Guild Ltd.
25 High Street,
Lewes, Sussex.

First published 1992
© Innes Hamilton 1992
Set in Baskerville
Typesetting by Ashford Setting & Design,
Ashford, Middlesex.
Printed in Great Britain by
Billing & Sons Ltd.,
Worcester.

A catalogue record for this book is
available from the British Library

ISBN 0 86332 705 2

AUTHOR'S ACKNOWLEDGEMENTS

That I was able to write this book at all I owe to John Parker, surely one of the world's most competent heart surgeons, who gave me a new life, and to those who subsequently looked after me: highly experienced, yet often seemingly so young as to be almost children. I remember being 'diagnosed' by one Amanda Tomkins in one of her rare spare moments (MANDY on her stethoscope). 'Stress' she pronounced, and she was probably right.

Once more I owe much to Basil and Phryne Bouzanis, their Greek history, civilized background, experience and friends in the diplomatic; to George Clark's unrivalled knowledge of the European Parliament; Bob Drummond of Zimbabwe's National Herbarium and Botanic Garden Department of Research; Roger Naumann's experience of Abyssinia; and Stuart M. Speiser, from whose writing on individual share ownership I, like many, have derived inspiration. Beverly Warren has kindly reminded me of certain Maltese spelling.

I am indebted to the Brooke Hospital for Animals, Cairo, and to Richard Searight, for permission to project forward for a hundred years the marvellous work of that devoted body, for which no publicity or support could be too great.

Finally, I owe much to Angela and Louise of Laservalue Ltd who have, always with cheerfulness and charm, wrestled with an unusual manuscript.

Virginia Water   I.H.
UK

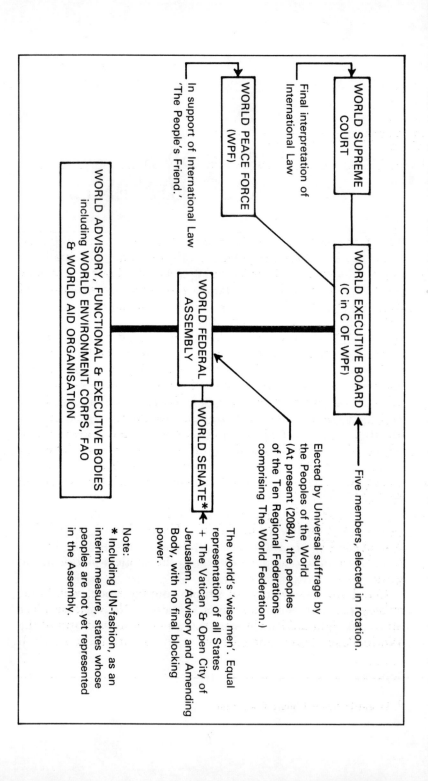

WORLD SUPREME COURT

Final interpretation of International Law

WORLD PEACE FORCE (WPF)

In support of International Law 'The People's Friend.'

WORLD EXECUTIVE BOARD (C in C OF WPF)

Five members, elected in rotation.

Elected by Universal suffrage by the Peoples of the World (At present (2084), the peoples of the Ten Regional Federations comprising The World Federation.)

WORLD FEDERAL ASSEMBLY

WORLD ADVISORY, FUNCTIONAL & EXECUTIVE BODIES including WORLD ENVIRONMENT CORPS, FAO & WORLD AID ORGANISATION

WORLD SENATE*

The world's 'wise men'. Equal representation of all States + The Vatican & Open City of Jerusalem. Advisory and Amending Body, with no final blocking power.

Note:
* Including UN-fashion, as an interim measure, states whose peoples are not yet represented in the Assembly.

1

The Churchill railway terminus. Europe's erstwhile least enthusiastic and least popular region had changed the station's name — tactfully — from Waterloo. Likewise, Lord Nelson now presided over Freedom Square. It was Napoleon's invasion of England that had been prevented at Trafalgar.

It was a spring Tuesday in early afternoon. The station concourse was crowded with commuters heading for home or recreation after a computer-assisted morning. Only would-be millionaires, the professional and industrial giants of the future, and those keen to improve their WISO[1] entitlement still worked a full day. A hundred years before, George Orwell's predecessor of the great multifaced clock overhead would have been striking fourteen. Now, in 2084, the new one played a few notes of music (Gershwin on Tuesdays); then with sanity struck two. The UK was a caring part of Europe in what was well on the way to becoming a complete new federal world. British trains were on time.

Jakko collected together his belongings, including a small suitcase inscribed with his initials. He read the neat panel of instructions by the carriage sliding doors, pressed the button to open them and stepped out on to the spotless platform. No gritty dust.

Our hero was twenty; of simple country stock, well-built, strong-featured, with blue eyes. Healthy. No varicose ulcer above *his* right ankle. He wore the walking-out uniform of the World Peace Force: the elite of mankind's institutions. Each

---

[1] World Individual Share Ownership

7

shoulder sported a small St George's Cross for England and the number of his Unit: EURO 2001.

Jakko had never been to London, or to any great city. The display on West Country Wednesdays of the district's best vegetable produce had been the highlight of his week, except on the rare occasions (he was a shy lad) on which he had been persuaded to drive to town on a Saturday evening when there was a modest knees-up.

He was about to make his way forward along the platform when he noticed a butterfly imprisoned in the stationary train, fluttering against a carriage window. Only the undersides of the wings were visible: shiny ash brown with a network of wavy black lines. Yellow markings and a cream border to the wings showed through from the coloured side. Jakko recognized at once a Camberwell Beauty, queen of British butterflies, of which large numbers were once again to be seen in the Home Counties. He put down his case, re-entered the carriage and, gathering the butterfly carefully in his hands, carried it out and set it free. He stood and watched for a few moments as the insect headed gratefully for the sunlight, then once more gathered up his things.

By now Jakko's fellow travellers had passed through the barrier, were greeting friends or threading their way through the crowds on the concourse. Some stood, baggage in hand, catching up with the latest world news from the telescreens. Already potential travellers out of the capital were heading towards him to secure their seats.

He passed on through the crowd. Ahead lay the widest set of marble steps that he had ever seen except on a TV screen, leading up to the Churchill VTO station above. It was an hour plus before take-off. To his left an illuminated sign announced MOON TICKETS HERE. Jakko, creature of the countryside and now committed with enthusiasm to an important role on Earth, had little desire to go there: all rock and dust and a few companies searching for mineral deposits. He directed his steps towards a coffee bar.

The commonsense idea of one World Money — like World Citizenship — had been mooted some fifty years before, and at last (but only recently) the change-over had been completed. The only people to suffer — in that they had to find something else to do — had been the veritable army of young people, many

8

of Earth's best brains, once considered elite, who had hitherto spent their days in the financial centres of the world, endlessly juggling with its many diverse currencies or shuffling other people's money and growing rich on the percentage that they or their firms retained for themselves.

Jakko extracted from an unaccustomed pocket the necessary World cents and, with coffee and a bun, set out to find an empty table. He had meanwhile to keep an eye on his belongings as, for all his progress, Man was still born with only two hands.

It was then that his eye caught sight of another figure in the same virgin uniform. Her back (for it was female) was towards him but he pressed on, eager for companionship in strange surroundings. He asked if he might share the table, gaining only a half, sideways impression of his fellow volunteer as he turned back to collect his case and bits and pieces. It was only when he had returned to the table and stacked his belongings safely at his feet that he cradled the coffee cup in his hands and looked up at his companion.

The intended words of thanks died on the young man's lips. Jakko put down the cup without drinking the coffee. He found himself unaware any more of time, place or occasion, gazing into a pair of hazel eyes. She was dark, her hair very fine and silky. Beautiful make-up. Mankind's new female recruit to the World Peace Force was the most beautiful thing that he had ever seen. She was older than Jakko; he guessed about twenty-five: with more experience of life. He noticed the St Andrew's Cross of Scotland on the shoulders of her uniform and that she too was destined for his unit: EURO 2001.

Jakko's mouth had become suddenly dry, but he managed to blurt out a simple 'Thank you.' Then 'I see we are in the same Unit . . . 2001.'

'Yes,' she said. 'It's quite an adventure, isn't it? I'm looking forward to the travel and to doing something worthwhile. There's no doubt it's the world's best career; for those who have got what it takes.'

The mixture of innocent embarrassment and youthful inexperience on the part of the young man must have touched his companion, for presently she stretched her hand across the table.

'My name is Jakko Mann,' he managed eventually, feeling himself flush.

9

'I'm Jamina,' she said. 'I came down from Edinburgh overnight. Isn't it awful about London? Did you see the posters in the Underground?' She was being friendly now.

Jakko hadn't seen the posters (Jamina had crossed London between main-line termini), but the world had long feared that eventually many of its low-lying cities, including the British capital, were doomed. 'It's to do with the Greenhouse Effect and everything, isn't it?' he ventured.

'Of course,' Jamina agreed. 'The world has known for a hundred years now that we were faced with serious climatic change. Countless warnings have been issued over the years, and at least *some* action has been taken. But even if, at the turn of the century, man-made emission of greenhouse gases had ceased altogether — which they didn't — *past* emissions would have continued the warming. But the UK has its own special problems and we are among the first candidates for flooding. You've heard of North Sea Surges, haven't you?'

'Yes, and of course I know about south-east England sinking and north-west Scotland rising,' Jakko added. 'But I thought the Thames Barrier and all those new defences would be enough.' He knew about those things from television.

'Of course construction of the Barrier was a prodigious feat,' Jamina agreed, putting her younger companion at his ease. 'Our governments of those days knew about North Sea Surges and that the UK was tilting. London was known to be subsiding into the clay, but only by about three-quarters of a metre every hundred years. Given luck, the defences would protect the capital for a century or more if all the adverse factors didn't coincide. But the rising sea level wasn't then uppermost in their minds. The Greenhouse Effect really ''arrived'' in world debate in 1988. It is the possible combination of *all* these things which is unique to south-east England.'

Jakko felt the girl's grip tighten on his hand. With no personal experience of London, he nonetheless felt an overwhelming sadness at the prospect of a great disaster. He drew comfort from Jamina and felt a sudden oneness with his new companion. He gazed into the hazel eyes. Slowly the Earth's terrible state, caused largely by Man, became reality. At least, maybe not at the eleventh hour but at two pm, *they* had both volunteered to do their best. No question of naivety. They were of a new WORLD generation.

Suddenly came the announcement 'WORLD PEACE FORCE UNIT EURO 2001 TO VTO CHECK-IN PLEASE ... WORLD PEACE UNIT EURO 2001 ...'

2

Jakko grabbed Jamina's suitcase, beckoning her to take their small things, and thus they made for the marble steps. These were so wide, so important-looking, that they looked to Jakko as if they must lead up towards another world — or to heaven perhaps.

The Churchill VTO station, spotless like the railway terminus below, was one of Britain's busiest. They checked in and passed through to the appropriate departure lounge, their arrival causing a stir amongst a score of new contemporaries.

Shoulder-flashes from other countries in Europe mingled with those from the UK.

Young men often mature and gain self-assurance later than do girls. Jakko, with his rural background, was no exception. It was only a few minutes since he had met Jamina but already, though still somewhat awed by her beauty and sophistication, he felt reassured that she was there beside him.

The trip to World College EURO 11 would take but a short while in a World Peace Force craft. The party soon embarked and, as the big blue machine lifted off and swung away to the south, excited conversation became general. It was the beginning of a great adventure.

The College, purpose-built thirty years before, adjacent to the city of Crawley, the international airport, and the eight-lane M23 motorway from London to the coast, had recently been modernized, indeed largely rebuilt. It was now a Euro Federal showpiece. The party landed a few yards from the main entrance, distinguished by an outsized version of the World Government logo: the fruits of Earth, scales of justice, and a white dove of peace cradled protectively in a semi-circle of linked hands.

12

The volunteers, carrying their hand baggage, stopped in twos and threes to read the wording on two panels set in the natural stonework on either side of the great doors. That to the left bore a quote from Benjamin Franklin:

> God grant that not only the love of liberty but a thorough knowledge of the Rights of Man may pervade all the nations of the earth so that a philosopher may set his foot anywhere and say 'This is my Country'.

Opposite, from a poster at the main gate of Portsmouth Dockyard on the eve of the Normandy Invasion a hundred and forty years before:

> The difficult we can do at once. The impossible may take a little longer.

On reading the latter, someone exclaimed *'Magnifique!'* There was a shout of *'Allez Monde!'* and they all entered the building.

* * *

The college had been rebuilt to a standard design resulting from a competition in the twenty-fifties.

The main entrance opened into a wide cross-wise walk, housing reception and administrative areas, thence through into a huge central hall-cum-theatre, with pillared aisles on either side, libraries, lecture and model rooms. At the rear lay a spacious panelled dining area and the domestic regions. Staff and students' accommodation occupied separate blocks

13

connected by covered moving walkways. Early in the life of the World Government, that body had encouraged all World establishments to display works of art by citizens of the Regional Federations. Thus the great hall, galleries, and passages of EURO College 11, like those of sister establishments the world over, were alive with beauty, colour and design: a contribution to the creation of a feeling of oneness in the peoples of the world.

Outside, a vast hanger-like structure housed a comprehensive selection of World Peace Force hardware for the initiation of successive units of its volunteers: aircraft, VTOs and gunships; armoured, scout and riot vehicles, trucks; repair and workshops; a complete mock-up of the latest MARK XXV Space Station with which the WPF was equipped for world surveillance, with it the last word in space flight simulators; and a big range for instruction in the use of STOP Guns and other weaponry. At all these things members of Unit EURO 2001 would have to become expert. They would *need* to be the cream of the world's youth.

College EURO 11 was equipped equally thoroughly for the training of volunteers for the World Environment Corps, with meteorological, forestry, horticultural and farm schools. The establishment generated a rich abundance of vegetables, fruit and produce to save World Government money and for its students' health, while (setting an example) much of its power came from the sun. Moreover, with every roof a catchment, the complex collected, purified and stored the world's most precious gift of rain rather than from the national grid of its host country. All World Colleges boasted their own hospital, worship room, and exceptional facilities for art, sport and recreation.

The new arrivals were directed to Reception to sign in. Jakko and Jamina joined a short queue, their World Identity Cards ready in their hands. Since World Citizenship had been recognized by the greater part of mankind, these had replaced regional (and a few remaining national) passports. The front cover bore the World Government logo and the holder's Identity and WISO numbers, prefixed (in their case) EURO to indicate their Federation.

On the inside of the cover, all mankind was called upon to safeguard its fellow citizen and the environment:

14

> The elected World Assembly representing the peoples of the Earth calls upon all whom it may concern to allow the bearer to pass freely upon their lawful occasions and at all times to afford to the Citizen of the World who bears this pass such comfort, assistance, and protection as may be necessary.
> Cherish thy brother and thy sister for we are all of one family and depend one upon another.
> Tread lightly on the Earth.

This exhortation was repeated in small print in eight other languages, for a world language had not thus far been universally adopted and not everyone yet carried a micro hand translator. The identity, description and photo of the citizen followed, with address, occupation, next of kin: details of health, blood group, immunizations and essential information together with the holder's wishes as regards receipt of organ transplants in the event of injury, or as a donor in the event of death. Convictions (for specific crimes) were recorded, these being removed after clean periods varying with the severity of the offence.

The telescreen was one of Orwell's most accurate predictions, even if his timing was awry, and — satirically — he saw it in 1984 as harnessed to the Devil's purposes. Now, a hundred years on, its uses ranged from World Government screens in the great city squares, stadia, and public places across every continent, to dissemination of news by Regional Federal authorities and — between whiles — national and other news, features and music. Nor was any worthwhile public body, utility or business without its own telescreen service and for many years the world's telephones had, unless negatived by push-button, transmitted pictures as well as voices during calls.

By now, the volunteers had reached the central hall. Here they stopped and put down their heavier cases as the big telescreen requested their attention and a tough father figure, the school's Principal, appeared framed before them.

'Ladies and gentlemen of Unit 2001, welcome to EURO 11. My name is Goodssen. I come from Norway and I have the honour to be the Principal of this College.' Goodssen spoke in English.

'All World Government bodies are important, particularly those concerned with the environment. Without *them* Man faces extinction. But — and this is not because I am a member myself — the World Peace Force to which you now belong is the "elite". It is we who keep the peace on planet Earth while Man gropes towards complete unity of purpose.

'The staff and I give a small reception on each Unit's first evening. Plain clothes: not uniform. Six o'clock here in Central Hall. So that we can get to know one another. We ask the ladies to wear play smocks and gentlemen a jacket.' (The play smock resulted from the world's ever-increasing leisure time and a craze to go casual at all costs.)

'After this evening's meal,' Goodssen continued, 'there will be a concert of popular light music from each of the Regional Federations which, so far, make up our World. During your time here we will be hosts to some of the world's finest musicians. Tonight's concert will be given by our own orchestra, of which we are very proud, and it is in fact a very special evening. Mandela Moses will conduct his own composition *The Saving of the Elephants* prior to its gala first performance by the LSO next Saturday in London.

'Meanwhile, in your rooms you will find your baggage and a pack containing timetables and details of your course with us, and a few necessary rules for the administration of the College. The latter are not irksome. They are designed only for the orderly and safe conduct of your course. As I expect you know, the use of habit-forming drugs and the smoking of cigarettes are banned in all World Government establishments.

'In a separate pack you will find details of three trips to different world locations. We send each course on two of these to get to know and to understand the problems, hopes, and fears of others; to see natural beauty in its wonderful variety, and man-made wonders too.

'If you have any problems, please ask any member of staff to help you. My own door is always open. I hope you will enjoy your time here and that you will go out into the world inspired by your calling and confident in your ability. I look forward to meeting you all this evening. Thank you.'

The picture faded and the telescreen reverted to quiet music.

3

Jakko's plain-clothes suit came from the market at home. It did not fit terribly well. He had once seen in a magazine a tough, good-looking male model wearing a colourful silk cravat, and had bought himself an expensive version with his farm wages to wear on special occasions. Thus far he had never worn it. The only occasion which had seemed to him special enough had been his Uncle Albert's funeral and, as the treasured cravat was a vivid green with spots, Jakko had felt that perhaps it wasn't suitable.

He had packed this treasured possession with his suit to take to EURO College 11. Now, after an agony of indecision, he had put it on for the welcoming reception being given to his Unit, but somehow he had contrived to get the narrow bit round the front of his neck so that he looked as if he had just managed to escape after receiving the last rites.

A female member of the staff reminded him from the small telescreen over his bed that it was nearly six o'clock. Jakko emerged from his room and ran straight into Jamina from a couple of doors further down the passage. The newly brushed dark hair and hazel eyes were set off by a silver play smock. Jakko felt his mouth go dry again. His new companion seemed more beautiful than ever.

'I don't think you've got that thing round your neck quite right,' Jamina said. 'Keep still,' she ordered kindly. 'Let's see what I can do.'

She untied the clumsy knot. As he stood momentarily with her arms around his neck, Jakko sensed her warmth, the trace of expensive scent. It was a new experience. 'That's better,' Jamina commented as she tucked the broad silk ends into his jacket. 'Come on or we'll be late.'

The College had perfected its routine; the reception broke a lot of ice. Most of Goodssen's staff were English, but Unit EURO 2001 was international. It wasn't long before a couple of suntanned colleagues from the Mediterranean spotted Jamina and began light-heartedly to chat her up.

'She's from Scotland,' Jakko announced.

'Too cold up there for beautiful girls, eh?' said one of the bronzed ones.

'We have warm hearts . . . for the right people,' Jamina said.

Further inconsequential conversation had to wait. Goodssen, preceded by an aide, made his way towards them. The College Principal shook hands with them in turn. They chatted in a group for a few minutes over their drinks (Jamina had asked for plain fruit juice), Goodssen enthusing about the Sahara vegetation which ARAB MIDDLE EAST and the Environment Corps had succeeded in producing, and the distillers and pumping stations along the North African shore. 'What is more,' he said, *there is no fighting anywhere in the world today.* That is the measure of World Peace Force success. Because the Force *exists.* Long may it last.' He turned to Jakko with a serious expression. 'You are English? We are sad here about London. A tragedy can happen any day now with the high tides. Have you read the story of Londoners during the Second World War? If you haven't, you should.' He addressed them all again. 'Nice to have you with us.' Then he was off to welcome other members of the Unit.

In due course the duty telescreen operator appeared to announce supper, and to request that Central Hall be cleared so that it could be made ready for the concert. Jakko and Jamina made their way together towards the dining area, to find the way blocked by colleagues who had stopped to stare.

As people took their places and the crowd thinned, the reason became apparent. Framed by beautiful wood panelling, a continuous mural two and a half metres high encircled the hall, depicting the moment when the flood waters receded from Mount Ararat, the Ark came to rest, and the creatures of the world took to the air or slithered down the gangplank lovingly made by Noah and his family, that those whom God had saved might repopulate the Earth.

When all were seated, Goodssen rose in his place at the head of the table. 'Friends, we are accustomed to appreciation and wonder when new arrivals see this dining room for the first time. You must not take too literally what you see. This is not the moment to debate whether God created all the species that share the world or whether, as Darwin would have it, we have all evolved to suit our particular environment . . . or indeed — as I believe — that there is truth in *both* these theories. Certainly we believe here in God. Equally, we *know* that evolution is a fact and that it is a process still continuing all around us. Speculation and thought are healthy among intelligent beings, but I ask you to consider in wonder all the inhabitants of Earth, that we are all dependent upon each other, that Man has the greatest responsibility in the preservation of the world for all to share. That is the message of this magnificent room.

'It is World Government policy to spend a minimum of the people's money upon nonessentials. But we are fortunate that the host countries in which these and other World establishments are sited have vied with each other in their generosity, so that the World's own buildings have become in many cases the most beautiful examples of what man can create.

'During a leisure moment I hope you will examine this mural in detail. You will find over four thousand species depicted besides Man. Whether they looked like this at the time of the Ark . . . indeed whether there ever was an Ark, I leave to you. It took five men two years to paint, under the direction of Carlo Bennini, the great man himself from Florence.

'I usually take this opportunity to mention two other matters to newly-arrived volunteers. First, I draw your attention to the note at the foot of the menu. There are always non-vegetarian dishes available for those who still prefer them . . . it is a free world.

'Secondly, there is the matter of religion. Freedom to worship any or no God is now enshrined in the World Constitution. Here, we have but one Worship Room, but — I am glad to say — it is used by all faiths and denominations: sometimes exclusively by members of one church, on other occasions by mixed congregations. If you care to attend services here or to visit the Worship Room quietly on your own, its doors are never locked.

'And now,' Goodssen bowed his head, 'the Grace adopted by the World Colleges: *Let us be grateful always for the blessings of the Earth and ever strive to make them available to all. Amen.*'

There was now time to look around them as conversation broke out amongst the fifty members of the unit and a score of staff, seated either side of the long dining table laden with presentation silver. In the centre, a magnificent rose bowl given by the City of London stood amidst a display of the fruits of Earth, much of it, for reasons already mentioned, grown by the College. Silver candelabra, ornamental glass and plate from Scottish, Welsh, and English cities, communities and business corporations evidenced the host countries' pride and belief in the purposes of the establishment.

By the end of supper, even the more sophisticated young began to appreciate that they had joined something special, a feeling reinforced by the presence of important guests. It was then that Goodssen once more called for silence. 'Ladies and Gentlemen; Mr Moses, our guest conductor in tonight's concert, is having dinner with my wife and a few members of the staff. As of course you know, he has long since lost his sight. God moves in a mysterious way. This lovely man has brought beauty and happiness into the lives of millions all over the world. The concert will begin in half an hour. Please take your seats in Central Hall in good time.' With this he left the table to join the party over which his wife was presiding in their private suite.

'Why do these things happen?' Jakko asked as he and Jamina left the dining hall.

'We'll never know until we have reached another world,' she suggested. 'Maybe he has done so well in this life that he is being tested to see if he is ready to move on in the next — to some higher place.' She squeezed Jakko's hand. 'See you in the hall in a few minutes.'

The evening's programme had been chosen carefully with — as befitted a World College — popular classics and music from four different Regions. Jakko, with his simple rural background, was inspired increasingly by each succeeding piece until, reminded in his programme of Gershwin's life and death so young, he became increasingly emotional: afraid lest his feelings got the better of him as he sat through *Rhapsody in Blue*, misty-eyed with a huge lump in his throat until rescued by the interval.

After the break, the audience of young Europe settled in silence and anticipation to await Mandela Moses, to rise applauding, one by one, until the whole assembly was standing as Goodssen led his guest to the platform. 'Friends, we welcome one of the world's best-loved personalities. Sadly, we see Mandela Moses only rarely in this country. That is not surprising. It is our loss. His heart is of course with the animals in Africa. Tonight, it is our great privilege to hear a performance — conducted by the maestro himself — of his new work *The Saving of the Elephants*. Our own orchestra, suitably augmented, has been rehearsing with a determination to be worthy of the moment. I have asked Mandela if he will be kind enough to say a few words to introduce his new composition . . .'

The old man held out his hands towards the crowded Central Hall as if physically giving to those present part of his soul.

'Thank you all for your kind reception. I come from Manica in Mozambique . . . but of course you know that.' He smiled. 'Manica is on the railway line to Beira, not far from the Zimbabwe border. My part of Africa has witnessed in three quite different operations the stirrings of European hearts, and later of governments, towards the problems of my continent: how best to achieve freedom and equality *in their own country* for the black people of South Africa; to feed the starving; to protect from evil exploitation the animals who are our friends and with whom we share the world.

'In those days, the front line states — that's what they were called — the bulk of whose trade depended upon South African railways, were powerless to apply pressure against the then South African regime without cutting their own throats. Meanwhile, Europe was spending millions to *destroy* surplus food and feeding to its livestock the world's basic crops which the starving should themselves have been eating.' There were tears in the sightless eyes as he added, '. . . It is not for me, now, to comment upon the godless inhumanity with which your food animals were treated . . . at the same time,' resuming his theme, 'exploitation of our wildlife for ivory and supposed aphrodisiacs threatened to wipe out for ever the elephants and rhinos.

'We all know of the differences between your country and others as how best to influence South Africa. Your then Prime Minister was isolated in that, as in other things. Meanwhile starvation haunted sub-Sahara, and slaughter continued in the bush. It is now history that substantial help from Europe tipped the scale in the end — although it took a generation — in all three of those spheres. Let me emphasize the gratitude of Africa. Now that we are well on the way to One World, Pan Africa is a vital part.'

The old man continued quietly. 'But, my friends, let us forget now those considerations. I wrote this music for the animals alone.

'You may find distressing the first movement of the piece that you are about to hear. You will be able, I hope . . .' — this with a little chuckle, then again seriousness — 'to distinguish the poachers' shots, the distressful crashes as the gentle creatures fall, the sounds made by the agonized survivors. In the second movement you will hear the airplanes, the vehicles, shouts and footfalls of protective patrols of Kenyan and Zimbabwe soldiers flushing out the poachers, and scenes in sanctuaries in which rescued baby animals are reared. Finally, in the third movement of the work, I have tried to capture the peace and the wondrous beauty of the vast continent which is Africa today, and the thrust of its now forward-looking people.'

Mandela Moses bowed gently to the audience, then turned as the leader of the augmented Euro 11 orchestra came forward to guide him to the rostrum. The old man raised his baton, then the great Central Hall was filled with sound.

* * *

'Let's go and have a look at tomorrow's programme,' Jamina suggested to Jakko as the gathering broke up. They made their way to the accommodation block. Jakko hesitated as they reached his door but found himself led to Jamina's. 'You have the armchair,' she suggested. 'I'll sit on the bed.' She turned on the music channel to provide a soothing background.

'Here we are,' reading from her information pack. '0700 PHYSICAL and PARADE GROUND. 0900-1030 and 1045-1215 our first lectures: THE STATE OF THE WORLD — POLITICAL. 1400-1530 'STOP GUN' INSTRUCTION. 1530-1700 ART — PAINTING AND SCULPTURE. 2000 DINNER. 2300 LIGHTS OUT.'

'What's a STOP GUN?' Jakko asked, but his thoughts were still with the elephants.

'You must have seen them on TV. They work on the basis of rays . . . causing temporary immobility: seizing up of the muscles in some day. Don't ask me the medical details! The point is that Peace Force personnel never *kill* in domestic situations if it can be avoided — but there are times, obviously, when people have to be stopped and apprehended.'

'So we sort of paralyse them — just for a few minutes.'

'You could say that. Incidentally, I'm not keen on the square-bashing; I'm not really conscious first thing in the morning.'

Jakko was thoughtful. 'In the recruiting ads it says we will be doing the most important job in the world. *Because Mankind has a large, effective, well-organized Peace Force to send to trouble spots, the world will be a safe place and individual Regions can put their arms away.* The billions spent on armaments in the old days will be spent instead to prevent climatic disaster and on all manner of things for the world's *people*. I didn't think we'd be involved in ... well ... sort of domestic police work.'

'We aren't really,' Jamina suggested. 'But we do much more than just *exist* as a force for good. The Units take turns in patrolling Space, providing Air/Sea Rescue Services, helping the civil power in the event of riots or natural disasters like earthquakes. Besides, there's always the chance that we may be called in to help the WAO[1] or the Environment Corps with water and food distribution in times of disturbances or drought. It's all very exciting. Of course, behind it all is the World Government's hope that the WPF will become recognized as everyone's best friend. That will make its job the easier to do.

'Don't worry, Jakko dear. We *have* joined the most important outfit in the world today.'

Jamina realized that her companion was still half the world away in Africa. She changed the subject. 'It's been a long day. Let's just switch on the News channel. Then I'd like to go to bed.'

She was upstaged, suddenly, by the telescreen. It was a different, middle-aged member of the College staff. 'Here is an urgent message for Unit 2001. The EURO Met Office has warned of a deep depression north of Scotland. Usually these continue north-eastwards to the north of Scandinavia, but this

---

[1] World Aid Organisation, a major World Government agency with its own command structure, depots, reserves, personnel and transport.

one has turned south over the North Sea. There is a ridge of high pressure to the west. Gale force north winds are expected: prime conditions for a major North Sea Surge. It is an accident of fate that this should coincide with exceptionally high tides and, of course, for centuries the UK has been tilting, south-east England gradually settling lower in the water.

'At the turn of the century some sixty square miles of Greater London were at risk, with a population of about a million and three quarters, protected by the Thames Barrier completed in the 1980s, and by wall defences below and up-river from the Barrier.

'I have explained this in some detail because there is now *added* to these already exceptional circumstances the gradual rise in sea levels, for which man himself is responsible. The EURO Met Office fears that this unique combination of factors could cause the disaster to the UK that has been feared. You appreciate that, while sea levels constitute but one factor, we may be among the first victims of flooding with world climatic change.

'Your unit has only arrived here today. Nonetheless, the College has offered to place Unit 2001 at the disposal of the London Flood Executive. We believe that you would not wish it any other way. If disaster comes, there will be much that you can do, and we know that you will live up to the Force that you have joined.

'Tomorrow's early morning physical is cancelled. Your lecture programme will be kept under review throughout the period of risk.

'You should have working uniform and wet weather suits ready, and be prepared to be lifted to London at short notice. You will be kept informed. I advise you all to get as much sleep now as you can. Good night.'

Jakko looked at his companion in silence for a moment as the picture faded: into the hazel eyes, at the silver play smock which emphasized a perfect shape, the beautiful hands . . . and suddenly he realized that it was *his* turn to be strong. 'I'm so glad that we met,' he said awkwardly. 'Don't worry. I will look after you . . .'

Jamina took his hand, straightened the strong fingers and, lifting the hand, gently kissed them. 'Thank you Jakko. I'm glad too,' she said.

4

Jakko lay awake for a long time, alternately moved, tortured, and inspired by a jumble of emotions. It had been a unique day in his life. His thoughts strayed back to the country, the goodbyes of his family; how he had hugged his mother, kid sister, and his dog longest of all because *he* couldn't understand, then hurriedly asked his father to drive him to the railway station lest his feelings got the better of him. They could do without him at the farm. British farmers, the most efficient in the world, were producing as much as their own country and the FAO needed to buy, and for which their reduced numbers earned, in world currency, a fair and guaranteed return. The pressure — at last — was off livestock. No longer any need for the barbaric extremes and deprivations of intensive factory farms. The kind, gentle, blind old man named after Nelson Mandela had recalled those things. Developing countries now ate the prime crops they produced, instead of exporting them to the industrialized world to be fed to livestock. The FAO and the World Health Authority hammered away constantly with their slogan FIBRE, FISH AND FRUIT. Heart and cancer deaths were rare.

He had learned from reading and from television that — for all the interim measures — Earth's future viability still hung in the balance. Shy but conscientious, he had decided to volunteer for the World Environment Corps, to play a part in helping the developing world to feed itself, in rain-making and irrigation, re-afforestation; preservation of the world's wild life and resources, wetlands and fish spawning grounds; in education to the dangers of continued global warming and over-exploitation of the land and sea, lest the Earth reached — for ever — the point of no recovery. To that end he had bought on market days as much reading matter as he could find until, one day, he had seen a recruiting advertisement issued by the World Executive calling for volunteers for the World Peace Force. 'IF YOU ARE FIT AND DEDICATED, JOIN THE "ELITE".'

Jakko was certainly fit, and he could be dedicated to a fault if he believed. There had been something of the frustrated ego of a late developer: of straightforward, honest youth awaiting a chance to prove itself. He had clipped the coupon and sent it off, filled out in his best handwriting, to the EURO HQ of the WPF. Efficiently, the reply had arrived by return mail. Jakko had been inspired — literally — by the wording: anything but stereotyped and formal . . . warm and welcoming to a great calling. The Environment Corps now forgotten, he had been determined to be accepted, probably added half an inch that day to his stature, and had awaited anxiously the call for interview and physical.

He recalled all these things as he lay awake, wondering about the threat to London and whether Unit 2001 would be sent to help . . . at least, he prided himself, he was a good swimmer . . . while, a few doors down the passage, the beauty with the hazel eyes whom he dared to hope was now his friend lay sleeping unruffled as bidden by the telescreen. Jakko recalled the coffee bar table when they first met, the hint of scent as Jamina straightened his cravat, her brushing caress of his fingers as they said goodnight. Tough, maybe . . . .but so beautiful. A mixture of pride and jealousy when everyone had noticed her at the reception.

Now he was drifting in and out of sleep to Gershwin's *Rhapsody in Blue* . . . Verdi's *Chorus of the Hebrew Slaves*, which had rallied a fragmented Italy, now unofficial anthem of mankind . . . and, with renewed emotion, Mandela Moses's music. Then once more back to Jamina . . . this time to her statistics about London.

Three quarters of a metre deeper into the clay every century, she'd said . . . *about twenty-four feet* in a thousand years. It didn't occur to him to doubt Jamina's word, but what if the whole process became speeded up . . . no-one could be sure. He began to visualize the likely effects of quicker sinking.

The tubes of the Underground would soon be fractured, tracks twisted and unusable even without flooding; sewers and conduits, gas mains and cables of all kinds fractured or buried. Old buildings would collapse altogether as their foundations

27

shifted, while those built with steel would lean at drunken angles as, distorted, they shed millions of tons of glass and marble cladding into the ruptured streets. There would be no alternative to the abandonment of a great part, if not the whole of the capital. Rats would be everywhere, escaping from their homes as ancient underground brickwork crumbled in the sewers and the water rose.

Such possible disaster to the capital of his own country while everywhere the world was shaking off the madness of the past, emerging with increasing brotherhood in its efforts to survive, suddenly filled Jakko with despair. He sat up in bed, a vision of Big Ben crashing in Parliament Square in his half-conscious mind. Immediately he was shocked into consciousness as the telescreen came to life and the College was filled with a loud, wailing alarm. He looked at his watch. He must have dozed off at intervals. It was 0500.

The screen depicted the same member of the College Staff who had told them the previous evening that the unit might be sent to London. Now they would know. Hurriedly, Jakko pulled on some clothes, knocked on Jamina's door, with 'It's me, Jakko. May I come in?' Jamina was already out of bed, sitting in the armchair, a rug around her shoulders, attention centred on the telescreen.

Jakko was taken off his guard momentarily by the quite different Jamina without make-up,.but as she beckoned him to perch on the end of the bed, his mind was rescued from renewed conjecture by an urgent announcement from the screen.

'This is a further message for Unit 2001.

'The London Flood Executive has, within the last few minutes, issued the Six Hour Warning. Our information is that serious flooding of the capital is expected shortly. The full force of the North Sea Surge is expected to coincide with exceptionally high water. Let me emphasize that only flooding is expected. I use the word *only*, to indicate to you that — while neither the time required nor the astronomical cost of repairing the likely damage and restoring services can be estimated — the pending disaster will be limited to severe and in some areas total disruption of communications, mains services, and transport. It is not expected that there will be permanent damage to the actual structure of the majority of modern buildings. I repeat: we are talking about *flooding*; not disintegration of south-east

28

England which may yet be between a hundred and a thousand years away. It may well be that if the present exceptional combination of circumstances is not repeated, the existing Thames Barrier and improved defences will protect the capital for a long time ... climatic change permitting. But that is another story. We have to deal with ''now''.

'There has already commenced during last night an orderly withdrawal from the threatened area, some sixty square miles and a further hundred beyond, of major equipment that is movable, and evacuation of low-lying property, records and so on. London Transport are already moving Underground trains and buses to outlying depots. A massive exodus of commercial vehicles and private cars is under way. Emergency cables are being rigged at first floor level to provide power for pumps, the Fire and Rescue Services.

'It has long been accepted policy that only low-lying property should be evacuated and that, where refuge can be taken well above expected flood level, the inhabitants of the threatened area should move to higher floors, taking with them only essentials and items of significant monetary or sentimental value. No difficulty is anticipated in the provision of food. Rations in pack form, inflatable rafts and line-throwing equipment have been held in outlying depots for many years, based on a likely maximum of two million people trapped in the flood area.

'All operations will be assisted by the Police and volunteers from various disciplined bodies including the WPF, under the control of the London Flood Executive. Object: to leave the Fire and Rescue Services free to deal with the flood water and emergency life-saving.

'Unit 2001 will be lifted by WPF VTOs to London Dockland Station III, leaving College at 0745. We have offered your services — and those of the college staff — in house-to-house search, to ensure that no-one remains below anticipated flood level. By the nature of this task, we will most likely be assisting the elderly and those who live alone.

'Finally, a word to those of you who come from countries other than the United Kingdom. It is appreciated that — without training and within a few hours of joining the World Peace Force — you are being asked to help in an all-British emergency. It is now one World and I am sure that I speak for the UK volunteers when I say that they would, and doubtless one day

29

will, be privileged to do the same for you.

'Breakfast will be an hour early . . . at 0630, when you will receive further briefing. Thank you.'

5

0800. 'FIRST LONDON WARNING.' Two VTOs carrying Unit 2001 and College staff were already in the air, followed immediately by two more with back-up personnel, rations, and equipment. It was essential to complete the lift before the Thames Estuary was struck by gale force winds. Goodssen, leaving a skeleton party at College, had put himself in charge.

Within minutes they were over Greater London, the city sprawling southwards from the river. There were exclamations at the sight below as the evacuation of thousands of vehicles continued to the surrounding, still floodlit orbital roads. Then down, down, in worsening conditions, to the Dockland station to which they had been ordered; morning light from the estuary highlighting the bold black WPF and identity letters edged with white on the blue hulls of the craft.

Before take-off, Unit 2001 had been divided hurriedly into small teams, each of half a dozen volunteers under a leader appointed arbitrarily (for as yet the College had no knowledge of their capabilities). All was hustle as they disembarked: thence to waiting personnel carriers and away to a building on high ground to the north, which was to be their temporary base.

0900. 'EMERGENCY SERVICES STAND BY.' Three hours before expected overtopping of the Thames defences. Daylight. Team leaders poring over maps; then the small groups — in touch by R/T with each other, their base, the London Flood Room, Rescue, and the Police — back towards the river to individual streets, business and residential tower blocks, houses, and shops.

Jamina: quiet, unruffled, older than most and appointed a team leader, had picked her little band from colleagues whom she had got to know briefly after the concert. Jakko had been

31

anxious until he was included. Now, as they made their way to their allotted starting point, he attached himself to his leader in the role of aide, carrying their street plans and instructions. With them were two more lads and two girls, all from the UK.

They soon found themselves in Newham, London Borough, of which — like Southwark on the south side of the river — at least half lay below Trinity High Water.

Instructions were to advise the public of the time factor: they must leave low-lying property, ground-floor and basement flats and offices, moving to higher levels. The final warning, one hour before anticipated flooding, would be given by siren, probably at 1100. Thereafter they should not use lifts lest power failures resulted in them being trapped. Telephone calls to relatives should be made as soon as possible. Telescreens and a home TV channel should remain switched on for bulletins and orders from Government, London Flood Room, and the Police.

The teams knew very well that the central part of the Underground would be paralysed; water, power, and gas supplies threatened; communications perhaps cut; drains and sewers so overloaded as to constitute a health hazard; but the public were to be reassured that the capital was threatened immediately only by flood. There was little danger or likelihood of loss of life.

Jamina ordered two of her team into the first buildings on each side of the street, keeping Jakko with her in the roadway. One man and a girl would work together on each side, the latter in case old people were reluctant to abandon possessions or to admit a strange male, even in uniform, into their homes. Progress would be speeded if someone responsible could be found in each block, to whom they might delegate the job of searching lower floors.

1100. Telescreen, TV, and siren warnings found Jamina's team with their allotted streets all but completed. The two groups together disappeared into the last buildings, an old tenement complex. Jamina and Jakko waited in the roadway; then grew anxious. Their colleagues didn't re-emerge.

The London Flood Room had reported the Thames Barrier closed at 0800, four hours ahead of the expected Surge. Now, as Jamina waited for her team to complete their last assignment, the Flood Room broadcast that the gates were being closed. She became concerned.

32

'Jakko, I'm going in to see what's going on. Call Mr Goodssen and report completion of our area bar this block. Then request instructions.'

Jakko had never used a handset except to be called in for meals when ploughing. His knowledge of procedure was confined to what he had learned from cops and robbers and *Star Wars* on TV. The wavelength was cluttered with queries and reports. He waited for a break; seized his opportunity. 'Calling EURO College Eleven HQ. This is Jakko Mann. Team Six.'

'Mann. Pass your message. Over.'

Jamina's aide-de-camp was taken aback momentarily. He continued with confidence increased. 'Team Six has completed search . . . except one tenement block. Request further instructions.'

'Team Six. Complete search of lower levels. Then clear streets of pedestrians. I say again *CLEAR THE STREETS*. Over.'

Jamina reappeared, beckoning. 'I need you inside.' Then, 'There are a couple of drunks in the basement and an old dear who refuses to move. You join the two lads and get the drunks out. The girls and I will cope with the old woman.' She led the way.

The entrance walls were covered with graffiti. The smell of stale urine and vomit made Jakko feel sick. He couldn't understand that Jamina, so beautiful, seemed to take all this in her stride but he pressed on in her support, then hesitated at the obscenities scribbled on the brickwork. BLACK SHIT . . . WOGS OUT . . . FUCK THE WPF . . . He was bewildered by the reference to the elite force for good that he had joined. Surely everyone stood to benefit from the world peace *that the WPF actually existed to preserve*. Jakko was glad that there was no-one to witness his discomfort. The honest-to-God country lad was out of his depth in a world he didn't understand.

His shocked senses suddenly became aware of a clear patch on the wall, about ten bricks in extent. There, amongst all the lewd epithets, someone had written in neat tiny letters BALLS TO THE POPE. It was as if — at dead of night when no-one was about — some inoffensive, henpecked little man had been determined to make his mark in the big world, to strike this tiny blow for common sense. Maybe he was the sixteenth child at yearly intervals in a family without enough to eat, protesting at idiotic anti-birth control dogma. Jakko noticed that, whereas most of the other illiterate scribbles had attracted counter-slogans, the reference to His Holiness had not been interfered with. Doubtless it was out of respect, but whether for the exhortation or the Pope he had no way of knowing. He dragged his thoughts back to the job in hand and plunged into the building.

A dank, cheerless lobby with pitted plaster walls once painted the colour of lentil soup gave access to two ground-floor dwellings. Bare stone stairways, walls decorated in similar style to those outside, led to higher levels and to the basement floor below. Jakko choked momentarily, the air overpowering with the smell of lavatories and sweat and just a suspicion of cheap scent, but his breathing was restored as he became acclimatized.

Jamina shouted from the lower regions, and he clattered down to her assistance. The doors of both basement flats were open. Inside the first, the two young men in his team were endeavouring to drag to its feet a large, struggling, intoxicated body, wildly protesting. Female voices could be heard through the other door. Jamina appeared. 'Give them a hand to hold that madman still,' she ordered. Presently the protests ceased, the singlet-clad frame heaving with deep breaths.

'Now, listen to me,' Jamina said firmly. Bloodshot eyes tried hard to focus. 'The river will probably overflow its banks shortly and much of London will be flooded. You have to GET UP and move to a higher flat. If you stay here, you may drown, do you understand? We are here to *HELP YOU*. Now *GET UP*.'

'You'm a very pretty lady ...' the corpse managed.

'Do you know the people upstairs? Would they take you in till the flood danger is over?'

'Course ...'

'And that goes for your mate in there? Now come on. We may not have much time. Right? *UP!*'

Jakko had most of the weight, but their protégé seemed suddenly to pull himself together. The heaving assortment of bodies made slow progress to the second floor.

Jamina knocked. 'Will you look after this character from the basement?' she asked urgently. 'The river may overtop its banks any time now. Keep your telescreen and TV switched on, and don't let him out until it's safe!' Their charge was handed over; then, urgently: 'Can you come down and help with his mate.'

As they hurried down the steps, water could be seen entering

34

the building. For a moment everyone stood mesmerized. Someone exclaimed 'Oh God!', then came an urgent message from the London Flood Executive that introduced a new and frightening dimension. '*CLEAR THE AIR. EMERGENCY.* CALLING ALL SERVICES AND VOLUNTARY BODIES *NORTH OF THE RIVER. THE THAMES DEFENCES ON THE NORTH BANK, DOWNSTREAM FROM THE BARRIER, HAVE BEEN BREACHED.* I EMPHASIZE, *THIS IS IN ADDITION TO THE OVERTOPPING WHICH COMMENCED AT 1145.*

'*CLEAR THE STREETS NORTH OF THE RIVER. I SAY AGAIN, CLEAR THE STREETS.* IMMEDIATE . . .'

Everyone gathered round Jakko and his handset. No-one spoke. The danger was now real, greater, immediate. If there was any light-heartedness in the capital, it would be at an end.

'Where's this other geezer?' one of the upstairs people asked. 'Best knock him out . . . it will save time.'

The message from the Flood Room was continuing. '*RESIDENTS IN NEWHAM, TOWER HAMLETS AND BARKING MUST MOVE TO UPPER FLOORS.*

'TO ALL THE PEOPLE OF LONDON: *KEEP CALM* AS YOU HAVE ALWAYS DONE. KEEP YOUR TELESCREENS AND TELEVISION SETS SWITCHED ON.'

The announcement continued in less urgent terms.

'In the affected areas, transport, electricity, gas, water, telephones, drainage, can now be expected to be more or less disrupted. In the rest of Greater London, the danger is less, but *precautions should not be relaxed.* That is up-river from the City of London and Southwark to the west.

'You can rely on the Emergency Services to do everything possible to restore the situation in the flooded area. Should the emergency be prolonged, ample food supplies are ready for distribution. Please conserve your drinking water. Fill baths and all available receptacles NOW, and *do not thereafter drink any tap water, to avoid risk of infection.* I will repeat the whole announcement . . .'

Within minutes the second drunk had been manhandled upstairs; likewise the old trout plus budgerigar, protesting till the last. Jamina and her team regained the street.

The water was now half a metre deep, but still flowing only

35

slowly to the north, the level kept down by huge quantities finding their way into the Underground, car parks, basements, and sewers. Nonetheless, they were cut off from professional Rescue Services and their temporary HQ. Jamina was in the act of calling 'London Flood Executive; this is WPF Team Six . .' when one of the girls suddenly cried out 'Oh God! *LOOK*!' pointing south towards the river.

Instantly they turned. Heading rapidly towards them was a wall of water which could have resulted only from a major breach.

* * *

Saturday evening. Exceptionally, there was no College weekend leave. Jakko and Jamina sat talking in her room as they awaited a telescreen appearance by the College Principal, which Unit 2001 had been warned was compulsory viewing.

Jamina had shed her uniform. She sat, seemingly in sisterly fashion, in a casual play smock with bare feet, brushing her hair. She knew what she was doing as Jakko took in the whole picture. To his appreciation of beauty there was now added admiration of no-nonsense leadership. He was in more than the first stages of love of a young man for the unattainable.

Jakko didn't know it, but the stirrings of admiration were affecting Jamina too. As the wall of death threatened to overwhelm them in London's Canning Town, she had flung her arms around an old lamp-post which should long since have been demolished, shouting to the others to hold on to her and to each other. Somehow they thus survived the first impact of the water, until the youngest of the team (named appropriately Susan Innocence) lost her grip and was carried away. Jakko had gone after her, half swimming, half stumbling, repeatedly submerged, in a frantic endeavour to reach the girl before she drowned or was crushed by the weight of water against some building or obstruction in the road. It was not until the evening when the College teams had gathered at HQ and Susan's body had been recovered, that the rest of them knew that Jakko Mann was safe.

Later at College, the telescreen came to life. Goodssen appeared.

'You all understand the combination of factors leading to the flooding of substantial parts of London late on Wednesday morning, and why the College offered your services. As you know, regular WPF units also took part in other parts of the capital.'

'To ensure minimum loss of life it was essential to clear lower floors and then the streets in an area of upwards of two million inhabitants. Only nine deaths have so far been reported; all of them caught in the open by the first wave when the defences were breached. That is a remarkably low figure. If, as seems the case, no-one has been lost in the heavily populated area for which our Unit was responsible, it is something of which we can be proud.

'As you all know, one of your Unit, Susan Innocence, was swept away and drowned. Her parents will be here in the morning, and there will be a short service in the Worship Room at which you may like to be present. Susan had been in the World Peace Force for just twenty-four hours. She gave her life that others might be safe. No-one — even in the WPF — can do more than that.

'As a mark of respect for Susan, there will be no Saturday night dance in Central Hall tonight.

'We are proud of you all, but I am sure that you will not take it amiss if I mention Mr Jakko Mann, who so bravely tried to save Miss Innocence. I have received word that he is to receive a Commendation.

'It will take a long time to restore London. Let us hope that there will not be another such tragedy for a long time. Doubtless by then the British capital will have been moved.

'Meanwhile, tomorrow morning your delayed WPF course will begin. A revised timetable will be available later this evening.

'Well done, all of you.' The screen faded. Jamina leaned over.

'Well done, *Jakko*,' she said.

6

After unaccustomed exercise, albeit merciful on the first morning, there were many aching joints as lectures got under way on Monday with State of the World — Political. The lecturer was an enthusiastic female member of the College staff assigned to the Unit during their course. The neat WPF uniform bore the insignia of a Captain and the motif for each of two Distinctions.

'Good morning,' she said. 'My name is Pippa Brightwell. I divide my opening lecture into three parts. First, it is essential that we understand what is meant by the word *Federal* . . . that is the key to this whole matter. Secondly, Regionalism. Then an outline of the World Government as it exists today and how the present World Assembly has come about.

'Let me first give you some definitions of *Federal*. Thus *Concise Oxford 2050*: "of the polity in which several States form a unity but remain independent in internal affairs." *Chambers 1901*: "of a union or government in which several states, while independent in home affairs, combine for national or general purposes." *Nuttal 1929*: "a union of . . . internally independent states under a common central government in which they are severally represented." There is an error there, of course. It is the *people*, not states, who are represented.' The Captain put the compilers of that work in their place. 'That hints at a *Confederation*,' she suggested.

'Here in College, we use more explicit terminology. *Federal means a getting together by states for specific common purposes, from which unity, it is agreed, all their peoples stand to gain: while leaving individual states to conduct their domestic affairs in their own way and to preserve their own culture and traditions.* The world would be a dull place without *that*.

38

'Before the Federal principle was accepted — particularly by Britain — there was much talk of *surrender of sovereignty*. There is of course no surrender, other than ability to veto action for the common good (a power of veto which did not exist in the first place).

'Citizens of a Federation acquire common citizenship and ability to move freely within the wider area. Industry and commerce acquire an enlarged restriction-, tariff-, and customs-free home market. The people enjoy peace within the union, since war between its constituent states becomes impossible. The "combining for general purposes" covers a multitude of benefits to be derived from unity . . . the list is endless . . . in which anyone can see the benefit of concerted action; in which independent, often conflicting entities and regulations must be detrimental. And we haven't even mentioned national security.

'During the twentieth century, the nation state became obsolete: unable any longer to compete economically or to defend itself. Hence grouping into progressively larger units for the mutual *and* individual benefit of the constituent peoples. These days the world understands these things.

'Respect for *national* interests, cultures, and traditions was expressed particularly at the time by France's Jacques Delors. He was of course speaking in a European context, but the principles are universal. "The emergence of a United Europe *and* loyalty to one's homeland;" —. my emphasis — "the need for a European power capable of tackling the problems of our age and the absolute necessity to preserve our roots in the shape of our nations and regions; and decentralization of responsibilities *so that we never entrust to a bigger unit anything that is best done by a smaller one.*"

'M. Delors' reference to the problems of the age and the need for a strong Europe were to be highlighted dramatically within weeks, as Communist governments in Eastern Europe began to crumble and everywhere the cry was raised for freedom and democracy. For every reason, a strong united Western Europe was essential: as an example of stability and co-operative prosperity, to aid the emerging democracies, and — importantly — for its own security in a period of uncertainty and rapid change. Further, German reunification would create one dynamic state of eighty million souls, larger than any of its neighbours. Their belief in European citizenship and a common purpose would be an absolute necessity.

'That the EC became, eventually, fully integrated; progressively extended meanwhile to include Malta, Cyprus, one by one the countries of Eastern Europe, Iceland, Scandinavia and the Baltic, is now history. *We are of course talking in terms of nearly a hundred years*: a long time. And yet, in the lifetime of our planet, in the light of justifiable anxieties and caution, mistaken nationalism, different speeds of advance, even bloody and brutal oppression and attempts at subversion, complex economic and financial problems and adjustments, it is not such a long time. A hundred years ago, an East European farm labourer could work days for the price of a taxi up the Champs Elysées. That, in those days, he was unlikely to spend a romantic weekend in Paris, isn't the point. That was a measure of the problem. Whatever the time scale, it was of supreme world importance that Europe should prove finally the Federal process when achieved freely, with equal regard for the common good and, in Europe's case, respect for such a veritable *host* of different nationalities, traditions, needs, and customs.

'Before we consider the present World Government, we would do well to consider the relationship between ever larger groupings and inter-unit war. The world had progressed from individual combat with bare hands or wooden clubs via tribal wars, the invention of gunpowder, to conflicts in which whole populations were involved and casualties were reckoned in millions. Finally, a few hundred nuclear bombs would have sufficed to eliminate many of the world's cities, bringing death to millions, a prolonged period of darkness, genetic mutations in human, animal, and plant life, decimation of the world's food, perhaps the end of all life save a fews subterranean and oceanic species.

'The early Federalists of 1945 were divided as to the means of attaining their objective. Many believed that, as a World Federation was then but a dream, *any* further grouping was desirable. Experience of working for the common good would be beneficial, leading to a desire for an extension of the process.

'Others held that fewer, larger units would lead inevitably to bigger wars: inter-bloc. In their view, a bold step direct to World Order should be made to bypass regionalism.

'Meanwhile the "functionalists" believed that if peoples worked together for specific purposes from which all stood to benefit, a desire for political union would grow out of the experience ... if, I would, add, they had not meanwhile destroyed each other and the world.

'A great tragedy was the forming of the UN on a *League* basis, based upon bargaining delegates of Governments of sovereign states, ever mindful of the supposed best interests of those states. Not *an elected* people's *Government* at all. But that was not surprising. The main concern of exhausted populations, their cities in ruins, economies destroyed, was peace, readjustment, and their own recovery.

'That we have an elected Assembly a mere hundred and forty years later is remarkable. We are fortunate that, during the age of blocs, peace was preserved by deterrence and fear of mutual annihilation.'

* * *

'There have been many remarkable developments during the intervening years: few greater than the progressive dismantling of hardline Communism in Eastern Europe, but an equally breathtaking success story is that of the GREAT FEDERATION OF THE EAST. It is often said that this century is theirs. Before that, the Nikkei-Dow index, covering a cross-section of 225 major Japanese companies, had appreciated *120 times* in forty years. Since then, brilliant Japanese technology, the speed with which their partners caught up after the Chinese counter-revolution, the inspired industrial relations, and *that vast mainland market hungry for progress*, combined to produce the world's most populous (and unstoppable!) Region. We are fortunate in the civilizing influence and policies that their Representatives and those of India bring to World deliberations: influence and policies founded on *success*.

'As remarkable has been the active participation of the reconstituted USSR.

'A hundred years ago, the Soviets had achieved overwhelming superiority in land forces then regarded as "conventional", strategic nuclear weapons, and in Space. Worldwide spread of Communism still remained the objective. Moreover, thirty years before, following confirmation yet again in World War Two of Mahan's assertion that, in the final analysis, sea power would always prove the deciding factor in matters of world domination,

41

Russia had commenced under Admiral Gorshkov a build-up of naval strength immeasurably greater than that needed for defence. This culminated in the 1984 "April Fools' Day" surprise (to NATO) appearance on the Russian left flank in the North Atlantic of an immensely powerful naval force.

'Even greater Soviet naval power was deployed in the Far East. However, for Communist domination of the world and to further the process in emerging Africa, this overwhelming strength in West and East still left a gaping deficiency in the central arena; the Indian Ocean.

'Hence Soviet occupation of Afghanistan and increased recruitment of Muslim troops with, surely, the eventual target of Karachi as a base for the missing central piece of the great Soviet naval jigsaw. Just look at the map! At the mercy of such power lay the Middle East and the vast potentially receptive sub-Sahara continent groping for survival, development, and wide open to friendly aid against South Africa.' The lecturer put down her cue.

'At this point a century ago, world history was completely re-orientated by the unlikely combination of the Afghans, Mikhail Gorbachev and the warming of the Earth.

'The tribesmen denied a quick advance to the Arabian Sea and prevented a world crisis over Karachi.

'The Soviets began a campaign of good neighbourliness and peaceful leadership abroad, calling repeatedly for arms reduction in order to divert their own resources to economic reform. Early manifestations of this policy were misinterpreted by a wary West. During Iraq's war with Iran, the Russians suggested a UN force to protect the world's merchant ships upon their lawful occasions, an idea rejected by the USA and Britain! Such suggestion would be obvious today: a job for WPF air and naval units on the world's behalf.

'In 1987, Mikhail Gorbachev and Ronald Reagan agreed "to promote international co-operation in the area of global climate and environmental change", further broadening Soviet leadership and good intent. The need to save the planet was beginning to assume importance as the ultimate *functional* spur for world unity of purpose.

'As important was the realization after seventy years that Communism had "failed to deliver", had impoverished the Soviet Union and its satellites. Whatever was then to prove the ultimate fate of Mikhail Gorbachev, his place in history was assured by the relaxation of world tension, of rigid Communist control; and a major shift of emphasis towards desperately needed economic reform. *That it was impossible to fill the shops the next day across half a continent, that economic purposes were overtaken by whirlwind demands in Eastern Europe and later within the Soviet Union, for freedom, democracy, and political reform, detracts not one iota from the courage of the man who made possible the opening of the flood gates.*

'We have in the College library film of the demolition of the Berlin Wall; of immense crowds in East Germany, and the capitals of Eastern Europe . . . crowds as far as the eye can see, as they, like the Baltic states, demanded an end to oppression, election of democratic governments, and withdrawal of Soviet troops. (The latter were to leave an appalling legacy of land despoilment which persisted for a century.)

'That we have an elected *World* Assembly a mere hundred and forty years later is remarkable, even if substantial numbers are — at present — still outside.'

The lecturer switched on a series of visual aids illustrating the Regions participating in the World Federation, their populations, and representation.

THE GREAT FEDERATION OF THE EAST
INDIA
PAN AFRICA
RUSSIAN
SOUTHEAST ASIA
NORTH AMERICA AND CARIBBEAN
EUROPEAN
THE FEDERATION OF ARAB MIDDLE EAST
LATIN AMERICAN
ANZFED

* * *

'Let me expand a little on the peace-keeping process, behind which stands in the final analysis the WPF to which you now belong.

'In the pre-One World regional era of the twentieth century, common defence (NATO for example) provided by deterrence the security that a nation state could no longer guarantee unto itself. That principle has now been projected on to a world plane; but with an essential difference. Whereas regional groupings pooled their national forces, *there now exist no national forces* other than domestic police; *only the WPF, guaranteeing peace and security for all Mankind.*

'Three essentials must be stressed.

'First, the absolute ban by the World Government of munitions sales (other than small arms for police work) to national governments, madmen, and would-be dictators.' Laughter. 'Amusing perhaps, but, I assure you, that is important. There have been supplies to both sides in the same conflict before now.' Silence.

'Secondly, and necessarily following from that ban, worldwide surveillance: a vital role for the WPF.

'Thirdly, the threat of World Sanctions. Any state seeking to flout decisions of the WG or the Supreme Court would be subject to sanctions at the hands of the entire world community. Not wishy-washy, only partially effective and therefore long drawn-out measures, such as were half-enforced against South Africa, sabotaged by those with substantial trading links with that country: particularly Britain, in defiance also of its own Commonwealth.

'WG Sanctions, mercifully never used to date, would involve *total, but total isolation* by the entire.World community. (That, within days at most, would have concentrated Pretoria minds wonderfully upon the means towards democracy, and saved years of anguish.)

'At last, with Mankind's carefully conceived institutions, the world can live at peace. Surely it cannot be long before *all* its peoples participate in the election of its Government.'

7

'Debate and decision-making,' Captain Brightwell continued, 'are of course properly functions of the World Assembly, elected by the *people* on a population basis. We take for granted that representation should coincide as accurately as possible with the votes cast, but it was not always so. Even in the UK — as recently as the later part of the last century — Governments with large majorities repeatedly represented only a minority. Large numbers were effectively disenfranchised. But that is in the past.

'As we have seen, the World Government Senate gives to states with small populations an equal say in an amending and approving Upper House. But as Assembly Representatives — like those in the European and other Regional parliaments — *have consistently voted upon party rather than national lines*, the World Senate has become, rather, a respected body of Mankind's most experienced citizens. It does not have a final blocking power, but the Assembly pays attention to its voice.

'College opinion believes that two telling features of the World Establishment concern the Executive and the physical siting of the World's political capital.

'It was widely felt that it was unhealthy to vest in one man the Presidency of a group of nations. It was a more than reasonable burden. And it had its dangers. The World's constitution-makers came up with the idea of a World Executive Board of five members . . . elected in rotation. By and large, three are always in the capital while two tour the Federations. This works well, and five different Regions are represented at any time in the final assent to World legislation. The Executive Board is, of course, the Commander-in-Chief of the World Peace Force.

'This is where you come in. The World Supreme Court is the final interpreter of the Constitution and of disputes. The WPF exists in support of the Supreme Court. It is the World *Police* Force, but the name is avoided as maybe provocative. Not surprisingly, since it preserves peace and is on hand in case of disaster and emergency, the WPF *has become the World's best friend*, like the one-time English bobby. You have a privileged position and a reputation to protect.

'In 1990/1991, the then UN had reached a unanimous decision in condemning the Iraqi invasion of Kuwait. *But the UN had no means of its own of enforcing its decisions.* The world was fed endless reporting by national spokesmen, their own country's flag ever prominent instead of, properly, the flag of the UN for whom they were fighting. Thus was cruelly divided and alienated much of world opinion. It was a sad lesson. If ever you young people have to bear arms in war, *you* will be *seen* to be doing so for us all.

'As to the geographical siting of the political capital and its administration (World *agencies* remain fixed), nothing has done more to convince Regional populations that they belong to One World than the moving of the capital every five years. The idea was at first described in some circles as insane, and the quinquennial upheaval has proved a temporary inconvenience, but one substantially outweighed by the goodwill.

'Since, a hundred years ago, there was a good deal of uncertainty in Europe on this question and, at that time, the EC had unique experience; it is relevant to remind ourselves that the then European Parliament had become "a kind of travelling circus", forced to work in three different places: Strasbourg (France), where the monthly plenary sessions were held; Brussels (Belgium), where Euro MPs attended committees; and Luxembourg, where many staff had their homes and offices. A report of the European Political Affairs Committee agreed that there was an overwhelming case for *one* working place where Parliament, committees, and groups could meet and where staff and libraries, etc would be located. "It would be possible to hold committee meetings in the morning and plenary sessions in the afternoon. It might be possible, not only to eliminate much travel, but to leave a full week each month 'for correspondence, constituency engagements, and contact with national (and Regional) parliaments, governments, and key organizations'."

Eventually, the European Parliament (by then strengthened) and its administration *were* concentrated in the same city.

'To its credit, and profiting from that early experience, the WG never contemplated siting the World Federal Parliament, committees, and administration separately.

'But, moved by a deep sense of responsibility to the whole world population and wishing to be seen to be so, the WG decided to move the entire organization every five years, and in so doing they highlighted a *new* problem. Its permanent staff would require quality accommodation in a succession of world cities. Further, the experienced services of at least some who did not wish to become itinerant would be lost.

'It has become a fascinating feature of WG organization — and one of extreme importance since it rendered the whole thing viable — that there emerged a World administrative "career person", not unlike the diplomatic, who — with pride and enthusiasm and a desire to be part of World order — gives their life to make the wheels go round. Without this hard core of elite experience and of course the Headquarters Corps, movement of the capital might well have created the shambles predicted by the sceptics.

'There is another plus. The world's senior administrators experience life in different countries, see and understand a succession of different peoples, problems and cultures, instead of becoming egg-bound by an entire career in the same city. In addition, important experience is gained by staff provided by the successive host countries, numbers of whom achieve promotion and themselves move to the next capital.

'In passing, I am myself delighted that the World capital moves to Harare in twenty eighty-five: a beautiful city at the heart of Pan Africa, with ample accommodation and one of the finest communications systems and airports in the world.'

* * *

'A word about the Headquarters Corps. It embraces an amazing mix of professions and trades: multilingual aides, interpreters, secretariat; computer and communications personnel; librarians, messengers; helipilots and drivers; security; electronic and other maintenance engineers; every instant translator, voting machine,

47

mail sorting, recycling, computer, time- or labour-saving necessity or gadget down to the last microphone and light bulb, meticulously kept in order. Not to mention a twenty-four hour catering service. You name it. And, at night the cleaning ladies, known of course in spite of their ages and shapes as the Angels; returning every inch to spotlessness once the auto dusters and waste machines have done *their* jobs.'

There were smiles at this well-deserved 'mention' accorded to the Angels. Of all unlikely people, they had formed their own orchestra in their spare time; were held in World affection. It was a logical enough activity, as the old dears had all day for practice and rehearsal. The very idea of an orchestra of the world's chars had scarcely been taken seriously until, some with their hair still tied up with dusters, and playing everything from violins to trombones, percussion, and Trinidadian oil drums, they had recorded a concert under the guest baton of Ludwig Strauss, no less, from Vienna, who happened to be visiting the capital. They had also, a hundred years on, returned ABBA's *I Have a Dream* to the top of the global ratings! '*I have Dream, a song to sing, to help me cope with anything . . . I believe in Angels . . . something good in everything I see. I believe in Angels . . . When I know the time is right for me, I'll cross the stream . . . I have a dream . . .*'

'They have done more for world togetherness than any formal treaty,' Captain Brightwell commented. 'I heard yesterday that the mums of Harare are already queueing for places next year in case any existing Angels (and there will be some) do not move there with the Government!'

She concluded her lecture in serious vein. 'The siting of the whole World Government machine in the same city was a unanimous derivative from Regional, and particularly European, experience. Whether to move the World capital was a more difficult decision. We can see now that the case is proven: the temporary upheaval more than balanced by the world-wide sense of "we belong".'

* * *

'Of course, the overriding problem in the minds of existing governments and individuals was how the *transition* might be

48

achieved from a bargaining delegate, league system, long established, to one of effective elected government, i.e. a *legislature*.

'It was here that, not by deliberate choice but by virtue of the most fortuitous "accident" in history, the world's Upper House or Senate came into being. *It already existed in the shape of the United Nations.*

'For opponents of the Federal idea; governments and peoples fearful that their voice or that of their Region would be drowned in the Assembly ... these included Britain, Israel, and others, and those with small populations ... here, in the Senate, where all states had equal representation regardless of numerical or economic strength, their voice would be heard regardless.

'Further ... and vitally ... states not initially participants in the World Federal structure, whose people were not therefore represented in the Assembly, would retain — as of right — a position in the Upper House, in which they could debate, advise upon and suggest amendments to proposed world legislation, during the interim before they *were* so represented, or indeed *for ever*, in the hypothetical event that they never joined the rest of us.

'If they, or anyone, behaved on the World stage, they had nothing to fear. If they suffered injustice in the eyes of the World, the World Supreme Court and WPF stood behind their rights, along with those of everyone else..It was the most important safety valve never devised.

'I would remind you at this point that there is representation in the World Senate of the Vatican and the open city of Jerusalem.'

8

By Friday evening, the members of Unit 2001 were exhausted but beginning to find new physical strengths to go with their increasing knowledge. Briefed first upon World Government institutions and their own role in World defence, they had been given also for their wider information the more important statistics, aims and achievements of the World Environment Corps in conjunction with the FAO. These ranged from soil preservation, the breeding of crop strains, food production and famine avoidance through co-ordinated global farm policies, guaranteed prices, food storage and distribution, to such basic matters as long-term preservation of the ozone layer, sea levels and congenial world temperatures.

Their first week's training had included an introduction to the command structure and deployment of the WPF, its surveillance Space Patrols (SPs), major deterrent weaponry, riot control, terrorist devices, and instruction in the use of hand Stop guns. Their introduction to weightlessness would follow and, after that, trips in WPF space craft on weapon trials, SPs, and to the world's potential trouble spots.

It had been a long day. Members of the Unit, now changed for the evening, some of them after a refreshing swim, began to gather in the Defenders Bar. Jakko and Jamina settled at a small table, she as usual with fruit juice. 'What about tomorrow?' Jakko asked. 'There's that big World Citizens Alliance election rally at the Olympic Stadium. I'd like to hear what they say. We didn't see much "live" in the country.'

Jamina told him that her family had asked her to spend the weekend in Edinburgh. 'My mother isn't well,' she added. 'Why don't you go, Jakko? You can tell me about it when I get back on Sunday night.'

50

* * *

Jakko made his way alone to the Stadium next day. If Jamina wasn't with him, he didn't want to be with anyone else. He was homesick, if the truth be known.

The rally was scheduled to begin at 1430. The Olympic Stadium held a quarter of a million people, but Jakko arrived very early to be sure of a good seat. Visible display of any political allegiance was banned in the WPF. He wore his plain-clothes suit to avoid any trouble. He inserted his World cents fifty, passed through the automatic turnstiles, was dispensed a glossy souvenir programme of the afternoon's proceedings, and took the escalator to a position in the south grandstand. He selected a seat immediately facing the platform erected specially in the huge arena.

In each of the great covered stands vast telescreens and loud speakers faced the thousands of seats opposite while giant floodlights, unlit in the bright afternoon sun, gazed down on the scene like huge muted animals. Enormous green, black, and white Party flags of the World Citizens Alliance fluttered from tall flagpoles around the stadium and above the central platform. All was quiet and orderly.

Jakko took in the scene, the atmosphere of a pending big occasion, then opened his souvenir programme at the centre spread. The afternoon would be introduced by the UK Secretary General of WCA; then at 1450 the guest of honour, Madame Li, President of the ruling Alliance Party in THE GREAT FEDERATION OF THE EAST, would release 1040 white doves of peace (one for each seat in the World Assembly) from the centre of the arena, formally to open the proceedings. Speeches would follow from the WCA's UK candidates in the forthcoming election; an interval of martial music to quicken the pulse; then a rallying call from Madame Li — one of the world's most passionate and dynamic orators. As a finale, a quarter of a million voices would be raised in the WCA anthem, hands outstretched in friendship to the peoples of the world.

By 1400 the trickle of people had become a flood, the great stadium filling rapidly as its monorail, coach parks, and helipads fed seemingly endless crowds through the turnstiles. It was the last major WCA rally in England before the world election.

The Party organizers were to pull out all the stops, turning

51

to good account the techniques which long ago had — by contrast — so brilliantly brought evil to power in Nazi Germany: use of huge numbers, slogans, and precision; the belief of millions in their leaders, themselves, and their own infallibility; rousing speeches, music, colour, inspiration; the spontaneous raising in unison amidst frenzied cheers of a sea of hands as far as the eye could see into the distance. The WCA with religious fervour was out to win a clear majority in the World Assembly. Nothing must stand in the way of that attainment. Half an hour before the scheduled arrival of the three UK Candidates, the Party's own band marched into the arena with an escort of green WCA banners, to applause from those already seated. Its task: with a selection of popular light music to put the huge crowd into friendly mood while they waited and the last places were filled.

Jakko was as susceptible to these devices and to reasoned argument as any of the many thousands present. All he knew of world politics he had gleaned from television and the news sheets. He had a vague idea that the WCA's policies were based upon freedom of the individual, equal opportunity, and people working together all over the world . . . and upon commonsense, like the Alliance government in his own country. That all seemed terribly obvious, like the need *to create wealth before it could be shared, or spent* to *provide the world's people with a full, happy life.* Now he sat in the sun, watching the last seats being occupied around him, contentedly listening to the music while he leafed once more through the programme; open to persuasion, if that was the way they wanted it, when he noticed two girls sidling their way towards him from the escalator. They deposited their two shoulder bags under the adjacent seats and settled. As they did so, the nearest, very fair with freckles, in jeans and a canary day smock, gave him a once-over with a 'Hi! OK if we sit here?'

With Jamina in Edinburgh, nothing was further from Jakko's mind than the chatting-up of any new acquaintance. He mumbled 'Of course' or something similar in non-committal tones and returned his attention to the preparations going on in the arena, but presently his next-door neighbour nudged his elbow. 'My name's Sylvie Mennin,' she said, holding out a bag of sweets. 'Have a bull's-eye.' She shook her head and the fair hair. 'Going to be hot,' she declared, unintentionally dropping her programme under the seats. The unsophisticated naturalness was so up Jakko's street that he felt compelled to be friendly.

52

He retrieved the girl's programme and took one of the proffered bull's-eyes with some difficulty because they were all stuck together in the bag. The bull's-eye had a stripe round it like the revolving sign outside a barber's shop. 'Thanks,' he said, parking it on one side of his mouth, 'I'm Jakko Mann,' adding proudly 'I'm in the WPF. We're not supposed to *have* any party politics . . . but of course we can vote as individuals like everybody else. It will be my first world election.'

'Me too,' said Sylvie. She seemed suddenly to remember her companion. 'Jakko, this is my friend Doris. Doris, this is Jakko . . .' proudly, 'Jakko's in the WPF.'

That body's latest volunteer sensed that he had already been 'adopted'; that he was being shown off by Sylvie Mennin as her very own exhibit A. The Doris character didn't seem particularly interested. She continued to gaze into space, chewing aimlessly like a retarded bovine; but it was of no consequence, because at that moment the music stopped and the giant telescreens sprang to life all round the ground with a head and shoulders picture of the WCA's UK General Secretary.

'Friends; welcome to the last World Assembly Election rally in England of the WORLD CITIZENS ALLIANCE.' Wild cheers from strategically planted pockets of spectators. As intended, this was infectious. The rally hadn't even begun, but the name of the party was enough. 'WORLD CITIZENS ALLIANCE! . . . UP THE WCA!' People were already standing, Sylvie among them, waving their programmes. 'Come on, Jakko!' she shouted. 'UP THE WCA! . . .'

Jakko was impressed by this spontaneous if naive enthusiasm, but he was too nervous to join in. In any case, he knew little about WCA policy. He was spared the necessity to make a decision because suddenly everyone sat down again. No signal had been given; the huge assembly appeared in some extraordinary way to be on their very own VHF wavelength. If one moved, so did the rest: a phenomenon better known in nature. 'Friends,' the telescreen figure continued, 'we have a few minutes before the programme begins. Let me set the scene for you.

'In the last World Parliament, the World Citizens Alliance — the Government party — held 438 seats in the 1040-seat Assembly: that is the lower, decision-making House, like our House of Commons. The Alliance was the largest single group, but it did not have a majority over all other parties. In the last Parliament, we witnessed on occasion a strange combination of extreme elements of right and left to defeat government measures designed for the common good, as if they wanted — for their own ends — to perpetuate the *divisions* among the peoples of the world. Here in the UK we are not unfamiliar with such tactics. A hundred years ago, our then Conservative and Labour parties — each financed largely by and answerable to one section of the electorate — resented equally the emergence of *our* Alliance. The two old parties behaved as if they had a divine right to govern alternately, each government seeking to reverse the legislation of its predecessor. Little wonder that our industry, industrial relations, indeed our whole life — even health and education — were starved of a creative sense of purpose; bedevilled with uncertainty as to the future after the next five years. It took a long time for this country to recover from such insane inhibitions and lack of the discussion and consensus so beneficial in Continental politics. Indeed, with its absurd electoral system, the UK was subjected to anti-common currency and anti-federal propaganda, besides uncompromising dogma and ill-considered domestic measures, by a Government which had never won a majority of votes. Moreover, minority voices, not to mention many of its own supporters, were largely unheeded. By contrast, on the Continent, measures usually reflected a majority view.

'In the World Assembly, the WCA has been supported by the Greens, and some minority groups with whom we are in enthusiastic agreement upon most issues. With their support we have placed valuable legislation on the World statute book. However, we cannot always be sure of their support. If we are to complete the REVOLUTION . . .' sustained organized cheers . . . '*if we are to complete our REVOLUTION, we must have a clear majority.* This election is vital for the peoples of the world . . .' More applause.

The picture faded, to be replaced immediately — to sustain the momentum — by that of a goodly assembly of trumpets as they blared forth a fanfare which must have been audible from Land's End to brave, stricken London. Then the World's unofficial Anthem, once *Chorus of the Hebrew Slaves*, as a quarter of a million of its citizens rose to their feet. Although in plain-clothes, Jakko found himself standing at attention: an automatic

54

reaction after his first intense, disciplined week in the WPF. Out of the corner of his eye he glanced at Sylvie Mennin — she would be about eighteen — in her canary-coloured smock. He was surprised that she too was standing, rigid. These people — even the very young — really *believed*. He suddenly realized how inspiring — and yet dangerous — it all was: thousands literally mesmerized by an idea. It was all splendid as long as the party in power really had the interests of the PEOPLE at heart. But what if power corrupted and that power was used for evil ends? Of course the answer, he realized, was that *they would be swept out at the next election.* Jakko was so absorbed in his own thoughts that he found himself still standing while everyone else was resuming their seats. He hurried to do likewise.

'Fellow Citizens. It is now my privilege to invite Madame Li to release one thousand and forty doves of peace.'

That lady took the mike, her familiar, petite but resolute figure portrayed on the screens. 'I regard it a privilege to perform this ceremony. In releasing these symbols of goodwill, I remind the people and governments yet to join the World Federation that — since its Assembly first came into being — seats for their elected representatives have been kept ready for them, awaiting their arrival.' She paused. 'Will you now all please be kind and remain seated and quiet for the doves. I release to the blue sky one bird of peace for every seat in the World Assembly, with the hope that those who have not yet joined us do so soon. Let it be ONE WORLD.'

Suddenly, the *whrr* of two thousand wings at full power during take-off. The birds rose from the arena, circling the stadium in the sunlight; then, getting their bearings, they headed away in groups one after another and were gone.

'Wasn't that lovely,' Sylvie exclaimed excitedly as the whole stadium broke into applause. Jakko felt her grasp his hand. They looked down simultaneously. Sylvie giggled. 'Oh . . . sorry! I sort of got carried away.'

The three UK candidates had been chosen for maximum combined appeal. Roy Springer-Smith, City figure and former England athlete, spoke on world finance; Di Davies, hill farmer from Wales, upon the environment: concerted action for the saving of the world; Moira Mackie, a fiery redhead from the Borders, upon preservation of World peace.

'We still live in a dangerous world,' Citizen Mackie concluded forcefully. 'I regret . . . we all do . . . that the WPF has to remain armed with weapons that should long since have been outlawed by a civilized society. *But as long as there remain unstable elements outside the world family of nations, and they possess hideous weapons of annihilation, so long must we retain a powerful deterrent WORLD FORCE FOR PEACE. That is WCA policy. That is common sense.*

'I stress the word "powerful". The WPF is no mere token force, and it is geared to instant action anywhere, its command structure constantly rehearsed. This is a far cry from units from various individual states of the old UN, with no proper chain of command or co-operative experience.

'*We cannot have ever again a situation in which those who support international law are widely believed to be motivated equally by purely national interest.* That divides world opinion at a time when unanimity is most essential. *Nor can we afford international discord resulting from unequal contribution to the common good.* That in the Iraqi context, did significant, if temporary, harm to European unity.

'Members of the WPF, those who wear its uniform, wear on their shoulders the insignia of their own countries. It is natural and with much pride that they do so. But *THEIR ALLEGIANCE IS TO THE WHOLE WORLD COMMUNITY. There are no national units in the WPF. ITS ACTION ON BEHALF OF ALL MANKIND CANNOT BE SUSPECT.*

'I look forward to the day when *all* the world's people are united, when every individual nation and faction has put away its arms. *Then* the World Peace Force — our defence by deterrence — can put much of *its* heavy armament away; but not until that happy state is reached and the world is a safe place in which to live. Let us hasten that day with courage, genuine friendship, and with understanding. Those who are well-intentioned have nothing they need fear.'

This sanity was well received, but the resulting wave of applause was drowned almost immediately by the Alliance band striking up a popular new march. The telescreens all round the arena were filled with shots of earlier WCA rallies: thousands of spectators, their hands raised in friendship to the World. It was the interval, but the fever must at all costs be maintained.

'Jakko,' Sylvie shouted suddenly above the hubbub. 'Don't go away, will you. Perhaps we could go on somewhere afterwards. I'm just going to spend a penny.' The phrase had survived long after the currency. She got up, prodding the reluctant Doris with 'You coming?' and they disappeared.

* * *

As the Party General Secretary returned to the screens to reintroduce Madame Li, Jakko suddenly realized that he had been too absorbed to notice that the girls had not returned. A long time to spend in the cloakroom. But it was no more than a passing thought. Maybe there had been a queue. Then he noticed out of the corner of his eye the two shoulder bags still there, under the seats. Reassured, he settled to listen to Madame Li on the WCA Revolution.

9

The introductory fanfare died away, with a quarter of a million world electors eager to hear Madame Li.

'I bring you greetings from the Great Federation of the East, where we — the World Citizens Alliance — do hold a clear majority of World Assembly seats.' Applause. 'That is as well,' — this with a twinkle clearly discernible — 'because there are so many of us.' She added importantly, 'But of course we vote on *Party* lines, like the members from every Federation.'

Thence straight into the attack, the diminutive figure punching the air to the delight of her huge audience.

'I have been asked to speak to you today upon WCA policy in the field of wealth and industrial relations or, as I call it, the treating of people as PEOPLE. This, above all, distinguishes the WCA from all parties and is a topic dear to us in the GFE, particularly in China after its hideous experience towards the end of the last century.

'Of course, all Men are not "created equal", but they should have an equal chance to develop and then to use the talent that they have, and (with emphasis) *to enjoy the fruits of their labours.* Basic rights and freedoms have been guaranteed — at least in theory — for a long time. In today's world we take these things for granted: the right of every member of the human race to health, education, opportunity; equality before the law; freedom of movement, speech, assembly, religion; from discrimination on account of race or sex; the *right to work* and *to be paid a fair wage.* All this was enshrined in UN charters, documents, and declarations, and has been spelt out more recently of course in the World's Bill of Rights. In passing, let me remind you that the World Bill of *Rights* refers also to *duties*: reflecting the rebirth of a creative society. That is a most important, indeed a quite vital parenthesis. Parts of the West in particular — forgive me — were sick with an obsession with what could be got out of life; as distinct from what could be put in. But . . . to continue . . . there is one glaring omission: *a required sharing by the individual in the fruits of his labour; required by law, as distinct from at the hands only of benevolent employers*: private, co-operative, *or* state.

'I am well-known for my next comment, but it is essential to Alliance policy. There was, basically, little to chose between old Capitalism and Communism in this context. The worker remained a hired hand — selling his labour to some corporation or other employer or the State, paid — in either case — at a fixed rate not as a general rule related to the success of the enterprise or to individual effort.

'It is hardly surprising that, in an atmosphere so lacking in incentive, the results under *both* systems were frequently so poor. In the capitalist case, of the three necessary elements: those who financed the business, directed and managed, or worked to produce the goods or services, only the shareholders always shared in the profits; sometimes senior management in bonus or incentive schemes; but rarely *all* those who had made the profit possible. As for 'State Ownership', that was the biggest swindle ever put across the human race. The *people* did not own their country, factories, the land, the goods they produced, transport, or other service industries. They owned their toothbrushes and a few personal possessions. We witnessed the failure of Marxism in Africa, South-East Asia, Eastern Europe, and in the USSR itself, and its disincentive effect; and of course later in China, with the shedding of much blood.

'Now is the age of the INDIVIDUAL CITIZEN,' the GFE Alliance President declared. '*PEOPLE MATTER, AT LAST.* Man has come into his own. This and WISO — World Individual Share Ownership — constitute a greater revolution by far than ever was achieved before. It took the WORLD CITIZENS ALLIANCE to bring all this about. Let the people *enthuse. We are advocating incentives for the whole world to create wealth . . . and then for it to be shared.* There is no limit to the benefits that this can bring. *We must have a clear majority* if we are to see this through.'

Madame Li then launched into detail, before considering WISO, as to how an Alliance majority World Government would lay down the basic principles to ensure worker representation on every board, profit sharing, and ownership of shares if desired, by everyone engaged in business. Every undertaking — starting with the world's largest — would be required to devise and submit for approval its own scheme incorporating the principles laid down ... or in impracticable circumstances it could request exemption. Its directors knew best their own industry, conditions, personnel. There would be no dictating as to detail by remote 'we know best' World or Regional authorities. It was the liberal, commonsense way to implement the principles: decisions by people, not for them. Public utilities would have to submit schemes like the rest.

'When we have finished,' Madame Li declared, 'everyone will be concerned — individually as a human being — and will care personally that the enterprise in which he or she works is a success. Moreover, those hitherto divided into two so-called "sides", employer and employee, will be *united* in their efforts in both state *and* private enterprise, *and* in work for the community and the humanities.

'I turn to World Individual Share Ownership: "Le Wiso", as I believe you call it in Europe.

'The idea itself is not new. What is new is Government action: instead of wishy-washy incentives, people — ALL the people — MATTER AT LAST. That cannot be said too often. This is nothing less than a NEW REVOLUTION. It leaves old-fashioned Capitalism and Communism far behind.

'Capitalism was supposed to provide jobs so that everyone earned enough to live, although the educated and ambitious would earn more than the rest. When there wasn't enough work to go round or individuals became elderly, handicapped, or disadvantaged, the State would provide welfare payments. Hence the term Welfare Capitalism. But where was the money to come from to finance all this ... and the necessary spending in those days on so-called defence? Answer: by mechanization, use of computers, robots and technology to increase profits, reducing still further in the process the number of human beings gainfully employed!

'Meanwhile, even a century ago, with social expenditure at anything up to a third of GDP, the existing system in your Capitalist West was already under strain. Health was the second largest "welfare" item, exceeded only by pensions, and *both* those elements were related to an ageing population. European governments were then estimating that a fifth of their populations would be over sixty-five within the next sixty years, with one in ten over seventy-five. In some other parts of the world — Australia, Canada, and Turkey were instanced — the over-seventy-five's were expected to *quadruple*. By 2050, more than one person in five in Germany and France would, it was reckoned, be aged eighty or over, with one in three over sixty-five. Moreover, health spending was four times as great per head on those over sixty-five as upon those under that age, and nearly *six times* on the over-seventies. And of course at that time, AIDS was still spreading.

'There were only three alternatives: the State could go on endeavouring under the existing Capitalist system to cope with the ever-increasing demand for welfare payments, until it — the State — went bankrupt. Secondly, it could "scrimp and scrape" — isn't that how you describe it — providing an ever-deteriorating service, leading to unacceptable human misery and degradation until the system finally collapsed. The third alternative was to introduce a completely new system, in which individuals — I refer to the majority who were not rich — *take care of their own needs, unemployment, sickness, and old age.*'

Madame Li paused and took a sip of fruit juice. The vast audience was attentive, silent.

'And what of Communism?' she resumed her theme; 'long regarded as the natural, indeed the only alternative; or maybe, as I am in England, I should use the word Socialism which in the political sense meant "common ownership of the means of production, distribution, and exchange." State ownership or nationalization was tried for fifty years and found wanting; not surprisingly since, in the final analysis, under that system *the individual owns nothing at all.* He is almost wholly dependent on the State, which — due to the disincentive effects of the system — is even less able to fund its welfare programme.

'We see therefore that WISO, *in which every law-abiding individual (besides what he earns) becomes a Capitalist, given an income-producing personal stake in the world's means of production*, was not simply a bright idea. It answered the question "Who was to own the robots?" It was new. It was exciting. *It was an idea whose time had come.*' Applause round the giant stadium.

'You will forgive me, before I enlarge on the eventual implementation worldwide of what at present is still functioning

61

in only some countries, if —, since I am privileged to be here in England — I comment briefly on your part in all this. Your governments of the 1980s, or to be more precise, your then Prime Minister, *demonstrated precisely how the problem should not be handled.* The problem was certainly recognized, and frantic efforts made for its solution: to raise the money by virtually any means and, in face of ever-increasing demand, to keep welfare spending within bounds. Your people were urged, even ''lectured'' upon the virtues of becoming self-reliant, while Government policies steadily *widened* the gap between rich and poor, making self-reliance even less possible for many.

'National assets were sold to those who could afford to buy them, and the proceeds used to lower personal taxation. Rather obviously, those who paid most tax were the most favoured, not the majority repeatedly exhorted to stand on their own feet.

'Once the merits of WISO became widely recognized and the concept began to catch on like a forest fire, came the ghastly realization that North Sea Oil and the previously nationalized UK means of production and income-producing services could have given your country a head start, unique in the whole world, in the implementation of individual share ownership. *Instead of those assets being distributed to the whole adult population or to People's Trusts, which have since become the pattern, in which units are distributed, they were in our context squandered: sold off to institutions and the minority who could afford to buy.* Lack of vision is surely the most generous judgement. *It was*, although realized by few at the time, *a tragedy on a gigantic scale.*'

Madame Li raised her arms, appealing to each side of the Stadium in turn. 'But let us now look forward: to improve and to extend individual ownership *so that everyone may hold up his head with dignity* and *everywhere the State be relieved of the burden that it cannot bear.* Simultaneously we have to plan a vast increase in cultural and recreational facilities that everyone will have the time and the money to enjoy. *Only WE believe enough . . . are bold enough.*

'FORWARD . . . *FORWARD WITH THE WCA*!'

At this, the claques planted around the stadium led renewed applause; thousands joining in, standing in their places, frenziedly waving their programmes.

* * *

62

Jakko eventually resumed his seat. Once again, it registered in his mind that the two seats next to him were empty. He reached for the nearest of the two shoulder bags, hoping that he might find some clue to the owner's identity or an address. There was hardly any weight there. He unzipped the bag. Inside was a light cardigan. Of course; in case in the evening it became too cool for those summer smocks the two girls had been wearing. Then a mini-camera.

Then he felt something solid underneath. He pulled it out instinctively. It took only a split-second of a young active brain to register what lay in his hand: the small, neat face of the timing device, the attached container which would hold enough of the world's very latest super-lightweight explosive to ensure death and mutilation over a wide area. There was no doubt in Jakko's mind. He had taken one of these deadly things to bits in class only the day before. But *Sylvie . . . whatever was she doing?* He returned instantly to the present. The stands held a quarter of a million unsuspecting souls . . . and there was the *other* shoulder bag as well, under the next seat. Inevitably his attention was focused once more on the dial. There were two minutes left.

* * *

Jakko stood motionless for a moment, numbed, rooted to the spot, holding the very latest terrorist bomb: a devastating killer. In all probability there was a second one under the seat not more than two metres away. In a crazy way his brain started to count the seconds remaining: a hundred and twenty . . . his thoughts were still coherent, logical . . . call it a hundred to be on the safe side . . . ninety-nine, ninety-eight, ninety-seven . . .

Most of the huge audience were standing, the attention of everyone on Madame Li. Jakko suddenly felt terribly alone with his secret . . . or did Sylvie know? . . . but in any case she couldn't help him now.

He made a conscious effort to motivate himself. There could be only about ninety seconds left. As a member of the World Peace Force, he must act quickly . . . set an example . . . somehow prevent a terrible disaster.

Providence had so organized it that he knew from the preceding day's lecture at EURO College 11 what he must do.

He reached under the seats and, without waiting to inspect the contents of the second bag, made for the escalator, the bomb still in one hand, the girl Doris's shoulder bag now in the other. Jakko was excellent WPF material. Already, instinctively, he had rejected the possibility of defusing the device, let alone two. There wasn't time. In any case, he did not have the necessary tools. He had to run for it . . . to get the bombs out of the stadium before they could explode. He thought quickly, remembering the vast coach park outside the gate through which he had entered the complex. The huge multi-seat buses would be empty except for a few drivers chatting and comparing notes; the rows of coaches would be capable of absorbing the force of the explosions. That was where he would throw the bombs. He ran headlong down the moving escalator, brushing aside two officials at the bottom with a cry of 'WPF . . . Look out! . . . *EXPLOSIVES* . . . LET ME OUT!'

He gained the open air . . . had lost count of time. There had to be a few seconds left. The bombs ought to be thrown in to the *middle* of the mass of metal and glass. He ran on, transferring the bomb in his hand to the shoulder bag; then swung the bag with all his strength and released his hold.

To his surprise, Jakko felt an almost irresistible desire to wait for the explosions; then in a split second his common sense reasserted itself. He turned back to save his own life if he could.

10

Crawley City Hospital. Casualty.

Jakko Mann opened his eyes. The Casualty Sister and a doctor in a white coat entered his consciousness. There were a number of other figures waiting in the background. There seemed to be one or two in Police uniform, but Jakko's vision was blurred. He tried to assess which pieces of him were still working. Things were a bit fuzzy, but he felt little pain. Then the doctor spoke.

'Jakko, can you hear me? You are in Crawley City Hospital. You are a very fortunate young man. You were knocked out by the blast of the explosions; you have extensive bruising where you hit the tarmac; you have a few superficial cuts from flying glass . . . but your distance from the explosions was such that their force was largely spent. We already know that you have no serious injury. Blast is an odd thing. You have been lucky. You got just far enough away. Terrorist Officers in the UK civil Police will want, urgently, to ask you a few questions, and Mr Goodssen of the WPF is here. Aside from a few minutes' conversation, we want you to rest.' He patted Jakko's hand that lay above the bedclothes. 'Well done,' he added before standing aside.

It was Goodssen's turn. 'We will have plenty of time later. The terrorist people want to talk to you now . . . if you feel up to it. I just came to see that you were in one piece and to congratulate you. Apart from preventing innumerable casualties in the stadium, you have — once again — done immeasurable good to the image of the WPF. The more people the world over realize that the Force is their friend, the more they will believe in One World. We look forward to having you back at College very soon.' Jakko managed 'Thank you, Sir', and Goodssen left him to the civil Police. ,

At this point the doctor returned to assure himself that Jakko could face questioning. The Terrorist Squad officers settled quietly round the bed, accompanied by a WPC to record Jakko's story. After he had told them in his own words the events of that afternoon, they asked him — naturally enough — to tell them everything that he could remember about Sylvie Mennin and her friend.

Jakko gave them a detailed description of each girl. It was obvious how the minds of the Police officers were working. The girls had planted the bombs and left on the pretext of going to the loo. They must have been miles away by the time the bombs went off. Had that been so, Jakko told himself, Sylvie had left him — deliberately and cold-bloodedly — to be blown to pieces. He just didn't believe it. Of course, he told the Police, some ill-intentioned maniac had planted the devices in their bags. He recalled the last thing that Sylvie said: 'Don't go away, will you. Perhaps we could go on somewhere afterwards.' And the bull's-eye with the stripes round it. So natural. She was just a kid. She would never have positively *asked him to stay*.

'I understand your feelings of course,' one of the Terrorist Squad reassured him. 'But if you are right, we have to discover everywhere those girls had been if we are to catch this madman.'

* * *

The initial diagnosis proved optimistic. True enough, no bones were broken, but Jakko's balance was affected, although it turned out to be temporary. A week under observation, however, provided anything but the prescribed rest. While not occupied by hospital staff, further questioning, or visits by his family and fellow Peace Force volunteers, Jakko's thoughts were in disarray.

His innocent mind couldn't understand why anyone should disrupt a gathering designed to foster the interests of the entire world population. It was 'Fuck the WPF' all over again. He hadn't fully grasped the details of WCA policy, yet was afraid to display his ignorance. But he could ask Jamina; she would be able to explain. 'You can tell me about it on Sunday', she had said, referring to the rally. But why had she not been to see him? Maybe she was detained in Edinburgh. He hoped fervently that that was so. Had it been Jamina who was injured, he would have been first at her side. It tortured him that perhaps, for all her gestures of affection, she didn't really care. And determination was evident in the Terrorist Squad that Sylvie was mixed up with the bombing. He found himself regretting, whatever his obvious duty, that he had ever mentioned her to the authorities. Yet, had he not done so, they might have suspected *him*.

As soon as he could get discharged from Crawley City Hospital, he would do two things: ask Jamina to explain urgently the detailed workings of WISO, opponents of which were prepared even to kill; and he would conduct his own urgent search for Sylvie Mennin.

Jakko returned to College after the following weekend. Jamina was still absent in Scotland, but he was reassured by a card that she would be back that night. Waiting letters from WPF EURO HQ Notified him formally of two Commendations.

He found himself the centre of attention, fellow volunteers eager to hear about the discovery of the bombs and how he had managed to get them out of the giant stadium in time, while Jakko was more concerned to discover what classes he had missed.

Thoughtfully, notes on the missing lectures had been left by Pippa Brightwell in his room, with a note offering to go over them in his spare time. He had missed discussion of political developments since the latter part of the previous century; the period had embraced the most momentous hundred years since the Creation; human behaviour at last matching progress in technology and a newly caring attitude towards the environment, living things, and the survival of the world.

* * *

'Let us be grateful always for the blessings of the Earth ... ' As, after grace, conversation broke out amongst those assembled for dinner, Jamina entered the great dining hall. Jakko's pulse quickened as she waited for a suitable moment to ask the evening's president if she might be seated, then he caught her eye as she made for a spare place at the table's end, and a noncommittal smile filled him with simultaneous longing and anxiety. He turned hurriedly to talk to neighbours lest they guess his thoughts.

At last the silver model gun carriage completed its circuit with port and cognac in two large ships' decanters, the WPF toast 'Ladies and Gentlemen, THE PEACE OF THE WORLD', and he was free to leave the table.

Jamina waited for Jakko by the mural of the Ark; greeted him with a good-natured 'Hello hero!' They left the dining area together until she disengaged her hand with 'Let's go to my room.'

She sat on her bed as usual, waving Jakko to the big armchair. The telescreen was silent. 'Well. Tell me all about it. Was your Sylvie *very* gorgeous? She looked pretty in the news sheets.'

Jakko had been waiting, after a personal welcome, to discuss WCA policy. The question was the last that the young man expected. 'Not *my* Sylvie,' he replied defensively. 'The Terrorist people have got it in for her, but I don't believe that she knew about the bombs.'

'Why then doesn't she come forward voluntarily?' Jakko sensed an unexpected hardness in the comment.

'I'm sure she's frightened. She is very young. I bet she's just lying low.'

'Not very clever of her,' said Jamina in similar vein. She changed the subject abruptly. 'Jakko, have you ever made love to a girl?'

'Well . . .' hesitantly, 'not exactly.'

She spared him further embarrassment. 'Would you like to make love to *me*? I can teach you, dear. You are a brave boy, and I would like to do that. Just let me lock the door.'

She took Jakko's hands in hers and pulled him to his feet. 'First of all you can undress me. That will stir the instincts; put you in the mood. Then we'll get into bed and do some exploring, and I'll show you what to do.'

Jakko, unbelieving, awed, stood gazing; emotions further kindled by the trace of scent; young, healthy, already aroused, but afraid to touch.

Jamina slowly took his hand, guided it to the shoulder button of her smock, then reaching for the dimmer switch, slowly found his mouth and entwined his body with her own. 'You can forget Sylvie,' she said.

68

11

Jakko joined Jamina after lunch the following day. They made their way to the College arboretum for a stroll before afternoon lectures. 'You are very beautiful,' Jakko ventured, feeling himself flush once again at her reply. 'And *you* are so natural, unspoiled, and so *strong*.'

They walked on without further conversation, taking in the beauty of the trees, new season's leaves of different species unfolding in their fashion; the occasional early bumblebee searching for spring flowers in the shafts of sunlight at their feet.

Presently Jakko broke the silence. 'Do you live actually *in* Edinburgh? I don't think I'd like to be cut off from nature and the countryside. One is sort of near God out in the fields, with the animals and the crops growing. It's a personal, friendly feeling. I suppose one has more time to think about it too . . . when ploughing, for instance. I nearly joined the Environment Corps, and then I saw the ads about the "elite". It was a challenge, really.'

Jamina squeezed his hand. 'Jakko, you *are* very special.' A pause. Then 'Yes. My family do live *in* Edinburgh. It is a proud, independent city — the St Andrew's Cross flies everywhere — unhappy and frustrated until the first Alliance Government at Westminster introduced a commonsense measure of devolution to Scotland, Wales, and the English regions. That was a reversal of the obsession by governments of the eighties to centralize everything and emasculate local decision-making.

'The Greater London Council was abolished simply because its *elected* policies for the time being were at variance with Whitehall, leaving London the world's only capital with no co-ordinating body; likewise the ILEA, which at least had the merit of protecting children in the poorer boroughs by spreading fairly the available resources. Yes, rightfully, Edinburgh is now a capital city, besides a major financial and artistic centre. But one is soon out in the country. Since the climate warmed we have grown maize in the south (for export to Africa), and we had to develop new tree species for the Highlands.'

They stopped and sat down among the pine needles. Jakko changed the subject, reverting to their college course. 'Pippa Brightwell asked me if I'd like to go over with her after dinner tonight the lecture I missed on Ulster ... how the problems there were solved ... and of course there's South Africa too.' Jamina disclosed that she also had been invited, adding, 'And then you and I have to get down to Le WISO ... funny how the whole world seems to have adopted the franglais, in spite of French efforts to keep their language pure.'

* * *

The Captain wasted no time as they settled in a small lecture room that evening. 'Let's deal with Ulster. Towards the end of the last century the British faced an impossible choice. Rightly, *they refused to abandon a population of which overwhelming majorities in successive referenda had opted to remain a part of the United Kingdom.* Indeed — apart from the Gibraltarians and Falkland Islanders — no population had ever by then more clearly or so often made such a choice. Additionally, the British *were determined to demonstrate that no problem could be solved by terrorism*, whether or not encouraged, financed, and supplied from overseas, as Ulster had been from the United States and Libya. In their resolve, successive British governments also believed — like those who refused to pander to kidnap, hostage-taking, and hijack — that they were setting an example to the world.

'But to oust the British and unite their country was a just cause in Irish eyes.

'On the British mainland, resentment steadily increased at the cost, both financial and in human misery: the barbaric maiming and killing by the IRA of innocent civilians, the Police, and British troops whose only job was to preserve the peace and protect the citizen.

'It took UK Governments until nearly the turn of the century to accept that neither side could ever win the ''war''. *Yet, simply* to pull out peace-keeping forces would be to surrender ... to prove that terrorism paid if pursued relentlessly to a conclusion.

'Undoubtedly, the eventual compromise was the best that could have been devised. As you know, the new British Government finally gave notice in 1997 that it was prepared *NEITHER to endure indefinitely the mounting cost in money, blood, and suffering, NOR to abandon to violence those with the declared wish to remain British.* In 1997 a three-year time limit was set for withdrawal of peace-keeping forces from the province, after which — as one UK MP put it, for which he was rebuked instantly and suspended from the Chamber — ''The Irish people would be left to their own devices: to kill and maim each other to their hearts' content.'' During the intervening three years, terrorism would be ruthlessly suppressed by peace-keeping troops, heavily reinforced. No quarter would be given. Meanwhile, citizens of Northern Ireland who wished to cross the Irish Sea and live at peace in the UK would be given every possible assistance: financial, in the purchase of homes, and to find employment. In 2000, all troops would be withdrawn. All prisoners and detainees in Northern Ireland gaols, other than convicted murderers and bombers, would be freed.

'Climbdown or no, *the UK Government would be seen to have kept faith with loyalty, while at the same time ridding itself of a terrible responsibility and assisting in the creating, at last, of a united Ireland.*

'I think we should remind ourselves too of the substantial gestures made towards united Ireland by the British at the time of their withdrawal. First, there was the grant of ten million then sterling pounds to assist in cleaning up what had been part of the UK: removal of rubble, slogans of hatred, and so on. Then the encouragement of two further large manufacturing concerns to site new factories in the former province; awarding of contracts to the Belfast shipyard for a frigate for the Royal Navy; to their aircraft industry for a prototype large all-purpose plane to be presented to Mankind by the new imaginative British Government for use in the mitigation of drought, famine, and natural disasters. She was christened *Penelope* — ever-faithful — and, importantly for the world, became the forerunner of the fleets of special aircraft now operated at World Government expense by the Environment Corps and World Aid Organization.

'Last, but to me not least, was the creating for the people

of Belfast of the/hundred acres City Park under the direction of the Royal Horticultural Society, at British Government expense. It was completed in 2004 and then handed over to the care of the Belfast Corporation. Now mature, eighty years on, the Park is exceptionally beautiful and indeed commercial. It draws large numbers of visitors to Ireland from all over the world.'

'Honest endeavour, surely,' commented Jamina.

'Yes, but *neither* side could justly claim a victory,' Pippa Brightwell continued. 'The hated "Brits" had finally withdrawn. Not much honour in that. For *their* part, the Irish were faced with realization that appreciable numbers of ordinary, decent, law-abiding folk would rather pull up their roots and leave than live amongst people so blighted with hatred that they were incapable of civilized behaviour. But after "Bloody Sunday" the guns at last were silent; the barricades were down; and a massive cleanup had begun. That was the victory.'

'What *about* Bloody Sunday?' It was Jakko.

'It was the final confrontation. The IRA planned vast "victory" parades in Dublin and throughout Northern Ireland. The hated British had surrendered and were pulling out. Demonstrations would be held on both sides of the border on an unprecedented scale even for the Irish: massed bands, parades, the carrying of thousands upon thousands of photo placards of those who over the long years had died "on active service", including those killed while putting together or planting their own bombs. Millions of rounds of then surplus IRA ammunition were to be discharged in volley after volley in honour of their dead. While thanksgiving services were being held in Dublin and Westminster Abbey and in churches all over the former province, the IRA planned their final bombing — mercifully detected — to decimate the Abbey congregation. It is difficult now to credit such an act, but Irish fanatics had shown their colours thirteen years before by bombing an Armistice Day gathering *of all people*, and later by their plans in 1988 to blow to pieces indiscriminately in a Gibraltar street troops on ceremonial duty, bystanders, and — inevitably — innocent children. The Westminster authorities had been prepared for the unspeakable.

'In view of their own honest endeavours, the British Government was not disposed to allow IRA "victory"

72

celebrations in the face of what it genuinely believed to be magnanimity and a civilized solution. Large reinforcements were deployed and clashes were inevitable. In a number of areas, security forces fired over their heads to disperse hostile crowds. It was inevitable that somewhere someone would be hurt. After being fired on by the IRA at two forbidden demonstrations, the security forces finally replied in kind, to the years-old cry of "Murderers". Twenty hooded, masked and armed IRA gunmen were shot down and several civilians wounded by stray ricochets . . . a not unexpected end to a long, long tragedy.

'The Irish Government, to its credit, did issue to the world a statement of gratitude to its UK counterpart for brave, sincere, efforts to assist the unification of their country and its regard for the rights and future of individual citizens.'

'One thing puzzles me,' admitted Jamina. 'Once both the UK and Ireland became members of the EEC, the inhabitants of both became Europeanized. Surely inter-state boundaries should have ceased to have their old-fashioned, traditional effect?'

'In the context of present-day Europe,' Pippa Brightwell suggested, 'or indeed of any fully-fledged Federation, we know that Common Citizenship means what it says: a degree of subordination of purely national interest to a greater oneness. National customs and traditions will always survive, as we saw in earlier discussion of the very word "Federal" — and a good thing too — but there is a feeling of belonging to the greater whole. But remember that, at the time of the UK withdrawal from Ulster, the British in particular still had absolutely no gut feeling about being Europeans. Indeed they were still, as always, insular: cut off from the mainstream of Community feeling in spite of holidays abroad and the new physical contact by the Channel Tunnel. Remember, too, that, earlier, EEC stood for European *Economic* Community; a matter in those days of business and elimination of barriers to trade, rather than the pooling in European unity of *feeling* and of hearts and minds that we have now. Remember, too, the English Channel! Philip of Spain, Napoleon, and Adolf Hitler failed in turn to secure command of the Channel, without which no invasion of England could be launched. Even God was in favour of isolation! Referring to the Armada, the Drake Memorial on Plymouth Hoe is still inscribed five hundred years later, "He blew with

73

his winds and they were scattered".'

'Well,' sighed Jamina, 'I am no lover of Spain because of the cruelty to animals, and I would never holiday there, but thank God we are privileged in so many respects to live in more enlightened times.'

'Here,' said Captain Brightwell by way of rounding off the session, 'are some notes for each of you on Ireland. As you know, the history books refer to "England's Vietnam", and it's not such a bad description. But the then UK Government had done much to restore Britain's honour which had been damaged so shamefully in 1989 over the people of Hong Kong.'

12

While in the lunch break other members of their unit researched in the perhaps uniquely comprehensive Euro College library, which was supported by an impressive variety of UK companies and institutions, a leisurely walk in the woods became for Jakko and Jamina a routine. 'We can study in the evenings.' It was Jakko who led the conversation during these rambles, identifying trees and plants, describing the lifestyles of the creatures that they met; still somewhat in awe of his companion and glad to make a knowledgeable contribution.

In the evenings they went over the lessons of the day, often with contemporaries, sometimes alone together in Jamina's room at night, where discussion of unlikely subjects was combined with love. One such was 'Le Wiso', in anticipation of the promised missing lecture.

'Of course I didn't hear Madame Li on WISO at that World Election Rally,' Jakko mused. 'I was too busy with the bombs! Before the interruption, she had outlined the World Government's — or, rather, the WCA's — ideas on incentive schemes in industry and commerce: a say in direction, a sharing of profits by all who help to make them, ability to buy shares in the businesses in which they work; in short, treating people as *people*: not mere units in a production process. I understand all that. Actually, I find the variety of methods a bit bewildering, but the important thing is that World Government legislation will be understood by the man in the street. These things are already widely practised in the developed world: ESOPs, partnerships, workers' co-operatives, employee "buy-outs," and so on. It's just making sure, isn't it, that the principles become worldwide.'

Jamina agreed. 'And all this has increased productivity, and

75

much of the resulting wealth has been put to good use. The purpose of all such schemes was, however, limited to the treatment as human beings of everyone creating the wealth and to spread the ownership of capital and thus personal income besides that which is directly earned. That had everything to commend it as regards human dignity and the ability of the citizen to look after himself; but it did nothing for those not employed, or disadvantaged, or for the huge numbers who worked in service industries where profit for its own sake is not — or shouldn't be — the object, or where there is no profit to share. Nor indeed for those engaged in work for the environment and for the humanities. *Those left out comprised a strange assortment: the people who earned the least, who did the dirty jobs, the unemployed, the chronic poor, and the most noble.*

'Of course, my dearest Jakko, you are an idealist. And thank God there are more and more of them around these days. You would have volunteered for the WPF — or the Environment Corps — *whatever* the pay. One can add to the list everyone whose effort makes the planet habitable, keeps it safe, and makes the wheels go round. The schemes you have been talking about were the beginning, but WISO is *totally different.* Already it has made a vital contribution to wellbeing and a saving to the state. Eventually, *it will ensure to every law-abiding citizen a stake in the world's production.* The producer needn't be afraid of robots and computers. Science and technology need no longer be ogres causing unemployment. They will still further reduce his working hours, but will *increase* his wealth. Vitally . . . *everyone else, too,* will be included in WISO.'

* * *

During the next morning's break, Captain Brightwell sent for Jakko and Jamina (and a third, female, UK member of EURO 2001 who had missed the WISO lecture). 'The first of your world trips will be announced today. I shouldn't tell you, really; it's one of Goodssen's little idiosyncrasies: making it a surprise on which trip you will be going . . . but it will be on the telescreens anyway in the lunch hour. You leave next week for the Caribbean . . .' 'Super!' (Jakko) '. . . flying to Trinidad, then partly by sea. WPF craft naturally. The World Government

76

also sees these expeditions as goodwill visits, like your Royal Navy in days gone by.' This with a glance at the UK shoulder-flashes. 'The WG never misses an opportunity!

'Units invariably enjoy this one. The whole area is as steeped in historical memorabilia as it is in beauty, bananas and goodwill. Being part of pioneer Regions in the WISO context, *the island populations have progressed in two hundred and fifty years literally the whole way from slavery to the ultimate: personal ownership of a slice of the whole world's wealth.* I find the great statue of William Wilberforce outside the WISO administrative building in Antigua a source of inspiration. I'm sure that you will too.

'The College organizers didn't forget the environment or indeed Darwin and the turtles, or the mural here in the dining hall lobby! You spend a day flying over the rain forests and the mouths of the Amazon — fabulous — and across South America to the Galapagos Islands. As you know, it was there that the idea was born which later led to the theory of evolution.

'However, the reason I asked you to come along now was in fact *about* WISO. I think we should complete that discussion before you leave next week ... or it will remain outstanding while we press on with other things. I'd like you to give up this evening if you will. Please bring your own WISO cards with you.'

* * *

Captain Brightwell met the three of them in the Defenders Bar that evening and then, after enthusing about the unit's forthcoming trip, they migrated in friendly off-duty fashion to a small lecture room.

'Well,' the Captain began, 'we needn't detail the principles again. We all understand that neither Welfare Capitalism nor Communism spread wealth to *every* individual. The former accentuated the gap between rich and poor, the latter — with state ownership — was the antithesis of *individual* ownership and human dignity. Under both systems, the robots and computers created wealth but did not ensure its widespread distribution. Finally, of course, people were living longer, placing a welfare burden on the State which, in the end, could lead only to bankruptcy. Something pretty drastic had to be done!

'Before going/into detail, let me stress just once more that WISO must not be confused with Employee Share Ownership and other profit- and wealth-sharing limited to those working in enlightened companies. "Bully for them," to use a very old phrase. They were being *paid* anyway. But not much bully for anyone else! So ... how did WISO begin?

'The lead was given not by governments but by organizations and individual thinkers, notably in North America and Britain. In both, there was a good deal of informed debate: politically, as far as the UK was concerned, by the centre ... those who eventually — after many false dawns — voted in the first of our "Alliance" governments.

'The problem was largely administrative, once initial objections had been overcome: "free hand-outs to people only too happy to be paid *not* to work" etc., when in fact the whole of society was being *saved from financial collapse* and much more human misery.

'Three factors helped to dispel those (perhaps natural) fears. First, the WISO allocation is made from *new* capital. *There is no confiscation from existing stock — or shareholders*, and *no increased taxation* to pay for the allotments. Credit is provided by the banks. The new stock eventually pays for itself, first repaying the banks (with proper interest), and thereafter the dividends accrue via the WISO funds to all the unit holders. And, of course, far from WISO creating a state *expense* — another fear — vast sums of public money are *saved* by the cessation of "Social Security", and no additional civil service personnel are required; actually *less* with the more advanced computers.

'Secondly, the system of allocation of WISO units ensures a fair and deserving distribution. The entire population receive their basic Alpha Units on their sixteenth birthday. These are supplemented with Beta Units based on points awarded for work, achievement, contribution to the public good, and personal disability or handicap. Gamma Units are allotted on World or Regional Federal Government recommendation to those — like you — who devote their lives to world order, the environment, and the humanities.

'Thirdly, WISO units do not have votes. It is the stake in the world's wealth and the *dividend* which they provide — *over and above more, less, or no earned income* — which is the object of the exercise. That income gives dignity to everyone in later life,

78

and relieves the state of a burden it can no longer carry. In any case, there is no guarantee that a vote would be beneficial in the hands of those with no knowledge of the companies over whose shares the WISO trustees have spread the money. WISO units are non-transferable, and revert to the trustees on death.

'Personally, I think the originators did a smashing job. After all, whose life is the more deserving? . . . well-paid brain-boxes . . . investors . . . the gangs repairing crumbling old sewers under our cities . . . people disadvantaged through no fault of their own . . . or the ''abstract'' creators: designers, thinkers, writers, painters, composers, who enrich our lives? What about Mandela Moses, for example, or indeed — since obviously Moses was named after him — Nelson Mandela himself, were he alive today? Can such men be compared with the Chairman of WCI[1]? Who would grudge *either* his entitlement?

'If you will have a look at your own WISO cards . . . they give you all the information that you need. Your number (which is also shown on your World Identity Cards); your Alpha, Beta, and now newly-allotted Gamma units as members of the WPF; the Regional Federation Trust of which your units form part, and the dates on which your dividends are paid. As you know, the value of the various units is published daily in the press, and each half-yearly report gives details of the world spread of the Trust's investments.

'So far, WISO is operating in the NA AND CARIBBEAN, EUROPEAN, and ANZFED Regional Federations, and in parts of others, particularly the GFE, INDIA, PAN AFRICA, ARAB MIDDLE EAST, and RUSSIA. It is a twist of fate that, where the system is most needed, its introduction is hampered by the very numbers and poverty of the human race involved, but — *however* prolonged the introductory process — the WCA in the World Assembly is determined to pursue the ideal to the end.

'This morning I mentioned the unique example provided by the West Indies' populations in this context: in many instances from slavery to a personal stake in the world's wealth for every citizen. The differing status and constitutions of the Caribbean

---

[1] World Computers Inc, the world's largest corporation.

79

islands provide also an example of commonsense in action once there exists determination to progress with an ideal.

'The history of the region involved Spain, Britain, France, Holland, latterly the United States and Russia; and mixed populations descended from the Arawak Indians, successive European conquerors, and slaves from Africa or (sadly) bred there for sale. By the time of the first World Regional groupings including EUROPEAN and NA AND CARIBBEAN, many of the Caribbean islands were already independent states (including most of the former British colonies). Some of the smallest were still governed on a colonial basis. By contrast, two: Martinique, with a population mostly of African descent, and the Guadeloupe group constituted French departments with direct representation in Paris.

'To everyone but the most determined of practical idealists, WISO introduction to the citizens of so diverse a region seemed like a madman's dream. Indeed, the very idea was so described, particularly in London, although attitudes even in Britain (by then part of Federal Europe) were changing fast. In the event, and looking back now, it seems so obvious that the independent states which had become part of the NORTH AMERICAN AND CARIBBEAN Federation should have been included (as they are) in WISO administration by that Region, while the islands virtually part of France, and those still under direct European administration, should have been included (as they are) with Europe. The essential is that the World Federal Government was determined that, once WISO was introduced anywhere, *no individual citizen in that area should be left out.*

'Once given the decision, computers made fast work of the administration. A highly beneficial side-effect in the special case of near neighbours drawing their WISO income from different Regional Trusts has been the healthy competition between the Trusts' investment panels, even if, understandably, many of the world's leading investments may well be common to both. You understand of course that, while it is the creation of *new* capital with which they are concerned in the first place, which takes time to commence dividends and to appreciate, the trustees are thereafter at liberty to trade their investments as they think best in the interest of the populations that they serve.'

Pippa Brightwell had reserved till then information that the Unit's Caribbean venture would include Antigua. 'As you know,

West Atlantic WPF naval admin and a repair yard are based there. What an island paradise! Full employment: literally *every* adult. Happiness; music; history preserved; a thriving tourist industry; rainforest inland; bananas and *Antigua Blacks*, the world's best pineapples; that white sand of theirs ... the sparkling blue sea. You will join a WPF frigate at Port of Spain, Trinidad, proceeding northwards from there to St John's.'

13

'You will be flying to Trinidad in an Entente IV[1] of WPF Training Command.' Unit EURO 2001 were being briefed on their forthcoming trip by a member of the College staff. 'There will be a number of additional aircrew and some relief personnel for the WPF frigate *Andromeda* besides a few civilian passengers taking passage on the flight.' Members of the Unit listened in silence. To Jakko, although now more of the world, it seemed like a dream.

'On D2 you fly south-eastwards to the Amazon, thereafter following the great river inland with a detour over the Trans Amazon Highway, across southern Columbia to Ecuador. That is 3,800 miles in all, taking in some of Man's most prodigious efforts at restoration of the Earth's forest breathing apparatus. I'm sure you will find that an inspiration. Your colleagues in the World Environment Corps have played an important part in it. The next day takes you over the "Islas Galapagos", the Panama Canal and back to Trinidad . . . a further two and a half thousand miles.'

Their instructor pressed a button, upon which there appeared a large map of Central America and the Caribbean. A model Entente IV then flew the route.

'D4 is a free day, during which you can explore the island. In the evening the Trinidad Government lays on a guest evening: a beautiful dinner, pan playing, dancing under the stars . . . they like to show you what a great life they have there. In the morning you join *Andromeda*. She sails later that day for

---

[1] A derivative from the Anglo-French Concorde of the previous century.

Grenada and your cruise up the Windward Islands to Antigua.'

Another button, and a model frigate passed through the Dragon's Mouth out of the Gulf of Paria; skirted Tobago; called at St George's in Grenada; passed the Grenadines to St Vincent; then northwards to Martinique; Basse Terre, Guadeloupe; Montserrat; to Antigua's St John's.

'Like Trinidad, all the islands give you a warm welcome, as well they might. Theirs is a big success story. You spend several days in Antigua, which is rich in history and now of course is an important WPF naval base.

'On your way out, please collect a check-sheet and tour information pack. Thank you for your attendance.'

* * *

The Entente IV was flying high, cruising comfortably at rather less than twice the speed of sound. WPF cabin crew. No jackets. Small flashes on their blouses: one English, one Scot, one Swedish. Jamina had coaxed Jakko into an outside seat so that he would see what was to be seen and have a good view as they landed. She was asleep.

Jakko Mann was watching the tail end of a movie . . . the credits . . . then the screen went blank. He glanced at his watch. Unaccustomed to passenger flying, he remembered the schoolboy joke: 'If you fly round the world faster than a spot on the Earth's surface, do you get back before you left?' Paper darts while the teacher wasn't looking. 'No, stupid! However fast you go you'll have taken a millionth of a second, so it will be that much later.' And so on. They were flying west. Anyway, the time in Trinidad would be behind. These harmless musings were interrupted by the appearance of a Euro Federal newsreader on the cabin telescreen.

'Newsflash! One of the two girls wanted in connection with the bombing of the WCA eve-of-poll rally at Crawley City, England, in the spring, is reported to have walked into a Police station in London early today UK time. The girl is Doris Wiggins, aged eighteen. She is reported to have made a statement to the effect that she had been in hiding, but that being ''wanted'' was getting on her nerves and she had decided to give herself up. She has stated that she knew nothing of the bomb in her hold-all; that it must have been planted there by some ill-intentioned person. It is further reported that she has so far refused to disclose any information about Miss Sylvie Mennin, her companion at the time. Meanwhile Wiggins is being held in custody while the UK Police and Terrorist Squad officers continue their enquiries. That is the end of the newsflash.'

Jakko felt himself being prodded from the seat behind. 'That your girlfriend, Jakko? Eh?' He turned and motioned to his colleague to be quiet. Of course everyone would be discussing the girl Doris, but Jamina was still dozing.

She stirred, but he did nothing to hasten her awakening. For all his physical desire for her, he realized once more in that moment how much he believed in Sylvie Mennin's innocence, how Jamina's 'Why then doesn't she come forward voluntarily?' had seemed to him unfair.

But chatter amongst his companions was inevitable. That Jakko's two Commendations during their Unit's first few days of training were accompanied by his natural, if shy, friendliness and total lack of 'side', had ensured his popularity. A number of his contemporaries now left their seats to gather round and pull his leg, waking Jamina.

'One of his Crawley girlfriends has given herself up,' said one.

'What are you talking about?' Jamina asked before Jakko could explain.

'There's just been a newsflash on the screen. One of the girls who left those bombs under the seats at Crawley has walked into a London Police station.'

'Your Sylvie?'

'Not *my* Sylvie. No. It was the other one: Doris something.'

'Wiggins!' This from someone. 'Sounds like a bit of a yokel.'

Jakko intervened, 'I remember, she didn't seem very bright at the time.'

'No,' said Jamina. 'Sylvie was the bright one, wasn't she!'

Jakko was upset by that. But already the WPF training had strengthened his character and self-assurance. 'Please let's have no misunderstanding about this. All I have ever said is that Sylvie Mennin seemed to me to be a perfectly natural, innocent, friendly kid. I just don't believe that she had anything to do with the planting of those bombs. That's all there is to it. OK?'

'If you say so, darling.'

Jakko flushed momentarily as, sensing trouble, their friends

84

melted away, returning to their seats. '*That* was bitchy!' Then, in a whisper, 'And please don't lay claim to me like that in public.' He turned with strangled, mixed emotions, and gazed out at the sky.

* * *

Gong. Silence. 'This is your captain speaking. We will be landing shortly at Piarco, Port of Spain's airport, about fifteen miles from the city. We hope you have enjoyed your trip. It is always a particular pleasure to carry new members of the WPF. The crew and I wish you well in your careers. Members of EURO 2001: tomorrow we fly you across South America; thence back via the Galapagos and the Panama Canal. You then have a day in Trinidad; there is much to see before you join *Andromeda*. All, please now fasten safety belts. Thank you.'

The buzz of conversation was resumed, normal relations between Jakko and Jamina outwardly restored in anticipation of the next part of a new adventure.

Touch down. *Au revoirs.* Garlands of flowers, cool drinks, and a steel band. Overhead — on a vast hoarding -

---

WELCOME TO TRINIDAD AND TOBAGO
PROUD MEMBER, NORTH AMERICAN &
CARIBBEAN FEDERATION.

Two minibuses over the lush green hills to the WPF base outside the capital, and a first sight of the Northern Range of mountains looming over the city and its skyscrapers. To the left, low-lying land stretching south-westwards towards the Gulf of Paria and mainland Venezuela.

14

Gear deposited in overnight cabins, the Unit was welcomed by the Officer Commanding the complex, a West Indian WPF Commodore.

'I'm sure that you are impatient to see the island, but these trips have a dual purpose. First, they are designed to widen knowledge of the world that it is our privilege to keep safe. Secondly, to constitute enjoyable breaks during your training. The Caribbean islands are ideally suited to both roles. They are steeped in history. Deservedly, after what they have been through, they now belong to one or other of the two most beneficial World Regions. Not least, they provide a moving tribute to peoples here, who — unlike some — have cared for and cherished their environment.

'Trinidad was discovered in 1498 by Christopher Columbus, who claimed the island for Spain, but the Spanish colony was destroyed by Sir Walter Raleigh in 1595. You remember from your school days the constant battles between European powers for the riches of the New World. The islands of the Caribbean and the convoys of merchant vessels, treasure and sugar ships were the prizes. The whole area constituted a battle zone for two hundred years. Much of the fighting between England and Spain and/or France was extremely bloody, involving powerful fleets and many thousands of troops. At one time, the British fleet reached a strength of 171 ships of the line, 85 frigates, 123 smaller vessels, and 70,000 sailors . . . a formidable force; and its gunnery, with incessant drill, was devastating. St Lucia changed hands between Britain and France no less than fourteen times. Maybe, as you all come from Europe, I should tell you that I do not take sides in these matters!

'*This* island was subsequently raided by the Dutch, the French (allied at that time with Spain), and finally by Britain, and was ceded to the British Crown in 1802. Perhaps the most noteworthy event or, more precisely, *non*-event, and certainly the most poignant, of our history was the arrival of the British under Admiral Nelson in 1805, hoping to destroy the French fleet in a repeat of the Battle of the Nile. But the Gulf of Paria was empty! The French under Villeneuve were at Martinique. Nelson had sailed south upon false reports and against his own better judgement. He was desperate to destroy the French fleet, which, had it joined French and Spanish squadrons in Europe and effected control of the English Channel, would have enabled Napoleon, with 150,000 men and more than 2,000 vessels already assembled, to invade Britain. History would have been changed. That command of the Channel and that invasion were of course finally prevented by Trafalgar. Long way from here . . . and long way from English Channel!

'Tobago was amalgamated politically with Trinidad in 1888. After the break-up of the ill-fated West Indian Federation, the two islands became an independent state within the British Commonwealth in 1976, subsequently opting out, as part of the New World, to join the NORTH AMERICAN AND CARIBBEAN grouping. As you are Europeans, maybe I should say that it was matter of geography and commonsense. Nothing to do with the past or slavery. These days we can talk freely.

'However, as a result of all this we have a very mixed population, so we are suitable people to talk about One World!

'Our major naval base in the area is in Antigua. You will be taken there in *Andromeda*. But we have a WPF presence here; mostly VTOs and surveillance.

'Trinidad prospers with its oil, tourism, and agriculture. After Puerto Rico, it is the most industrialized island in the Caribbean. Some of its skyscraper buildings are very impressive, and the Golden Gates Hotel in Port of Spain city is one of the wonders of the modern world.'

At this point the Commodore revealed a wall map. 'So far I have not mentioned the beauty of Trinidad itself. The buses will take you on a tour this afternoon. The island was, long time ago, part of the South American mainland. It lies between ten and eleven degrees North latitude, and is a tropical gem treasured by its people. The land, the clear waters that surround us, even the sky, our wildlife, tropical vegetation, will entrance those of you who have not been here before. Everywhere there is colour: flame trees and jacarandas, bougainvilleas, hibiscus, and — in the more wooded area — wild poinsettias: Trinidad's national flower. We have more than 700 Orchid species. The birds and tropical fish, and over 600 species of butterflies, add to the enchantment. All this the Trinidadians cherish and protect: not *only* for love. They know the importance of our tourist industry.

'Your trip this afternoon will take you first of all to Arima, then north to the nature sanctuary at Blanchisseuse. How many of you have seen humming birds in their natural habitat? — then down the east coast to the Navira Swamp. This is a bird-watchers' paradise. Then across to our second city, San Fernando; the Pitch Lake, a natural phenomenon of self-replenished asphalt; then northwards to the Caroni Swamp. Your tour is timed to arrive there before sundown to witness the unforgettable sight of formations of scarlet ibis, our national bird, flying in to roost.

'So much for what we arrange for you. In your spare day on the island you are free to choose your own amusements. I suggest that you include the shopping district in Port of Spain, the very fine Botanic Gardens, the Art Gallery and National Museum. One word of warning: rum is strong stuff!'

Evening at the Golden Gates. Members of Unit EURO 2001 relaxed with cool drinks in one of the most beautiful dining-cum-ballrooms in the world: tables set in a sea of flowers amidst the palm trees surrounding the huge swimming pool, stretching out from the building far into the gardens; to the west, over the Gulf, the sunset flame subsiding; the air full of scents, the gentle rhythm of steel bands. Girls, suntanned, flowers in their hair, looking after the guests.

Jakko and Jamina each toyed with a tall glass of some rum and fruit concoction. In spite of the new experiences crowding one upon another, excitement, and beauty of that afternoon, their conversation was muted following their differing reaction to the news flash. Jamina spilled some of her drink. 'Oh shit!' The expletive, amongst so much beauty, struck a jarring note.

'Would you like to dance?' It was the bronzed one who had chatted up Jamina at the Euro College welcoming reception.

'Of course. I'd like to.'

Jakko found himself alone. He got up from the table, made

his way round the dance floor. Colleagues in the water waved in friendly fashion as he skirted the pool and made his way outside.

He had walked a little way, stopped to admire a hibiscus, had cupped one of its flowers in his hands, when he was startled by a gentle 'Hullo Jakko'. He turned, and there was the youngest member of the Unit. 'I'm Danielle,' she volunteered. 'Danielle de Croix. Isn't that flower beautiful?' She held out a hand. Jakko released the flower and took her hand instinctively.

'I know,' he said, for he had noticed often this small fragment of France with the tricolour on its shoulders, who seemed often to be by herself. 'What are you doing out here all alone?'

'Oh . . . it is just me . . . the boys seem to want — how you say it? — just one thing.'

'Are you warm enough?' asked Jakko. 'Shall we wander round for a bit?' She didn't answer for a few moments, and he was able to take in the nature of his fellow volunteer. Short. Not much more than one and a half metres. Fair. Hair loose, gathered in a little bow. The whole picture one of guileless naturalness. He rather expected a French girl to be more complex and sophisticated. But here was someone he could understand: a perfect recruit to the forces of the World. She would never do anything but offer help to another soul in need, would lovingly sacrifice herself if ever it was necessary. A picture of Sylvie Mennin flashed through his mind, then one of Susan Innocence. She, after just one day in uniform, had *done* just that. They had entered his life for only a few minutes. Then Susan, at least, had gone for ever. Here was another of God's children cast in the same mould. They were no longer so rare. Danielle — he liked the name Danielle. Already he believed in her. WPF recruiting were no fools. He hoped that she was strong enough to hold down the duties and cope with the hardships that must come their way. Jamina was beautiful but — by comparison — Jamina, he realized suddenly, was *tough*. And yet . . . maybe that was a good thing. Life in the service of the World would be no sinecure.

'Yes, let's.' Her agreement brought him back to earth.

'I'm so sorry,' releasing her hand. 'Of course.' Then, 'I was just thinking nice things about you.' They linked hands again in the gathering darkness and set off amidst the palms. Jakko, eventually: 'We have a very long day tomorrow. Maybe we should get a taxi back to base.' Then, 'And I ought to find Jamina.'

'Must you?'

There was only one answer. 'I don't *have* to.'

The steel band was still playing. A few couples were still on the floor, the lights amidst the flowers now dimmed; late gamblers, laughing, leaving the casino. 'I don't dance very well,' Jakko said. There was no reply, just 'We don't have to!' They were both tired. Instinctively they held each other closely: two young people from another continent, lost on a tropical night to the World they were pledged to serve.

* * *

It was the sheer width of the Amazon which next day awed them all as the aircraft slowed and headed inland. By comparison, the river's length — all 4,050 miles of it, second only to the Nile — was merely a statistic.

And soon the rainforest: the last lush natural areas preserved; vast tracts of now matured planting, resulting from Man's near panic towards the turn of the last century; dams, pumping stations, irrigation: huge projects needed to stop irreparable soil erosion where earlier the land had been so wantonly denuded. Interspersed, mile upon mile of man-made tree species bred for good ground-holding and rapid growth. The Trans-Amazon highway. Westward once more; touchdown at the great Environment Corps base. Specialized aircraft and VTO's parked. An atmosphere of infectious enthusiasm and controlled efficiency. A tour of the museum: maps, working models, engineering wonders. The Environment Corps nursery, in conjunction with the Brazilian Government, with — lined out — millions of micro-propagated baby trees of both proven and experimental species. Observers from Indonesia on an exchange mission. On again to the west, with new horizons and new knowledge gained.

En route from mainland Ecuador to the Galapagos early next day, a crew member distributed to his charges copies of a leaflet describing the historic five-year second voyage of the British brig HMS *Beagle*, under Captain (later Admiral) Fitzroy, who was accompanied by Darwin. As they neared the islands, he called for everyone's attention.

'For some years now, the Caribbean trip for WPF trainees during their course has included this detour after seeing the rainforests. Basically, the *Beagle's* world voyage was one of survey and chart-making, at which Fitzroy was particularly adept. It was intended as a three-year operation, but it took five in the event. *Beagle* also boasted no less than twenty-two chronometers and was to carry GMT around the world, checking previously recorded longitudes. Additionally, Fitzroy acquired deservedly the title ''Father of Meteorology'', so expert did he become in interpretation of barometric readings. Darwin accompanied him as the expedition's scientist.

'Fitzroy had taken all but four years by the time he had surveyed the coast of Patagonia and the extremely intricate and dangerous waters off the tip of South America, a prodigious undertaking. The results were on their way to England and now in October 1835, under less pressure, he had landed Charles Darwin and his party in the Galapagos. It is here that was sown in Darwin's fertile mind the germ of his theory on the *Origin of Species*, later to lead to debate the world over, which has continued ever since. You will, of course, be familiar with the famous mural in Euro College 11. It is my loss that I have not seen it. In a few minutes we will fly round the Galapagos and finally low over James Island in the centre of the group, where Darwin spent nine days ashore while *Beagle* completed her survey of the islands.

'So you can chalk up a little more history and experience . . . then back to Trinidad. We have enjoyed having you with us.'

* * *

The members of Unit 2001 set off in groups for their free day: further exploring Port of Spain city and its history; sea fishing; sightseeing inland and along the coast; boating and swimming; a contingent of skin divers nipping across to Tobago to see for themselves the coral gardens of the Bucco Reef, where three hundred exotic species of tropical fish abound in the crystal water.

By evening, a tired but happy assembly of young people converged once more upon the Golden Gates Hotel. In a setting so beautiful, early attachments soon mature. WPF volunteers — the cream of the world's youth, resulting from the most sophisticated of selection methods — developed nonetheless along well-proven lines. It was always so. Those who play their duties by the book, if rarely inspired, become the reliable, successful, future officers. The tough, sometimes but not always loved, thrive on respect because they never command others to do what they themselves cannot. The considerate, often inspired when need arises, are followed because they care about those that they lead, and share with their own the latter's achievements, hopes and fears.

Inevitably in affairs of the heart, like attracts like, and Jakko Mann had already begun to understand that he and Jamina had been thrown together only by circumstance: their first meeting at London's Churchill railway terminal, when neither had yet met any other of their colleagues. He suspected now that he had been *used* by Jamina because he was well-built and strong; not because they were compatible, but because — whatever her undeniable sheer beauty — she was tough, highly-sexed and physically demanding. She had needed him.

That early evening when he and Danielle had strolled hand in hand down to the harbour for a better view of *Andromeda* as she rode quietly at anchor offshore; there stood Jamina posing for photographs, wet clothes clinging to her beautiful body, one arched foot upon a kingfish that — with help — she had managed to land after a long struggle: the king mackerel's mouth ajar, gills bloody from the long battle for its life. The whole picture was so striking as to be worthy of an Annigoni portrait, had that genius survived into the further century. Indeed a large crowd had gathered, mostly silent, to take in the spectacle.

Jakko felt his companion's grip tighten, and they had turned away.

15

By 0900 the next morning, all were fallen in on the New Mole, the most recent addition to a busy harbour, temporary team leaders (Jamina among them) out in front. As the Executive Officer of the WPF complex arrived in his car to say farewell, the Unit was called to attention. A few local civilians, accustomed to the WPF presence, were nonetheless impressed by their smart bearing.

'Stand them at ease, please.' Then, 'In a few minutes, boats will take you out to *Andromeda*. Your gear has been sent on. I hope you have enjoyed your short stay in Trinidad. I congratulate you on your excellent behaviour here. It reflects credit upon your Euro College and upon you all. Have a pleasant cruise up to Antigua. Good luck in your careers. Come back and see us some time. You will always be welcome.'

Attention again. Salutes. The WPF staff car moved off. Fall out to await the boats.

Two motor cutters rounded the Mole, girl boats' crews in spotless white, boathooks at the ready. Trinidad and Tobago flashes on four pairs of shoulders, one Stars and Stripes, one Maple Leaf. Immaculate drill as they came alongside.

Danielle: 'Oh, Jakko. *That's* the life for me!'

Jakko: 'I expect they have hard times as well. What about hurricanes!'

'Right!' This from the cox'n of the leading cutter. 'Twenty-five in each boat. Spread yourselves evenly on the thwarts. Face for'ard. No elbows on the gunn'l!'

'Bear off, for'ard. Let go, aft!' More exhibition boathook drill. They were away.

There is always something beautiful about a fighting ship, however purposeful her weapons, even if her role is defensive

93

and her lines ruined by camouflage, multiple fitments, aerials, and gadgetry. *Andromeda* was no exception. Sleek, tropical light grey. NA & C 21 in bold white-edged black letters on her side. A precisely cut-in water line. Deadly small-size ship to ship, ship to air, and underwater weaponry replacing the more cumbersome versions of a century ago. A forest of aerials. VTO aircraft on its pad. An array of life rafts reflecting a 'good citizen' and air/sea rescue role. Very fast. Powered by the latest jet thrust engines.

Members of the Unit saluted as they stepped aboard, greeted by the duty officer and a brass plate on the bulkhead.

WPF NORTH AMERICAN AND CARIBBEAN 2nd ATLANTIC FAST FRIGATE SQUADRON	
ANDROMEDA	21
ACHILLES	22
APOLLO	23
CERES	24
CHIRON	25
HERMES	26
ICARUS	27
MELPOMENE	28

The duty officer: 'We sail for Grenada in two hours' time. Meanwhile you should familiarize yourselves with the ship and your own quarters, and stow your gear. When you hear "Hands to stations for leaving harbour", I want half of your Unit fallen in smartly on either side of the forward deck with' — he consulted some notes — 'Mr Jakko Mann in the eyes of the ship ... that is right for'ard. You remain at attention as we weigh and leave harbour.'

'Why me?' Jakko mused as they made their way forward.

'It's the two commendations, Jakko boy,' said someone. 'You're a marked man!'

Andromeda weighed and turned towards the Dragon's Mouth, Jakko rigid, alone, right forward; the sea breeze in his face, the crystal-blue water and gathering bow wave beneath his feet as the frigate increased speed.

Then, presently, 'Hands to cruising stations. Unit 2001 fall out.'

It is just over one hundred miles from Port of Spain to St George's in Grenada: a comfortable two and a half hours in smooth water. *Andromeda* was cruising quietly north at forty knots, and had completed half her journey. The young people, off duty bar two of their number gaining experience as additional watchkeepers on the bridge, were relaxing on deck when suddenly came an urgent broadcast. 'This is the Captain. An airliner with six hundred passengers aboard is reported down in the sea in flames, south-west of Barbados. VTOs from Bridgetown and Grenada besides two merchant vessels on passage are headed for the reported position, but *Andromeda* is the nearest — and certainly the fastest — ship. We are proceeding to render assistance.' With this the frigate altered course sharply, heeling over, shuddering as speed increased. Her sharp bow sliced through the water as she reached fifty knots.

'I always thought it was crazy to build these bloody great aeroplanes,' someone commented, shouting to make himself heard in the slipstream and holding on to the guardrail. 'How can you hope to pick up *six hundred* people out of the drink before a goodly number of them have drowned.'

'There are very few accidents these days.'

'Yes, but when there *is* one, they make sure it's a major disaster, don't they? It's this craze to do everything faster or build it bigger or whatever. You'd think the world would have *grown up* by now. We're still just like a bunch of kids. Would you like to live in that bloody Space Station that's been up there for *ten years*?' Shouted conversation continued with difficulty on these somewhat rambling lines until all were silenced by the ship's Executive Officer.

'Green watch to muster. Prepare VTO for lift-off. Prepare all boats, floats, ladders and scrambling nets. Boats' crews to muster. All seamen personnel provide life jackets. When all is ready, I will stand down the off-duty watch until we reach the area. Unit 2001; you are about to see the WPF in a do-gooder role, and an important role it is, apart from the lives we save. It will be experience to watch the crew preparing for an emergency. *Watch*, but please do not hinder. We will advise you of practical things that *you* can do. Meanwhile, you too provide life jackets.'

As the ship sped north-eastwards, members of the Unit, keeping out of the crew's way, witnessed preparations to retrieve survivors from the sea. Presently their own attention was called for. 'Unit 2001 assemble aft. Team leaders please fall in separately those experienced in first aid: particularly as regards burns and drowning. We carry only one medical officer and three men of our own. The rest of you can act as stretcher-bearers — the after mess deck is being prepared as a casualty station — and please detail a few of your strongest men to assist survivors up the ladders and nets. Thank you. Ship's ratings: ''Cooks to the Galley''!'

The Captain again. 'We have instructions to proceed to Bridgetown with survivors. I have no need, any more than Nelson had, to call for your best efforts. I would get an equally dusty reaction. But we are part of a force dedicated to the peoples of the world. Today, we have a chance to live up to that. Six hundred survivors will be all but three times our own complement! We have the aircraft on the screens; it is still afloat. *Allez Andromeda!*'

'The spirit is infectious, isn't it?' Jakko commented to a colleague as they collected life jackets and hurried aft in the wind.

Jamina — of course — and two older volunteers were already taking charge. 'Jakko Mann,' — she had to shout to make herself heard — 'please assemble ten men to assist at the ladders and nets. All girls with first aid training over here please. Remainder pair off and report to the crew as stretcher party. Come on now, let's get sorted out!'

Presently the frigate lost way, stopped engines, head to wind, for VTO lift off; then on again at her best speed until once more she lost way, 'astern' jets checking her forward drift as she entered the wide area covered with inflated dinghies, bobbing heads, bodies and small debris. The remains of the aeroplane had disappeared. Smoke, thinning, drifted overhead; the flames

— their deadly work done — extinguished by the sea.

Andromeda's VTO and two from Grenada hovered over the water, crewmen suspended beside swimmers, attaching harness in which they could be hauled to safety. Apart from an occasional cry, there was a strange silence, a dignified performance by the human race.

Within minutes the ship's boats and rafts, overburdened, awash, were alongside, but few of those dragged from the water were capable of the effort needed to climb the ladders when urged on by the crew. Even as survivors did their best, others still in the water grasped despairingly at the boats' sides. Individual swimmers, some helping colleagues to remain afloat, clung to the nets and ropes suspended over the ship's sides until hauled inboard by willing hands or, exhausted, they lost their grip and drifted away. Some, calling upon the last of their strength, or already burned or injured in the break-up of the aircraft, reached the ship, only to drown entangled in the nets.

Jakko had positioned himself on the starboard ladder where he could grasp survivors as they began their climb and help them to reach the deck, but all of them were waterlogged and most so exhausted as well that he had virtually to drag them upwards with brute force. Nonetheless, profoundly moved by the appalling sight below, where the injured and exhausted lay in the bottom of the boats heaped amongst the dying, he said a silent prayer for the strength to carry on. But presently he called up to a Swedish colleague stationed above, 'Gustav ... This is too slow ... *This is too slow.* We need more stretchers and boatswain's chairs to be lowered — one at a time — into the boats. Then they must haul them up as the next empty one is lowered. Tell them on deck: Faster! *Faster! They must get a "routine" moving.*' He turned back to the scene in the nearest boat. '*Andromeda* fellows; can you please allow on to the ladder *only those who can climb it.* Take off some of their heavy clothes. That will speed things up. I have asked them on deck to be quicker lowering and hauling up stretchers and boatswain's chairs for the rest.' Jakko realized suddenly that he had virtually shouted an order to the ship's men, but was reassured by their acknowledgement and by renewed activity above.

As the 'faster routine' for which he had called got into its stride, he was able to take a look further afield. By now, survivors had for the most part collected in groups centred upon a float

97

or a life raft, hanging on round the outside; others clinging together or supporting an injured colleague where one or more had life jackets. Bodies floated away singly. Lone swimmers still struggled on their own towards the ship. It was obvious that *Andromeda*'s boats, crammed with survivors alongside, were in no position to cast off and take these outlying groups in tow. The ship's officers had responded to the need. Already their own VTO, controlled by the Captain on the bridge, had a line secured to the largest assembly óf survivors centred on one of the ship's rafts, and was towing them all towards *Andromeda*. The Executive Officer, amidships with line-throwing guns, had grappled several groups, these too being hauled steadily to safety.

Jakko took in the scene and with it the scattered small groups and individual swimmers who — correctly in any staff course questionnaire — must be left to fend for themselves while available resources are concentrated on saving the greatest number. The Unit had as yet done no staff course, but commonsense decision-making came naturally to disciplined, enthusiastic youth. Jakko Mann weighed up consciously the need for his presence on the ladder, that he had been ordered there in the first place. But he had himself ensured efficient clearing of the boats and floats. That might save the lives of those buried under their colleagues who would be hauled inboard last. There was no more that he could do for them. By contrast, hope faded minute by minute for lone survivors scattered in the sea: particularly the injured, those without life jackets, the old and very young as, tiring, they disappeared or were carried away. Other rescuers were coming — if they arrived in time. He shouted once more to those on deck: this time that a line be thrown down and tended at the inboard end; quickly secured the line to his life jacket and, jumping clear of the boats into the sea, struck out for a small group of survivors. Grasping one of their number, he shouted back to those on deck 'HAUL AWAY! … HAUL AWAY! … SLOW AND STEADY. *S L O W   A N D   S T E A D Y* … it is only a light line.' Then to his charges, 'Those who can manage it, kick out with your legs; help us to reach the ship. All of you … *hold on to each other*. You mustn't … let … go … now.'

Suffice it to record that Jakko repeated this feat twice, retrieving a further small group on each occasion; then, tiring, he rested for a while in the water before clambering on to a float for a final glance to seaward. Several more VTOs had by now arrived. A number of small aircraft patrolled round the area. He had with reluctance decided that there was no more that he could do when he noticed a lone survivor some distance from the ship, swimming very slowly, all but spent. It was a girl with long dark hair which, between feeble strokes, she tried repeatedly to push to one side so that she could see where she was heading. Making sure that his light lifeline was clear, he struck out from the ship for the last time.

It is impossible to cite emotions that Jakko Mann did not recall as later he reasoned with himself what he should do. As he reached the lone swimmer, she held out an arm instinctively, only for the skin to come away in his fingers as he grasped her hand. He saw that one side of her face was burned as if she had instinctively turned away from an explosion: fuel tanks perhaps. It is extraordinary how much detail, seemingly irrelevant, the mind can absorb in seconds. The other side of her face was unscarred and freckled. And that wasn't all. The dark hair, sodden and matted, hung so that blonde roots were exposed.

The girl's eyes were wide. In shock she showed no emotion, made no sound. It was as Jakko made a conscious effort to drag *his* tired mind back to essentials that suddenly she seemed to see him, clasped her arms around his neck in a last despairing effort, and let out a stifled cry . . . 'Oh, Jakko! . . . Oh God . . . can it really be you? I must be unconscious . . . NO; I am dying . . . Oh God; I was trying to escape to South America, but now I am coming to you. Help me . . . *please*. I didn't do it. *I didn't do it. YOU* know that I didn't do it . . . Into *thy* hands . . . '

16

Before Sylvie Mennin lapsed into unconsciousness she had believed that she was dying: indeed — like Jesus at the last — with unsullied simple faith had, aloud, committed her spirit to God's care. Jakko, incredulous and himself near the end of physical endurance, began to wonder whether he too had lost his senses. His brain felt as if somehow it had become detached. He started swimming on his back: mechanically, like a clockwork toy whose spring had all but run down; towing the body of the girl, oblivious to all else. Of course, and he blamed himself, he had attempted one rescue too many; he must have been out of his mind. And yet it was unfair that a survivor should be lost because he or she had not been near a life raft, a matter of mere happenstance.

In the plea to her God the girl had mumbled something about trying to reach South America. Of course that could make sense. It *could* be Sylvie, following the example set by the Great Train Robbers and other villains since who had, over a century or more, eluded capture in the United Kingdom. But that was before modern co-operation of which INTERPOL had been the worthy forerunner. And what about her World Identity card? How had she got on to the aircraft? And her WISO dividends: they'd only continue to be paid into her Bank until the date came for someone to attest, *à la* Samuel Pepys, that she was still alive.

He couldn't see *Andromeda* behind him, but now he could hear undisciplined exhortations urging him on and feel the line, still attached to his life jacket, half dragging him through the water. Then suddenly he was alerted to his own problem by a still functioning brain. He alone knew the girl's identity. Her simple dying cry to God of her innocence when she believed herself about to meet Him, must dispel all lingering doubt. But in the absence of the real culprit, who or what jury, what Court of Enquiry, would believe her story? She had every right to be scared. But if innocent, she had every right to freedom from pursuit.

Now he was nearing the ship. There was a time when he would have confided at once in Jamina. Not any more, and certainly not about Sylvie Mennin. Willing hands were now lifting his charge out of the water. He must contrive to stay with her and remove all evidence of identity when she was stripped of her wet clothes. Anyone who noticed would think it strange behaviour, but he had no choice. Then, as soon as she was conscious, he must warn her not to give anything away. As with unseeing eyes he clambered, aided by companions, to the deck, came the realization that Sylvie would be landed at Bridgetown with all the other casualties, while *Andromeda*, having landed them, sailed on.

The after mess deck was so crowded that Jakko's immediate fears were stilled. He threaded his way amongst the stretcher-bearers to a makeshift casualty reception area. Here volunteers from his Unit were assisting ship's personnel to instil a state of order, segregating immediately the exhausted and near-drowned, the injured and burned, and those for whom without question there was no further hope. The latter, available particulars listed and with large named labels attached, were being removed at once to the open deck to make room for the living.

Everyone was occupied. Jakko followed the two seamen who bore Sylvie on a stretcher. 'This one's got burns,' one of them volunteered as they paused momentarily and were ushered on by one of the ship's qualified ratings. 'The doc's the other end of the mess deck.' They soon reached the first-aid area. The stretcher was set down. Two girls from the Unit — Jakko at once recognized Danielle — turned their urgent attention to the newcomer, to check breathing and pulse and gingerly to cut away what remained of her clothing.

Presently Danielle extracted a note case from an inner pocket as Jakko bent down with 'Let me have it . . . I will hand it in.' A lot of world currency in sodden notes of large denomination, and a World Identity Card. Nothing else. Printed beneath the IC photograph was the name Suzi Mendoza.

* * *

There comes a moment when the Captain of a ship in *Andromeda*'s position must decide to proceed at utmost speed to land large numbers of survivors for skilled medical attention, leaving to others the rescue of isolated survivors and the reclaiming of bodies from the sea. The problem is akin to that faced by convoy escorts a century and a half before when depth-charging enemy submarines and, in the process, swimmers from merchant vessels on their own side or by the captain of a rescuing vessel — on perceiving a new threat — ordering the engines to be put full ahead and cutting to pieces with the ship's propellers of those days, survivors no longer able to hold on to the nets.

The WPF had in the first place the great part of mankind from which to choose. Its training was based upon a proven mix of humanity, selflessness, and the finest staff courses ever devised. There was now no hesitation; no doubt of the correctness of the action. The Captain, informed that — besides twenty-six dead — he had on board a hundred and eighty-six souls, the lives of at least thirty of whom were in danger, ordered his main engine jets to 'Slow Ahead'. Once clear of the area, he increased to full speed, ordered the ship's VTO to land in Grenada, and broadcast a report to Bridgetown, to all those proceeding to the area, and to Antigua naval base.

* * *

'Suzi Mendoza' was conscious, her brow furrowed with pain. She looked up, and the expression softened.

'Oh Jakko, what can I say to you?'

He knelt down beside the stretcher. No-one but Danielle would hear. 'You concentrate all your strength on recovery,' he urged, gently taking the undamaged hand. 'Then, if it really is you, we must clear you of suspicion once and for all. You mustn't run away like this . . . there is so much to do in the world. Can you say something to clear all doubt from my mind . . . please . . .'

Tears immediately stood in her eyes in the presence of affection, overflowed, mingling with the burned tissue. 'Do you remember the bull's-eyes with stripes round them? . . . before we went to spend a penny.'

17

'Mr Jakko Mann of Unit 2001 to the bridge, please!'

The order was repeated.

Apart from first aid attention to survivors and exchanges between crew and those fully recovered, over hot drinks, WPF buns and a special rum ration, a degree of normality had been restored aboard the frigate. The Captain removed his cap and sat back in his bridge chair out of the wind as Jakko Mann reported and the Officer of the Watch scanned the horizon.

'Well, young man, how do you feel?'

'A bit wrung out, Sir.'

'I am not surprised. I have sent for you to commend your conduct. I propose to send — via Antigua — a report to Euro College 11. One piece of advice. A fine line divides inspiration from a lack of tact. Be careful lest some superior takes initiative of yours amiss.'

Jakko thanked the frigate's CO, adding 'I was only doing what seemed best to achieve the object. At college we have studied the Battle of St Vincent[1]; but thank you, Sir. I meant no disrespect.'

He hesitated, debating within himself whether, in the presence of authority so balanced and so friendly, to seek guidance on the Sylvie problem. He had, he realized, changed his mind a thousand times already. Now — by his silence — he could prejudice his own career. But that was an unworthy thought.

---

[1] Nelson had turned out of the line without orders, an unprecedented act in those days, and headed off the Spanish fleet so that it could be brought to close action.

The girl's behaviour must add to the doubts by which she was surrounded in official quarters. Her return voluntarily to face questioning could free her to live a normal life.

'Would it be in order for me to ask your advice on a completely different matter?' He reminded the Captain of the Crawley bomb attempt; that according to news bulletins the girl Doris had given herself up. 'You have the other girl in your sick bay, Sir.'

The Captain, astonished, asked, 'Are you sure?'

'She was hoping to hide in South America, but the plane crashed.' Jakko pulled the Identity Card from a pocket.

'But this belongs to a Suzi Mendoza.'

'I'm sure it's a forgery, Sir. I doubt if there is such a person.'

'Why is she so desperate to get away if she has nothing to hide?'

'That is the question that everyone asks. She is young and frightened and, in the absence of arrests, convinced that no-one will believe her.'

'Is Miss Mennin attractive?'

'If you mean am I influenced because she is a pretty girl, the answer is that she is — or was — just a normal happy teenager as far as one could see. But if ever I had suspicions, they were dispelled this afternoon. I feel that I am breaking a very personal confidence, but when she believed that she was going to perish, she cried aloud "*You* know that I didn't do it." Anyone who heard that could have no further doubt. It was God that she was talking to.'

The Captain turned to his watchkeeper. 'I'll be in sick bay if you need me.' Then to Jakko, 'Come on; this must be sorted out.'

The ship's Medical Officer and Danielle de Croix stood up simultaneously as the Captain threaded his way through the injured to where Sylvie Mennin lay.

'Well done, Doc. Sorry I haven't been able to get aft before. What's the situation?'

The MO kept his voice down. 'There are three or four in a bad way. I've got my fellows keeping an eye on them. There appears to have been an explosion of some kind. All the "burns only" cases will survive; the sea cleaned them up for us — that's important — and we have enough of what we need.' He indicated a series of drips suspended from the bulkhead.

'Changing the subject, Captain, I am most impressed by members of the Unit under training. They saved a number of drowning cases. This little lady for one ...' he indicated Danielle, '... got at least three survivors breathing again, to my knowledge, while we were busy with other things.'

The CO kneeled down beside Sylvie. 'Miss Mennin, can you hear me? I know you are in pain, but please listen carefully.

'Don't be afraid. We are all your friends. That is our job: to look after the world's people and to help them. Mr Mann here assures me that there is no question of you having placed those bombs. *You only cause suspicion by running away.* Remember: even if they do not find the bombers, they have to prove your guilt, and *that they cannot do if you are innocent.* This ridiculous nonsense ... your unhappiness, Miss Mennin ... has gone on long enough. *Do you understand?'*

Tears flowed again. A faint 'Yes ... thank you.'

The Captain of *Andromeda* continued. 'I have already decided what I will do. You will be transferred to hospital in Barbados until you are fit to travel. You will then be sent back to England under escort. I'm afraid that is our duty. Meanwhile, I will ask the Admiral in Antigua to press for an enquiry to be held immediately on your return and, assuming that there is no case to answer, *you will of course be freed at once.* That is the law, Miss Mennin. It was our privilege to rescue you today. Please don't let us down ...' Then, softening after the firmness, 'Make the most, my child, of the life you have been given.'

* * *

Bridgtown.

Unaccustomed to man-made as distinct from meteorological disaster, the Barbados people turned out in large numbers with a fine blend of efficiency and curiosity. First ashore: the Captain to report to the authorities. Survivors disembarked, injured were whisked away to hospital, the dead landed with quiet dignity. *Andromeda*'s crew were busied collecting and stowing replacement life-saving and medical supplies and replenishing temporarily the ship's depleted rations, while full use was made of her enthusiastic passengers to restore the ship to pristine cleanliness, whereupon shore leave was granted.

105

Later, with all back on board, the Unit's attention was called to amendments to the cruise. 'We will now be proceeding direct to Martinique where, I need hardly say, the French nationals among you will be particularly welcome; and from there direct to the WPF naval base in Antigua. The Unit will be landed on arrival and you will be accommodated at the base until you return to Europe, but before you leave you will see all eight ships of our squadron together, assembled for a major exercise. Normally they act singly on goodwill missions, showing the WPF flag, holding themselves in readiness to support international law or provide help in any part of this widespread command. The whole squadron together makes a brave sight. So ... Martinique next.'

Fort de France.

'You should learn to speak more languages, Jakko Mann! Even after all this time, you expect everyone to speak English. It is a lazy habit.' Danielle turned her attention to Martinique. 'To Frenchmen, it is the pearl of the Antilles. The population is nearly half a million: mostly of African decent. I'm afraid that we too indulged in slavery on the plantations. The island still exports sugar and bananas. It is a province of France. That is how it became part of the EUROPEAN Federation when the independent, formerly British islands joined North America ... sorry Jakko! I pull your leg.'

Together they explored the largest city in the French West Indies, Danielle now effervescent, talkative throughout. They hired a car, driving in turn to tour the plantations and extinct volcanoes; hand in hand, the wind in their hair, gazing from vantage points over the sea. Danielle, naturally perhaps, asked eventually about Sylvie, only to be reassured. 'I met her only once before ... at that famous WCA Election Rally. I have sympathy for her, because in the eyes of so many people she is suspect. Jamina hasn't helped. I don't mind her being tough, but she jumps to conclusions without *any* evidence. That is unfair.'

Danielle: 'Jealousy! Don't you see. But you are so kind.'

They were now on high ground towards the north-west end of the island, looking across the blue water towards Dominica.

Jakko took a long searching look at his companion, took both hands in his. 'Jealousy? *You* are not like that, are you. *You* could never be bitchy in a million years. Besides, I am a very poor catch.'

She looked up, all one and a half metres and a bit, genuinely awaiting a reply. 'What is this ''poor catch'' business?'

Jakko told her much later, when they had reached the stage of exchanging innermost thoughts, that he didn't *blow a fuse* at that moment. The circuits had just *melted* . . .

* * *

So, to Antigua with — once more — the young volunteers lining the foredeck, Jakko Mann in the eyes of the ship, as *Andromeda* steamed close by three of her squadron off English Harbour, exchanging flag signals and verbal pleasantries: 'Hi, sister' . . . '*Bon jour, mes enfants!*' . . . 'Welcome from the Asteroids, O Constellation' and the rest . . .

Thence round the coast clockwise, to join the remainder of the squadron off St Johns. Here, having saluted the base Flag Officer, she anchored amidst more signalling, a more serious 'Well done' from the C-in-C. Her Captain hastened ashore to wait upon the Admiral.

Boats from the base, manned as before, were sent out for their gear, and in due course two cutters came alongside to collect the party.

The incident that followed demands to be recorded. It expressed to the young people something of the comradeship permeating those who had given their lives to the World's service. Their intention unknown to anyone but the Executive Officer, whose approval had been sought but who had been sworn to secrecy, *Andromeda*'s ship's company now lined the guardrails. As the boats shoved off, there was a shout of 'WELL DONE', followed by three cheers.

Immediate reply was needed if it was to be effective. Jakko Mann stood up on a thwart, shouted to the second cutter, 'THREE CHEERS FOR *ANDROMEDA*.'

He turned to the boat's Cox'n. 'Forgive me!'

'That is OK,' she said. 'I understand. We have heard all about it.'

18

Jakko and Danielle walked hand in hand towards the giant statue that dominated the wide square in the newer part of St Johns. The square itself was spotless; swept and garnished. It was their last afternoon before they were due to return to Euro College 11.

Already, given shore leave from the naval base, they had experienced together the unique contrasts that characterized the island of Antigua. Forts, four hundred years old, some original guns still in place — at least one bearing Queen Anne's crown — looked down protectively upon Falmouth, English Harbour, and Nelson's Dockyard; while a bare ten miles away, St Johns Deep Water Harbour — necessarily for an island economy — was one of the most efficient small ports of the world. There too were gathered administrative and repair facilities in support of naval units of the WPF, whose *raison d' être* was elimination forever of forces with national allegiance.

Likewise they had climbed Boggy Point, from which could be seen on a clear day the entire coastline, and Fig Tree Hill with its unequalled scenery; inspected Betty's Hope, the then colony's first full-scale sugar complex, established by Codrington in 1674. Two windmill towers still stood, hard by the surviving arches of the old boiling house. Not ten miles from this site with its slave labour memories now stood a building unique to the Caribbean, housing one of the most complex computers in the world: a major WISO centre, serving some fifty million unit holders of the NORTH AMERICAN AND CARIBBEAN FEDERATION.

They approached the statue, looked up first at the proud figure, then down at the inscription.

> # THE RT. HON. DR VERE CORNWALL BIRD
> Father of the Nation.
> This statue was erected by the people of
> ## ANTIGUA AND BARBUDA
> in fond and everlasting memory.
> 'Each Endeavouring — All Achieving'

The sides of the square boasted a long line of seats and park benches. Each bore a brass plate inscribed with the donor's name or that of the personality in whose memory it had been gifted to the city. Jamina would have been reminded of Princes Street. On a busy week day most of the seats were empty save for a few children playing, but on that nearest the statue sat, somewhat huddled, a very, very old coloured man. His clothes had seen better days and, though threadbare in places, they had obviously been cared for. The patched trousers had a distinct crease. Frizzed white hair protruded round the edges of an ancient hat, but there was a distinct air of respectability. The gaze of the two volunteers followed downwards that of the old man, and there on ancient feet was a pair of new, bright red socks.

The moment demanded some kind observation, and no two members of the world's younger generation were more fitted to make it. Danielle, least inhibited, opened the conversation. 'Those are beautiful socks. May I ask where you got them?'

The old man pulled up his trouser legs so that all might have a better view. 'My son bought them for me out of his WISO money. That WISO is a splendid thing. He doesn't need his dividend at the moment. I am one hundred years old. I was born in 1984.'

'You look remarkably well,' Jakko observed. 'I suppose it's because you live on such a beautiful island, with the fresh air and all the fruit and vegetables and everything.'

But the old man was only just getting into his stride. 'You see Doctor Vere Cornwall Bird up there. Well, I was five years old in 1989 — I can remember it — when the Antigua Trades and Labour Union celebrated its Golden Jubilee . . . that is fifty years . . . it was formed in 1939 . . .' He warmed to his young audience; at peace with the world, contentedly sitting in the sun while the population, long since boasting zero unemployment, busied itself with its prosperity.

'By 1989, Doctor VC Bird had worked for the people for fifty years. It was a double celebration: as much his as the union's. I have studied the history. It was a long fight. First the union led our people in their demand for better wages. They were very badly treated. In those days it was only sugar, and when the bad times came there was no other employment. Then Mr Bird led us to independence from the colonial power and to develop a mixed economy. Japan, Singapore and Hong Kong had all developed rapidly without raw materials of their own. Antigua, he said' (there was a suspicion of Gershwin in the *he said*), 'must do the same. In the old days, secondary education was reserved for the white people. Doctor Vere Cornwall Bird was determined that it should be open to all ... including university. Education and St Johns Deep Water Harbour were the keys to our prosperity and future, with a mixed economy in which tourism would play a major part. Yes, truly Doctor Vere Cornwall Bird was the Father of the Nation.' He used Dr Bird's full names yet again with affection and respect. 'More than that, he achieved it all without violence. He was an example to the world.' The old man spread his arms wide to indicate the magnitude of the achievement.

'I was very glad,' he mused, changing the subject, 'when eventually our Government renamed Codrington in Barbuda. It is now known as Freetown. You see, Codrington leased the island of Barbuda from the British crown. There he bred and sold slaves and supplied stores and draught animals to the sugar planters on the islands. Even the poor horses were ill-used; they were unsuited to the climate. But I suppose, really,' reverting to the theme, 'the two biggest triumphs for our island were the siting here of the WPF base and the WISO centre. Of course the Americans and Canadians said that they must have all the WISO centres, but our Government said ''We are part of the Federation, same as you, and we have the educated young people, same as you. Besides, *the World Government itself* moves every five years so everyone feels that they belong.'' That was one of the best ideas the world ever had. We all belong now. So they built one of the WISO centres here. The others, they are all on the mainland.'

He leaned back on the wooden seat. 'I do a lot of reading.

110

I am not sure what good it does! I often wonder why God didn't make it possible for young people to begin their lives where the old people leave off. Then knowledge and experience would not be wasted. By the time most people know enough, they are too old to lead the world.' He chuckled. 'Maybe I tell the good Lord when I get there!'

Jakko, was moved equally by the philosophy and by the simple faith. 'I hope that won't be for a long time.'

'I'm not afraid. My wife Martha; she's with the Lord, so she can introduce me. No; I am not afraid.'

Jakko turned to his companion. 'I think we should ask our friend to have a drink with us.'

The old man answered first, 'It is very kind of you, but I don't drink during the day. It sets off my old bladder. But thank you just the same.'

Danielle: 'Well, it was nice talking to you.'

'And to talk to you too . . . before you go, let me show you what I found a few days ago in an old junk shop.' With that he extracted with great care from a jacket pocket an ancient paperback book. The remains of a strip of sticking plaster held the cover together, the pages yellow with age, but the lettering on the outside was still legible.

'This copy was printed the year I was born.' He carefully turned back the front cover and held the precious volume to the light. 'It says inside, ''First published 1949''. (Reading) ''Reprinted *thirty-one times*(!). *This edition 1984.*'' That makes it one hundred years old, like yours truly.' He replaced the front cover. The title was unblemished:

GEORGE ORWELL'S
NINETEEN EIGHTY-FOUR

The old man rose to his feet with some difficulty and held out a hand. 'There'll be no Big Brothers while the WPF and you youngsters are around. God bless you and keep our world in peace. Like it says on the Identity Cards, we are all one family now.'

Danielle leaned forward and kissed him. 'We'll do our best,' she said.

19

Unit 2001 returned to Crawley. Fame had preceded them. A new Environment Corps intake, fifty strong, appeared excitedly to have taken possession of the College. With congratulations from staff and admiring questions from these younger colleagues, the returning WPF recruits might have been forgiven for believing briefly that they were seasoned troops, had their course not been resumed with a new — frightening — intensity. On the very first evening, a Friday, they were called by telescreen to assemble for a special briefing. The lighter aspects of their experiences were soon to become sweet memories.

They rose as Goodssen himself appeared, accompanied by Brightwell and a Professor Emden, a senior member of the World Government staff. The College Principal: 'A quick word first about your trip. I am sure that you all found it of value. We expect the sort of behaviour that you exhibited aboard *Andromeda* but that does not lessen our satisfaction in College as the story unfolded on the screens. I am told by HQ Europe to expect one or two Commendations. These may indeed be the least awards to WPF Personnel, but they are not lightly given, particularly as they carry a small bonus of WISO Beta units.

'What I have to tell you now is at present confidential. The reasons will be obvious. Some months ago, the World Government commissioned an urgent study by a group of eminent persons from all ten Federations — and indeed from outside. They were to report, first, upon progress towards One World and, secondly, upon the measures they deemed necessary to ensure that we continue to have a world at all. I have to tell you bluntly that in the group's findings on both counts, the WG got more than it bargained for.

112

'Your course is to be expedited so that you may pass out from College, volunteer for the arm of the WPF in which you wish to serve, and be posted as soon as possible to your units.

'A crash expansion of the WPF has been ordered. There is basic contradiction in the WG's desire always to minimize expenditure of what is in the final analysis the people's money and, on the other hand, the *absolute need* for the WPF to be large enough and competent to do its job. If it failed in that, the world might revert — at least in some areas — to armed inter-nation or inter-faction conflict. The people of all nations are not yet within the World Federation. There are still some States that are dissatisfied with the status quo. Additionally, there is still widespread maldistribution of wealth: a continuing source of tension.

'In round figures there are twelve billion human beings on the Earth today. Sadly, many of the great population concentrations are in the poorest — and environmentally threatened — parts of the world. In the face of persecution and fear of extinction, the elephants began a hundred years ago to limit their own members. Likewise the human birthrate in the more advanced Regions was limited by the fear of nuclear war. By contrast, it was seen as necessary by the most disadvantaged to have many children to ensure the survival of *any*.

'Besides, those with neither work, recreation, nor the means to pursue culture, had little save scratching a living to occupy their time and such energy as they possessed. It will be a daunting task to ensure a personal stake in the World's wealth to the deprived and backward, of whom unhappily there are still so many, and to those whose land — due to the Earth's warming — has become desert.

'In 2084 we thus still have a great divide or, more precisely, three divisions: World Citizens who share personally and individually in the World's wealth; World Citizens — in that they belong to the World Federation — all of whom *do not* yet share in its wealth; and those *neither* yet World Citizens *nor* wealth-sharing. Meanwhile there are still millions of refugees, and as many who have no individual say in the direction of affairs.'

* * *

113

Goodssen returned to world security.

'The Middle East and Arab/Israeli mistrust constituted a threat to the world's peace. There existed not only interstate tensions but huge inequalities in individual wealth and quality of life.

'Israel's desire to retain the West Bank was natural enough. Any country with a "waist" barely twenty miles in width, bordered on one side by the sea and surrounded on the other by supposed potential enemies would be a strategic nonsense. Additionally, miraculous Israeli development in largely hostile terrain had earned enormous admiration. That being so, it was particularly regrettable that their harsh treatment of the Palestinians during the military occupation of the West Bank and Gaza Strip forfeited much of that sympathy and understanding in the eyes of the civilized world. I find it difficult to equate the tragic history of the Jewish people and their passionate craving for a home of their own with their apparent lack of understanding of a like desire in others.

'At all events, "no way", to use a twentieth-century expression, would the Israelis have given up the West Bank. And "no way" would the Palestinians — indeed anyone else — have been excluded from Jerusalem.

'It was none too soon for the peace of the world that, at Egypt's initial instigation, THE FEDERATION OF ARAB MIDDLE EAST designated Sinai a Palestinian Home within the group, under its protection and thus — importantly — *also of the World Government and the WPF*; and, at World instance, Jerusalem itself was declared an open city, where *all* may worship according to their faith.

'Israel retained the entire West Bank but withdrew from the Gaza Strip, which had never divided their country geographically nor threatened its security. The area west of and the road itself from Gaza to Elat was ceded to the new State. Final recognition of Israel, peace, and consolidation of all *de facto* Israeli territory further north was for Israel a favourable deal. As an interim measure, Elat was placed under WG administration as a free port.

'For the Palestinians, it was to become a modern miracle. Aid of every description from a sympathetic world, grateful for elimination of a major threat to peace, poured in to build their beautiful new capital city backed by rugged escarpment, facing

114

the sea; and to create a viable if diverse economy where once was but sand and salt and rock. Meanwhile Israel finally introduced a Bill of Rights, following the World pattern, guaranteeing equal, civilized, treatment of *all* its citizens.'

* * *

'Once more we owe much to the Federal idea, both for security in the region *and* hugely improved quality of life. The present ARAB FEDERATION, pioneered initially by Egypt and Saudi Arabia, the Gulf States and Libya, was then joined by Jordan. That was as important as it was logical, uniting in the Federation, alongside New Palestine in Sinai, Jordan's predominantly Palestinian population. Syria joined later.

'As regards quality of life, hitherto so grossly unbalanced, the Federation united the oil-rich Gulf states; Egypt with its tourist industry, Canal dues and dam power; rapidly evolving, green food-producing Libya; and the Palestinians, recipients of massive World aid and development finance. Common citizenship, mutual understanding, and the beginnings of WISO introduction have totally changed the potential for the individual.

'Peace thus secured in the Middle East remains of supreme World importance. Nonetheless the World Government has its anxieties. The "great awakening" before and around the turn of the century, and the establishment of democratic institutions in areas previously under hard-line Communist control, created its own tensions. To majorities impatient for freedom and reform, the pace often seemed too slow. To hard-line conservatives it was seen as being too fast. Europe was awash with refugees seeking a new life in the West. Later, China was awash with blood. Pan Africa's democracy was but feeling its way after a century of oppression in the south. *It was vital for the World's new, inexperienced, more liberal governments to succeed.* Not all members, even of the existing World Assembly, have long backgrounds of tolerance and individual liberty. Indescribable misery still exists in South-East Asia and part of South America.

'There is still a great deal to be done.

'And now, my friends, as if all that was not enough, we are faced with new climatic problems on an unprecedented scale. The measures taken by Man around the turn of the century to save planet Earth may prove to have been too little and too late.'

115

20

Goodssen introduced Professor Emden. 'The Professor is one of the most respected and knowledgeable students of the likely future of our planet Earth. He is a member of the World Government's think tank on the Environment, and its Chief Permanent Adviser. Professor Emden is uniquely qualified by nationality, experience, and observation.

'After university in his native Germany, he volunteered to join the team of scientists then collating information for the World Government prior to its international conference "Action by Man," the most important get-together since 1957 International Geophysical Year, the Montreal Protocol of 1987 and International Space Year 1992. He has visited Halley Bay Research Station in the Antarctic, which first spotted the hole in the ozone layer over Antarctica, the Mauna Loa, Hawaii, monitor of gases in the atmosphere, besides most of the world's other important atmospheric and climatic research stations from Pole to Pole: Greenland and Canada to Chile's Punta Arenas on the Straits of Magellan, the Falklands, Cape Town and Tasmania; Japan; Russia; and a host of universities. He has been involved in research into the Earth's warming, the role of the great rainforests, the warming of the oceans, effect on the world's wind patterns, storm routes and hurricanes, the spread of deserts, major changes in the great food-producing areas, the breeding of new crops to adapt to drier — and often saltier — conditions, melting of the polar ice and possible drowning of many of the world's most concentrated centres of population. Finally, Professor Emden, who is already a Nobel Prizewinner, is Chief Scientific Adviser to mankind's biggest projects. At present he is undertaking a lightning tour of World Colleges. As chance would have it, we have as our guests tomorrow night one of Berlin's great orchestras, and I have persuaded the Professor to stay with us for the extra day . . . Professor Emden . . . '

'My friends,' he began. 'I am glad to be here. I have already visited two Euro Colleges. It is a serious message that I bring. You young people have a big responsibility and an important part to play.

'Before I talk about the need for increased determination if we are to save planet Earth, I would like to refer to your Captain Brightwell's first lecture to volunteers who pass through this College . . . and her comments upon San Francisco, 1945.' He turned to the Captain with a little bow of chivalrous acknowledgement. 'There is no doubt that had there existed towards the end of the last century a World *Government* with executive powers in vital areas . . . or even one capable of ensuring effective co-operation . . . the likelihood is that immediate concerted action would have been taken to protect the Earth: to cease the release of harmful emissions into the atmosphere, for example, and to stop the burning; a crash programme for survival of the human race. I mean *immediate*; not percentages or by distant dates. Of course my country suffered most from *Waldsterben*. I tend to be emphatic! But there existed only the UN, a collection of bargaining delegates of sovereign States, not an executive body . . . an organization with, in any case, little influence in important parts of the world.

'Your Captain Brightwell maintains correctly that there were four choices open to those at San Francisco: election immediately of a World Assembly as a nucleus open to all to join in their own time; an intermediate stage of regionalism; the functional approach; or a mere talking shop like the UN. The Captain was correct in her assessment of the alternatives, but of course after the World War in which much of the civilized world was reduced to rubble and casualties were reckoned in millions, national recovery was — understandably — the uppermost desire. It was no time for fundamental changes involving the sovereignty or security of the survivors. It was an ''idea whose time had not yet come''.

'And so a combination of regionalism and functional considerations led to the first major step forward: when Robert Schuman, the Foreign Minister of France, put forward the idea of a European Coal and Steel Community. I quote from the

117

Declaration of 9 May 1950. ''World peace cannot be safeguarded without the making of constructive efforts proportionate to the dangers which threaten it. The contribution which an organized and living Europe can bring to civilization is indispensable . . .'' *There* is the regionalism. ''Europe will not be made all at once or according to a single general plan. It will be built through concrete achievements which first create a *de facto* solidarity.'' *There* is the functional. ''The French Government proposes to place Franco-German production of coal and steel under a common higher authority, within the framework of an organization *open to the participation of the other countries of Europe.* The pooling of coal and steel production will immediately provide for the setting up of common bases for economic development *as a first step in the federation of Europe.*'' That is my emphasis. *There* is the functional as a means to regionalism.

'My message now is that THE EMERGENCY MEASURES FOR THE EARTH'S SURVIVAL CALLED FOR IN THE 2084 REPORT TO THE WORLD GOVERNMENT AND WHICH WILL BE ENACTED AT ITS INSTIGATION, PROVIDE THE FUNCTIONAL REASONING FOR THE RALLYING BEHIND THE WORLD ASSEMBLY OF THE ENTIRE HUMAN RACE.'

21

'A few comments to remind ourselves of the causes and effects of the greenhouse and damage to the ozone layer before we consider the present emergency, the announcement to be made to the whole world population by the World Executive, and the reasons for the "telescoping" and early completion of your course . . .

'Much of the gas in the atmosphere, including oxygen and nitrogen, which make up about ninety per cent, does not affect our climate. Radiation passes through it. By contrast, the greenhouse gases, which include water vapour, carbon dioxide, nitrous oxide, methane, and chlorofluorocarbons (CFCs) have a major effect. Radiation from the sun passes through the atmosphere and warms the Earth's surface, including — importantly — the oceans, inland seas and waterways; but radiation from the Earth in the reverse direction is prevented by the carbon dioxide from escaping into space. Hence the warming of the lower atmosphere around the Earth and Man's responsibility since he created, or caused, most of the harmful gases in the first place.

'Life on land and in the upper ocean layers is protected from ultra-violet radiation by the ozone layer, a thin covering in the stratosphere around the Earth. As every human being must now know, the first hole over Antarctica in that protective layer was discovered in 1985 by the Halley Bay research station, set up by Britain as part of this country's contribution to International Geophysical Year.' Another little bow. 'The gases responsible had been released into the atmosphere by Man *many years before . . . and were still being released in gigantic quantities.*

'The Earth's warming is particularly dangerous nearest to the Poles because, as the ice melts, reflection is reduced, more of the Sun's heat can be absorbed, and as warmer water washes around and under the ice shelves, so fragments of the ice break away and augment the melting. In the event of *substantial* break-up of the shelves, we would be talking about a rise in sea levels *of the order of ten to twenty metres, and the drowning of cities in which live a hundred million or more souls.*

'These facts and estimates were known a hundred years ago. Had so much damage already been done, that life on Earth was doomed? What should be done, in case it was not too late? What were the most l'kely earlier effects of global warming? Would other holes appear in the ozone layer? . . . And where? Even if measures were agreed on the whole world's behalf, could they be enforced?'

The Professor caught the eye momentarily of Danielle de Croix as she sat beside Jakko in the front row of his audience. 'Ah! . . . young lady . . . of course! The WPF and the World Environment Corps . . . had they existed, *and* been many times larger than they are today!' He turned to Goodssen. 'How well you teach them. They are young *missionaries*!'

For all his knowledge, experience, and no-nonsense manner, Emden appeared also a humanitarian . . . to have been moved by the gentle child volunteer for the World's service with whom he had exchanged a glance. He resumed his theme almost paternally, then once more got into his stride as professionalism reasserted itself. 'Towards the end of the last century, scientists were piecing together a vast mass of data which seemed to be connected: the rise in global temperatures; falling levels of the inland seas and rivers; drought and starvation across Africa (by then the drought could not be immediately prevented, but the starvation was a scandal); dust bowls, forest fires, increased skin cancer in Australia, nearest to the first ozone "hole"; the vast parched, drought-hit North American grain belts; sickness in our trees in Europe and in North America; the rise in sea temperatures and important changes in wind patterns; hurricanes of unprecedented ferocity; floods; disappearance of fish from traditional grounds to more congenial waters; wholesale changes in farming and food patterns as the warmth spread from the Equator Polewards; migration, unemployment, ruin, and, most alarming of all, beginnings of the feared rise in the level of the sea.' He paused before continuing with renewed emphasis.

'Unquestionably, *the Earth was entering an uncharted future* . . .

and all this millions of years after its creation, when common interest and caring were spreading at last over its surface at the hands of Man, and individual members of the human race were beginning to acquire, as of right, a personal stake in its wealth, future, and good things. I can conceive of nothing more tragic than the possible end of it all at such a time.' He paused again, contemplating anew the audience of Europe's most dedicated youth as they sat in silence, awed by the magnitude of the world's problems.

Then, explosively, 'Faced a hundred years ago with the unknown and possible extinction of life as we know it, one would have expected *action*, total, immediate, and enforced as far as possible, from the then inter-governmental bodies . . . such as they were. Not so! Emissions of carbon dioxide have *continued*.'

At this he threw up his arms. Silence in the hall was absolute once more.

'Nor was time on their side. Much of the world's power was still derived from fossil fuels and from nuclear power stations which could, accidentally, destroy the world. Agricultural land in Scotland is *still* affected a hundred years on by radioactive fallout from Chernobyl. Everywhere, scientists were working feverishly to produce economic *fusion* power to replace timber, coal, oil *and* those dangerous reactors, with energy that was *clean and cheap and safe*. But the battle was being fought not by world agencies funded by mankind but in the main by universities, small teams, even individuals.

'It was generally accepted that the Earth *was* warming. Typical projections suggested $2° — 6°C$, that is $3.6° — 10.8°F$, by this year (2084). Chemicals *already released* into the atmosphere were expected to persist for a hundred years. Virtually all were agreed that sea levels would rise, with three feet by 2084 a popular consensus. That would cause flooding: for example in Bangladesh, the Nile Delta, and a number of important cities. Moreover, in 1988 the world had a foretaste of other possible effects. In that year, for example, consumption of grain exceeded production by sixty million tons, due to the parched earth.

'However, all scientists rarely agree. The view was also held that the world was heading — and soon — for a new Ice Age. These occur every ten thousand years, and the Earth was at the "right" moment for the next! Increased evaporation would result from the warming, the moisture falling as increased snow falls at higher latitudes; each fall being "overtaken" and augmented by the next before it had time to melt. Hence the spread towards more temperate zones. Others maintained that Ice Ages are caused by the Earth's "wobbles"; the Milankovitch cycles.

'The effect of conflicting views and estimates was to strengthen the hand of those advocating delay in the taking of any major action, because "the case was not yet proven". And remember, much of the world was in turmoil; millions preoccupied: in the Soviet Union and Eastern Europe with the throwing-off of Communism; in Africa with newly-elected governments and — in some areas — starvation; in parts of South-East Asia with survival. Western Europe, still hindered by Britain, was striving for complete integration for its common good while preserving the character and traditions of its several parts . . . not an easy matter, in spite of the ideal and the necessity. That the undivided attention of man was not concentrated upon continued survival of life on this unhappy planet is not entirely surprising.

'It is fortunate for us that sufficient measures *were* taken during the intervening hundred years at least to *slow down* the effects of global warming.

'The "developed" nations did succeed — over ten years! — in prohibiting the emission of harmful gases from the exhausts of motor vehicles, but it took a generation even for that measure to become, supposedly, worldwide.' Emden noted surprise amongst his audience at the 'ten years'. 'Well, it was an *achievement* without a world legislature!'

He continued, 'I refer, too, to the vast tree-planting programmes the world over, resolute action to stop the destruction of the rainforests — you saw some of this during your recent stopover in Amazonia — and determination by individual governments to reduce deadly emissions from industry and power stations. In face of wholesale coal burning in China and Eastern Europe in the years around the turn of the century, it is little short of a miracle that we still have a chance to save the Earth.

'As for the ozone layer, CFCs were banned more quickly. But methane . . . that was more of a problem. Production of methane in nature — notably by the world's multi-billion termite population, wild animals, and in swamps — was boosted dramatically by Man's waste disposal problems, rice fields,

122

factory farms and eating habits. Human beings are not naturally carnivores, but — while vegetarianism was spreading rapidly in "developed" countries — meat-eating continued with all its related problems: heart disease, constipation, and bowel cancer: the latter a particularly nasty killer. The world's cattle population was at its height. "Exhaust gases" from the processing of vegetable matter into meat, and from dairy herds, constituted a major factor in methane release. Similarly, the world's rubbish dumps. Waste disposal (not to mention nuclear, or dangerous chemicals) had become Man's dominant environmental problem.

'But now let us consider *our* responsibilities.'

* * *

'I turn now to the 2084 Eminent Persons' Report: "ACTION BY MAN".

'Basically, we have to harness and distribute, worldwide, power from "clean" sources; to make possible an *absolute ban on production units emitting harmful gases of any kind whatsoever*, or based upon old-type nuclear plants. There are no technical difficulties now that fusion power has been mastered. Already, substantial ring mains exist regionally: first pioneered by the Arab world, Europe, the Americas, Russia and Japan. Nothing stands in the way, bar the sheer size of the projects and physical construction. No half-measures will do.

'The Report is equally concerned to halt the spread from the Equator of further unproductive desert, and thirdly with the rising level of the sea. The Eminent Persons stress the common factor: that if the seas are "overflowing" and water is needed desperately inland, two of the three major possible courses of action will assist solution of *both* problems. The first involves diverting fresh water from selected rivers, so that reduced quantities reach the sea in the first place, the water being used to create inland reserves and for irrigation. Secondly, sea levels can be lowered by pumping water ashore, first removing the salt. Thirdly, related only to the sea level problem,, salt water *without* desalination can be pumped inland into existing depressions, where it may also prove to be of unexpected further benefit: in evaporation, cloud formation, even rain-making, and

123

fish farming.

'Of course these ideas are not new. The Russians had been considering for more than a hundred years the diversion of water from north-flowing rivers southwards into the rapidly drying Aral and Caspian Seas. Sadly, the turbulent first quarter of this century in the Russian Federation and its sphere of influence was not conducive to unprecedented expenditure on huge labour-intensive enterprise, but it is to Man's credit that the World Executive internationalized the problem and organized massive assistance to Russian Federal Government in the interests of us all. The Aral/Caspian depression had dried to such an extent that its filling, without endangering Baku or Astrakhan, negated an estimated twelve years of predicted rise in sea levels. Together with other measures, this ambitious project provided essential breathing space for the planning of further action by World agencies.

'The Aral/Caspian project is, of course, immense. It proves that virtually nothing is impossible, given the necessity. It helped to delay the drowning of the Earth's land mass, and diversion of fresh water permitted huge expansion of existing irrigation. The allied project: diversion southwards of water from the Ob, Yenisey and Lena rivers helped the sea level problem, *and* began to feed immense fresh water schemes in Central Asia precisely when the spreading Polewards of global warmth finally destroyed the great grain-producing belts of the Ukraine and North America.

'The connection between the diverting of rivers and the ring mains will not have escaped you young people. We can look forward to substantial contributions of "clean" power from new dams to augment that from fusion plants. There are many other excellent examples, such as the La Grande Riviere projects in north-western Quebec, with the partial reversal of the Caniapiscau; Zimbabwe's Kariba; and, more recently, the construction of fresh water reserves in the Rockies; to name only a few.

'In 1984 it would have been asked how immense projects of this kind could be financed where sites important to the world occur in territories which are themselves unable to bear the cost. I need hardly remind you that the very existence of a World Government and Constitution, backed by a World Police Force (for, let us not mince words, that is what it is), has enabled

124

elimination of by far the greater part of one-time national weapons of defence and, with them, the crippling drain on the budgets of the world. Besides, where great new profit-making utilities are to be created, they will be candidates for WISO . . . just as North Sea Oil, British Gas etc. should have been here. They will eventually prove to be self-financing and thereafter, once the initial loans have been repaid, will distribute income to the WISO Trusts and through them to their unitholders, the people of the world.'

At this point Emden handed his audience back to the College Principal.

Goodssen thanked the Professor for his talk and announced that a World Government film would be shown each evening in the week following, outlining the emergency programme of new projects.

'I have seen a preview of some of them,' he commented. 'Even in the times in which we live, they will take your breath away.'

22

'Monika Brandt and Jakko Mann of Euro 2001 to the Principal's office ... Monika Brandt and Jakko Mann please ...'

Jakko and Danielle, dressed early for Saturday guest night dinner and the concert, had commandeered a small corner table in the Defenders Bar.

'Jakko! What have you been doing with that always efficient German lady?' There was just a suspicion of forced hilarity in the question: anxiety, perhaps. Danielle put down her glass. They were the only two in the bar, but it made no difference. Jakko's reaction was spontaneous. He took both her hands in his over the table. 'Nothing! I promise. Of course Monika is attractive, and she *is* efficient. Everybody accepts that. But I hardly know her; only to say hello, like anyone else in the Unit. I believe she did a good job in *Andromeda* when we picked up those survivors. She was on the other side of the ship from us.'

Danielle, relenting, then excitedly, 'That is a clue, isn't it? Oh Jakko, perhaps it is another Commendation. I couldn't be more happy if it was me. I wait for you ... for ever.'

Their mutual affection had deepened since Trinidad, further since Antigua, but Jakko was still moved by the 'for ever'. 'I'll come straight back.' He left the bar quickly to comply with the telescreen's instruction.

By the time he returned, now accompanied by Monika Brandt, the bar was full of WPF and Environment Corps trainees, shoulder flashes from all over Europe, happy laughter, and the clink of ice in glasses. The whole WPF Unit had heard the telescreen order. Now there was silence as they waited for news.

'Well?' somebody asked.

Monika raised Jakko's hand in boxing-ring fashion. 'I am

happy to tell you that Jakko and I are to receive WPF Commendations for life-saving when we were in *Andromeda*. I am pleased for my country. But we both know that these Commendations belong equally to you . . . to all of us . . . to Europe. Jakko and I are very happy to be your friends.'

Instantly a number of volunteers from Germany broke into *Lilli Marlene*, sung a century and a half before by desert soldiers on both sides and, uniquely, ever since. Soon the whole bar was filled with voices. The chorus subsided, there was a shout of 'Something for Jakko', and an enthusiastic if somewhat garbled rendering of *For he's a jolly good fellow* as a number of staff entered the bar, the evening's conductor and Professor Emden in their midst.

Silence . . . broken by Pippa Brightwell. 'I think it is as well that this announcement was made *before* dinner! You can rest assured that Unit 2001 will become part of the history of the College.'

As staff and their guests were besieged around the bar, Jakko disengaged himself from well-wishing colleagues in search of Danielle. Presently he felt a tug at his sleeve and there she was beside him, looking up with, 'I thought you had forgotten me. Oh Jakko, I am so proud of you.' He bent down and whispered in her ear amidst the fair hair and the hubbub,

'Let's finish our drinks . . . if they are still there. I suggest we go in early and bag good places for dinner.' Apart from the evening's President and members of the staff, seating was a matter of first come, first served.

'What is bag?' Danielle asked, recalling instantly for Jakko the magic moment in Martinique. There they had been alone together, the wind in their hair, gazing northwards across the crystal water towards Dominica, most unspoiled island of them all. He had put his arms around the little girl from Normandy and they had shared the first gentle kiss, even in the twenty-first century, of the young and inexperienced; each believing that — unless, later, fate otherwise decided — they had so early found their affinity in their first love. Now in the crowded bar they could only grasp each other's hands again, inconspicuously this time, and hold on so tightly that nothing *but* fate could ever part them.

'I just mean that we make sure of places near the top table so that we can hear the toasts and speeches.'

127

Jakko was still in a state of reaction from his education at Jamina's hands in the art of sex for its own sake. Given his simple unsophisticated background, that she was the most beautiful thing that he had ever seen, that they met when he was alone in a great city for the first time, embarking on a career that was to change his life, it was hardy surprising that he had been completely captivated. But suddenly in Trinidad, at the Golden Gates Hotel, he had been shocked by Jamina's disregard of loyalties following her tough possessiveness. He had been surprised at his own instant rejection of a so intense relationship, but — looking back — it now seemed to him so crude.

With Danielle his instinct was, by contrast, one of respect for her innocence and complete naturalness, which was in accord with his own. He stood now, still holding her hands, oblivious to the excited chatter by which they were surrounded; his eyes misted, heart filled with affection and protectiveness. And then a secret plea that, each having volunteered for the service of the World, they might be allowed to serve together.

* * *

The last notes of Verdi's *Chorus of the Hebrew Slaves* brought the evening to a tumultuous conclusion, the entire guest night audience in Central Hall standing as they sang the unofficial anthem of Mankind. Prolonged applause for the Berlin orchestra and its conductor. Professor Emden, led by Goodssen to the stage, given a warm, respectful sendoff.

'Let's go to my room and I make some coffee,' Danielle suggested, 'unless you want a nightcap. Anyway, we can put some cognac in the coffee.' Jakko fell in at once with the suggestion. Soon they were at her door.

Jakko: 'Oh ...' — awed and surprised — 'you have made it *beautiful*.' Threaded at the centre through a gold ring on the wall, a draped tricolour in muslin framed the single bed. Matching curtains. A print of Napoleon and a rugby 'cap', tassel dangling, perched on a hook.

'My brother Jean-Pierre lives in the south ... near Toulouse. He played number eight for France last time we won the Grand Slam. We have won it more times than anyone else. You see, I am what you call "Rugby fanatic". In the Five Nations, only

Scotland play fast, open rugby like France. Sit down, Jakko. I make the coffee. It is better than they give us in the dining hall.'

She motioned Jakko towards the regulation armchair, increasingly talkative now. 'Some Camembert? My family keep me supplied from Normandy. Or is it too late at night? I think I have a few crackers left. But perhaps it would keep you awake.' Jakko was overcome as much by the patriotism as the decor.

You are passionately French,' he volunteered.

'Of course! Are you not passionately English? ... no, I suppose not. It is your weather! It must be difficult to be "passionate" when it is always damp and miserable. But maybe things will improve now the Earth's warmth is spreading northwards!! Jakko, you put in the cognac ... not too much for me.' She pointed to a bottle on the shelf under Napoleon. 'You are growing grapes in England now, of course.'

The little fragment of France changed the subject, tossed back the fair hair, became suddenly more serious. 'I have listened attentively to all the talk here about Federal structures and sovereignty,' she declared between sips of coffee. 'But it all seems to me what you call "common sense". My family lost soldiers killed in all three wars: 1870, 1916 and 1943 with the Resistance, but they were as enthusiastic as anyone when the German people were reunited ... can you imagine France cut in half or England with a Berlin Wall through the middle of London? The important thing was that Western Europe was strong. I think your Prime Minister was very wrong to oppose closer integration. It was so important at that time. Amongst loosely associated sovereign states, Germany would have once more become dominant. Paradoxically — is that how you say it — the Germans taught Europe too, about *de*centralization, with their *länder*: strong at the centre, with regions preserving their identity and handling local affairs. Like your Scotland and Wales now ... and just like our Jaques Delors said.'

Jakko couldn't help contrasting the Danielle now commenting upon Europe so wisely and, being French, indeed bravely as he saw it, with the little girl holding his hand as they gazed across the sea together towards Dominica; who had instinctively bent down to kiss the old man in the square in St Johns, Antigua. But then, of course, in *Andromeda* she had proved herself not only caring but extremely competent. He recalled for a split second his earlier doubt whether she was strong enough for the

WPF. How unjustified he now saw those fears to have been. But Danielle was continuing, her eyes fixed on her companion over the coffee cup now held in both her hands.

'It wasn't only because of German reunification that Europe needed to hurry. The countries to the east as they obtained their freedom needed, immediately, an example of democracy: free, *stable*, prosperous, and *strong*; a united Europe, of which in due course they could become a welcome part if their people chose. Meanwhile they needed the help which was so readily given, to establish democratic institutions and to restore their mostly impoverished economies.'

She put down the now empty cup and poured two liqueur glasses of cognac. 'Jakko, let us drink to the future! I wonder what the films will be about that we are to see next week. Are you glad to be part of the future? *I* am.' It was for both of them one more inspired, unspoiled moment.

'*Vive la France! Vive l'Angleterre! ALLEZ MONDE*!' Then, 'Let us not forget our Russian friends!' She threw back her head, drained her glass, then . . . gasping for breath . . . smashed it on the floor. 'Water! . . . water . . . please . . . quickly,' pointing to the handbasin.

Danielle recovered slowly . . . then, 'Jakko, you are so brave . . . and yet so shy. I *love* you ., . . I think it better if I get some vodka for the next time!'

23

Monday evening.

The entire College staff and members of both Units under training assembled in Central Hall. The introductory first part of the World Government's emergency film was to be screened. The series itself would follow on successive nights. Training schedules of both Units had been revised. Weekend leave was cancelled.

To Danielle's amusement, Jakko had 'bagged' two good seats in advance. The assembled company was hushed, then silent. Goodssen appeared.

'Tonight we are to hear a special introduction to the WG film *Action by Man* being shown to the World Assembly and Senate, all WG agencies, Regional Federal and national Governments within the World Federation, and to all WPF and Environment Corps Units and Colleges. Courtesy copies have been supplied to governments outside the Federation for reasons of goodwill and because the fate of their territories and peoples depends — like ours — upon resolute action by *all* mankind. Disaster knows no frontiers and its prevention is in any case, as we have seen, the most compelling functional inducement of all time for all Earth's inhabitants to act together for the common good.

'The preface that we are to see this evening is not being shown to the public.'

Goodssen continued, changing the subject, 'Members of Euro 2001; when you return to your rooms tonight you will find forms, usually distributed only at the end of courses, on which you are asked to state your preference as to the arm of the WPF in which you wish to serve. There is no guarantee that your wishes will be met, but — subject to manning requirements — HQ usually does its best. Subsequently your instruction here will be

131

specialized accordingly.'

Danielle nudged Jakko's arm. 'Can we fill in our forms together?' He took her hand as the Central Hall lights were dimmed.

ACTION BY MAN

AN INTRODUCTION TO THE EMINENT PERSONS' REPORT COMMISSIONED IN 2084 BY THE WORLD EXECUTIVE UPON THE RECOMMENDATION OF THE WORLD FEDERAL ASSEMBLY AND SENATE.

English Edition

Representations, technical forecasts, and advice have been sought on behalf of the world's peoples from all Regional Federations and from territories outside. Participation by the latter was warmly welcomed.

On behalf of the world's peoples, the Executive expresses to the twenty-one "Eminent Persons" and to the nine hundred and sixteen scientific and other advisers, sincere appreciation of their endeavours and co-operation in the urgent preparation of this report. The valuable co-operation of research establishments, universities, computer personnel and secretariat in every continent is likewise warmly acknowledged.

The names and countries of origin of participating individuals, establishments, and universities are given in Part IX at the end of the Report.

THE REPORT IS PRESENTED IN NINE PARTS AND IN TEN LANGUAGES, AND IS INTRODUCED IN EACH LANGUAGE BY A MEMBER OF THE WORLD EXECUTIVE.

THIS EDITION IN ENGLISH INTRODUCED BY
NELSON BANANA II
(Zimbabwe. Pan African Federation)

I   TERMS OF REFERENCE AND FORECASTS

II   PREVENTION OF FURTHER GLOBAL WARMING

1 Artificial Volcano Dust
2 Cessation of harmful emissions
3 Absorption of Carbon Dioxide
4 Extension of 'Clean' Power (see also VI 6)
5 The Earth's Forests (see also VI 3)

III   PREVENTION OF FURTHER DAMAGE TO THE
OZONE LAYER

1 Cessation of harmful emissions
2 Methane
    i Cattle
    ii Rice Fields (see also V 3ii)
    iii Waste Disposal
    iv Infilling of Swamps

IV   SEA LEVELS

1 Cities and Deltas under immediate threat
2 Further threats
3 Calving of ice masses
4 Physical defences against flooding
5 Reduction of amounts of fresh water reaching the
oceans
    i Creation of fresh water reserves (see also VI 4 ii and
    iv and VI 5 ii)
    ii Irrigation (see also VI 4 ii and iii and VI 5)
    iii Additional Hydro-electric power (see also VI 4 iv
    and VI 6)

6 'Clean' Power
  i Fusion Power. Ring Mains programme, Pumps,
     and Distillers
  ii Hydro-electric power
  iii Solar Power
  iv Wind Power
7 Crops
  i New Grain Belts. Canada and Central Asia models
  ii Research. Continuation
8 World. Continuous monitoring and review

VII ACTION FUTURE

1 Follow-up procedures
2 Kariba projects. Selected locations
3 New Depressions. Selected locations
4 Underground Water Reserves. Selected locations
5 Lake Chad. Research
6 World. Continuous monitoring and review. World
  Federal Government and Agencies/Regional
  responsibilities

VIII COST

1 Of monitoring, review, planning
2 Of Projects
3 Of Research

IX ACKNOWLEDGEMENTS[1]

* * *

At this point there appeared on the screen the respected father
figure and current Member of the World Executive, Nelson
Banana II.

* * *

---

[1] Acknowledgement followed of one thousand two hundred and sixty
individuals, research establishments, and universities, besides those
responsible for the compilation and distribution of the Report. These are
omitted in the telling of this story.

24

Nelson Banana II: 'It is my privilege to introduce the English edition of the 2084 Eminent Persons' Report.

'My four colleagues and I, Members of the World Executive at this historic time, have agreed that each of us shall introduce in his own words — I should say ''our'', because we have one very charming and competent lady Executive member from India at present — the editions of the Report for which we are responsible.' The smile that had captivated peoples everywhere produced from Danielle a whispered 'He is lovely! No wonder he is the World's favourite!'

'So, I am permitted a few comments of my own,' the old man continued, serious again. 'The map of the world is usually drawn with Africa at the centre. If you look at the atlas, you will see that Zimbabwe, which is itself heart-shaped, is at the very heart of Africa and of the World. When next year, 2085, the World Assembly moves to Harare, the Earth's heart and mind will be at one. If I may comment with proper modesty, that is far from inappropriate because that beautiful city has exceptional facilities. Importantly also, it is Africa upon which is centred much of the emergency action outlined in the Report.

'Every century has seen changes. But in the last hundred years since 1984, Mankind has witnessed in the blossoming of World Citizenship, opportunity, the sharing in peace of created wealth and the good things of the Earth, the most important advances that it has ever known.

'Man's biggest problem since he began to live in communities has been to establish the ideal relationship between the individual and the ''State'' or the community. He has tried tribalism, oppression, slavery, feudalism, caste systems, so-called Welfare Capitalism and Communism: the latter the generally accepted

136

alternative to Capitalism until discredited and abandoned in a series of whirlwind popular uprisings towards the end of the last century.

'Importantly, "socialism" does not define the state at which we have arrived. In our modern context, the word socialism is by definition flawed. Something went wrong with the English language.' He smiled his smile again. '*My* favourite word is "social", from which I assume is derived *Socialization*. The dictionary says of social, "of or concerning human society, its organization, or *quality of life*". This is what we have today: Quality of life.

'Marx and Engels proposed *socialization* of the means of production, but they never defined what they intended. Lenin he got it wrong, advocating *state ownership and control*. It was left to Karl Kautsky, one of the authors of *Das Kapital*, to point out that Russia had gone off the rails. "Certainly," he wrote in 1932, "it is the aim of socialists to deprive capitalists of the means of production. But," he said, "we must also determine who *is* to control these means of production. When another minority takes the place of the capitalists and controls the means of production, independently of the people and frequently against their will, the change thus accomplished signifies, last of all, socialization . . . In Russia, it is the government, not the people, which controls the means of production. The government is thus the master of the people . . . We must oppose those forces aiming to destroy capitalism only to replace it with a barbarous mode of production . . . What we see in Russia is . . . not socialization but its antithesis. It can become socialization only when the people expropriate the expropriators . . . The fact that in Russia the expropriating expropriators call themselves Communists makes not the slightest difference".

'I have presumed to substitute Marx and Engel's word *socialization* for socialism in that quote. That,' — with a twinkle — 'is usually what you call a "not done thing". *But it was the vital distinction between social ownership on the one hand and, on the other, nationalization or ownership and absolute control by the state, that the writer was seeking to make clear.* "Socialism", as distinct from socialization, is defined as "any of various beliefs (sometimes considered to include Communism) aiming at public ownership" — *that is ownership by the State* — "of the means of production and the establishment of a society in which every person is

137

equal''.

'That definition seems to me as badly worded as the American Declaration of Independence, which holds that all men are created equal. That all men are *not* created equal is self-evident. What matters is that all men shall have equal rights and equal opportunities, and in particular not be reduced to a common norm or be subservient to the state. THE STATE WAS CREATED FOR MAN; NOT MAN FOR THE STATE.

'The achievement of the most recent hundred years is that, hand in hand with freedom, opportunity, and incentive, there will now be eventually a sharing in his country's wealth — and in the wealth of the world — by every individual so that he can always with dignity stand on his own feet. Common ownership "of all means of production, distribution, and exchange", to quote the constitution of the old British Labour Party, was dedicated to a *denial* of the system that has now evolved.

'Equally inadequate as we now see it exposed was so-called Welfare Capitalism: to preach the virtues of self-reliance while the poor, the old, sick, unemployed and disadvantaged had insufficient means with which to look after themselves. In any event, State handouts do little for human dignity. Inevitably, too, they must bleed white a humane society if the benefits are meaningful . . . and if we all continue to live longer! Nor was the old UK-type "privatization" an answer to this problem, where the big institutions and the well-off took up most of the stock. After years of bribery and intensive lobbying — financed incidentally from the public purse — only a minority owned shares, and many of those owned a stake in no more than a single enterprise.

'Just a brief word on trade unions in this context. Ownership of stock by the unions is also basically flawed. It certainly gives voting power to the unions but, once again, is distinct from ownership by individual citizens.

'Now we have the World Government's Bill of Rights, the Employment Charter pioneered by the WCA following the Social Charter of the EC, and steadily spreading Individual Share Ownership, in which — one day — all will participate. I am proud that my country is one of those in Africa in which WISO is already operating, due at least in part to the huge educational programme that we pursued after Independence. I admit that we had a bit of luck because — as we felt our way

138

politically — suddenly Communism was exposed and we were able to bypass the era of rigid state control and ownership which others, less fortunate, experienced for three quarters of a century. We have a free, happy and united people. Above all, we have dignity as individuals, as do all those who have the incentive to pioneer, to work and themselves achieve success, and who also — as of right — share in the wealth of their country and the world.

'It is difficult to say in which continent the changes have been the most remarkable. Europe, the Soviet Union, Africa, the Middle and Far East must all be candidates. The dream of Monnet and others of a United States of Europe finally became reality: spurred first by the need for common defence, in NATO; needs economic, in the EEC; and finally political, in what is now the enlarged EUROPEAN FEDERATION including in turn a reunified Germany and later much of Eastern Europe, as the establishment of democracy and economic recovery gradually permitted.

'A century ago, creation of the FEDERATION OF ARAB MIDDLE EAST including the prosperous state of Palestine was not yet on the agenda. The Soviet Union, partially fragmented, was in the throes of economic revolution and the early stages of the greatest ''tanks into plough shares'' operation ever, other than at the end of a World War. China had not yet joined in the momentous political upheaval resulting from the failure worldwide of rigid state control and ownership. Who, then, would have believed that so soon — in relative terms — the GFE would have been born of China's counter-revolution and Japan's tremendous enthusiasm and success?

'And Africa, free at last; driven first by a lukewarm West into initial flirtations with Communism; now uniting; heart of the world; but under the gravest environmental threat.

'After long periods of colonialism, oppression, or stifling political systems, it is impossible for those advocating freedom and prosperity to ''deliver'' overnight. In my country, when Independence was achieved in 1980, there were some who expected to be given land the next day. In Eastern Europe, the throwing-off of Communism could not — on a vast scale — modernize industry overnight or fill the shops with goods. These things, with all the goodwill in the world, take time.

'My Colleagues and I of the World Executive, on your behalf,

139

pay tribute in particular to Mikhail Gorbachev, who with immense personal courage initiated what we now call the Great Reform, and to all those who have pioneered the dignity of individual members of the human race and the complex social and financial mechanisms by means of which we have eventually achieved it.

'As we will see in a few minutes, the World Community must now embark upon a number of projects of a magnitude hitherto undreamed. A hundred years ago, the cry would have been raised that we were all insane. How could such immense tasks be financed? *The scrapping of national defence budgets has released countless billions now that we have a rule of law supported by a world police.*

'We say to peoples still outside the World Federation, "We are not interested in the *imposition* of isms or fanaticism. Big Brother is dead. We are free, each with our own opportunities, religion, customs and traditions. That is the federal way. *We are united by our mutual tolerance.* NOTHING IN EXCESS. Come and join us. Together — all of us — we must now act to save the Earth: to make up for lost time".'

25

Nelson Banana II turned to the Report.

'The earlier parts outline the Terms of Reference laid before the Eminent Persons, and a summary of forecasts as to likely climatic behaviour. The World Executive made no attempt to arrive at precise conclusions. There are as many predictions as there are scientists. There is, however, no doubt about three basic developments. The Earth *is* entering uncharted territory. It *is* warming. Sea levels *are* rising. *The days are over when people and indeed governments can defer meaningful action on the basis that there is no universal agreement on these basic facts.*

'It was of course based upon such consensus as existed that a number of governments *have* taken action. We should be profoundly grateful. I need not remind you again of the Aral/Caspian project, physical measures taken to prevent flooding, action to safeguard fresh water supplies, the vast forest programmes, and constant research, not only into our likely future, but how to deal with it . . . for example with new strains of rice and other crops to adapt to expected conditions and to reduce methane release.

'The Report will speak for itself. I propose to refer in outline to projects concerned with sea levels: the greatest threat in which, in any case, the WPF is most likely to be involved. They are dealt with in Part VI.

'There are four of these, all to be put in hand immediately. All are in Africa. All involve pumping sea water ashore. While in all four projects the water will come ashore in Africa; in one case, the Qattara Depression infilling, it will come from the Mediterranean; in one case, the Zambezi/Sabi project, it will come from the Indian Ocean; and there are two locations in the Red Sea, Port Sudan and Amfile Bay, feeding the Nile and

141

Lake Asale.

'The most obvious and straightforward is the filling of the Qattara Depression. The operation will be based on El Alamein, and we are talking about pipelines of some sixty miles only. The Mediterranean will simply be pumped ashore without desalination. While sea levels reassert themselves, water will be taken from a threatened area of major importance, adjacent to the Nile Delta, in which live some nine millions of Egypt's population.

'The other three projects are more complex. All three involve huge distilling plants so that, while sea levels are lowered, *fresh water* is pumped ashore.

'It will be readily apparent why the three locations have been chosen. Two of them achieve no less than four vital objectives simultaneously, and the third two. In the case of Lake Asale, we are filling a natural depression with water from the sea, at the same time creating a fresh water lake a hundred miles long and some forty miles wide at the widest part, and this in Tigray, where starvation has repeatedly over the past century decimated the population. Once this supply of fresh water has been created — *and it will be subject to constant replenishment* — it will be for the world's most experienced experts upon irrigation to take it from there. Fish too. Here again, while the distilling is a major undertaking, the distances involved are small: some forty miles in all from the sea.

'The Port Sudan/Nile plan is controversial and, while it is one of the two most complex of these four operations, the risk could not be taken that the Nile flow may be appreciably reduced. Discussion goes back a hundred years to the conflicting opinions regarding the headwaters. The devastating floods in the Sudan in 1988 were regarded as a freak occurrence, conflicting with the long-term probability of reduced flow and the risk to the entire irrigation of the Nile valley, to Aswan, and clean hydro-electric power. There is an additional threat: that with insufficient fresh water the salt accumulations will simply kill the crops in spite of all the research into new strains.

'Fresh water is to be pumped from the distillers at Port Sudan to Atbara, following the route taken by both road and railway. This is a formidable project, involving something over 250 miles with back-up pumping stations at intervals, but — for the very reason that it will take time to complete — the WG believes that it *must* be put in hand.' Then came the old man's smile again. 'You may like to know that, at the suggestion of the Executive — we are rather proud of that! — the entire system is to be *reversible*, just in case those 1988 floods were *not* a freak and the predictions of the experts turn out to be wrong! As a second, later, stage it is proposed to extend the pipeline upstream to Khartoum.'

He resumed his outline of immediate projects. 'I turn now to the Zambezi. Zimbabwe has always set an example in the use of dams. *We* use the word "dam" to describe our fresh water reserves and reservoirs, of which we have a large number, as distinct from a dam wall . . . but the terminology is unimportant. What matters is that the Zambezi flow, like that of the Tigris and Euphrates, is gradually diminishing; likewise many of our smaller rivers, which are already in many cases seasonal.

'The Kariba dam provides essential power for Zimbabwe, Zambia and — on occasion — to South Africa as well. Zimbabwe is exceptionally well-supplied with electricity, and environmentally is one of the cleanest countries in the world. Cheap electricity meant an end of the burning of trees, while millions of new ones were being planted: a lesson well-taught a hundred years ago by a young government. The mere threat to this, the heart of Africa, was enough. To the credit of the Eminent Persons and the World Government, both saw the need for immediate action. Unlike those in high places who dithered a century ago, they were not prepared to wait until it was too late.

'Fresh water is to be pumped from Beira, following the road and railway route for something over 250 miles to Mutare, thence westwards, where it will feed simultaneously the upper reaches of the Munyati and Sabi rivers. The former is a tributary of the Sanyati feeding Lake Kariba. The Sabi, downstream, supplies important areas of irrigation. Both also have falls in their lower reaches.

'This is by far the most extensive and complex of the four immediate projects, but it is essential to safeguard the clean power supply. The Sabi irrigation is a vital bonus. Once again, of course, sea levels will reassert themselves. Nonetheless, the intake at Beira will draw sea water from the Indian Ocean to add to the effect of the intakes at Port Sudan and Amfile Bay from the Red Sea. The hope is that these three projects will

143

combine to assist in at least a small way in saving the Maldives . . . if indeed that is now possible with the *in*creased flow of a number of rivers, notably the Brahmaputra. Those islands may soon have to be evacuated. There is no more that Man can do to save them.

'Other viewers of this introductory film will forgive me if I say a few words to members of the WPF and the World Environment Corps. The lead contractors in each case (doubtless we will be talking about international consortia) will of course co-ordinate the work. The WG is however concerned for the *safety* of each project and those working upon it: from possible deliberate interference, climatic extremes and phenomena, accidents, and sickness. Remember: the weather is no longer predictable, and even the mosquitos range over much more of the Earth.

'WPF VTO aircraft, helicopters, and ground forces will be deployed over sometimes great distances. The Environment Corps will be concerned with the conditions in which the contractors have to work, with wildlife displaced or threatened, although in the first generation of operations not on a scale comparable with the original Kariba "Operation Noah". That will come later when the new Kariba sites have been agreed.

'That, ladies and gentlemen, is all that I have to say in my introductory capacity. When you have seen the very comprehensive World Government films that follow, I hope that you will do *your* best to save the Earth. It is — in spite of all the space exploration — still the only Earth we have.'

26

Members of EURO 2001 were awed, yet simultaneously inspired, by the World Government's so comprehensive an outline of its determined bid to save the Earth. They looked forward eagerly to the following parts of the film. As they gathered later in the Defenders Bar, by now an established routine for friendly discussion, the atmosphere was nonetheless muted and restrained in face of the enormity of proposed projects and realization that it was perhaps the world's last chance. They realized too that — whatever the rights and wrongs, actions and inactions of the past, differences amongst scientists and excuses among governments — the buck had finally stopped with their generation.

It was a sober moment, particularly perhaps for the young people from the UK. It had been their forebears who once stood alone, unflinching, in defence of freedom: to save the world from tyranny. There had followed, with the exception of the Falklands war and support for the old UN in the Gulf, a lack of vision abroad and decline in domestic caring and behaviour. Jakko and his colleagues had heard of these things, but they were part of a reborn United Kingdom. There was no question but that they would play their part. Many, like Edinburgh's Jamina, were natural leaders. Others, Jakko Mann included, from a totally honest if more simple background, were excellent material, needing only the increasing confidence that comes from experience of life.

Jakko and Danielle settled eventually in her room, gay with its French decor; in their hands the forms on which to record 'the arm of the WPF in which they wished to serve'. And here Jakko, as he had done with those calls to the boats' crews and his colleagues in *Andromeda*, once more displayed the beginnings

145

of instinctive leadership.

Danielle, pouring two cups of her special coffee, started to read aloud the headings on the form . . . 'WPF Space Personnel . . . Scientific .. . Earth Land Forces . . . Navy . . . Air Arm . . . Projects and Operations Security . . . Transport Corps . . . Administration . . . Medical . . .' Then, returning to the Navy Section, she read over the subtitles: 'Ships' Complements . . . Base Personnel . . . Boats' Crews . . .' she paused for a few seconds, then continued, 'Secretarial . . . Stores and Pay Branch . . . Nursing. I will never forget those boats's crews in the West Indies. They were so proud and *smart*. Oh Jakko, I would so much like to volunteer for the WPF Navy. It would be doing a good job, surely: helping to keep the world's peace and . . . and . . . *helping* people. There will be more hurricanes. But of course if I *was* sent to the West Indies, or any other station far away, we might be separated.' Tears stood in her eyes. 'Jakko, what shall I do? What are *you* going to do?'

The little girl from Normandy was pleading now for assurance that she was choosing a worthy role whereby she might serve. The tricolour, the watching eye of Napoleon, her brother Jean-Pierre's rugby colours — Toulouse and the French back row, she'd said — the intense pride in her country, even the camembert and cognac, with — simultaneously — her passionate desire to help *everyone*, were too much for her companion. Jakko, no historian, recalled reading at school about Joan of Arc. Intensely moved, he took both Danielle's hands again and held them very tightly. This had become their private communication of the bond between them. The possibility of separation was in danger of clouding reasoned judgement, but he replied logically enough. 'I think we should wait until we have seen the WG films and we know more about the things that must be done. If some of the projects are as vital as I think they are . . . in preventing the drowning of whole populations, for instance . . . then maybe we can find essential work that we can do together. Remember, too, in the final analysis we are being trained for *war* in the defence of peace.'

Danielle cried a little then. 'Of course you are quite right . . . *cher* Jakko. I should have known better. It is no time for selfishness.' There was a little sniff of misery.

Now it was his turn, instantly concerned. Her immediate reaction had been to volunteer for something that was fun.

146

Nothing wrong with that: the most natural thing in the world *and*, he realized, it would have involved long hours, often soaked to the skin in bad weather, would on occasion have been dangerous, requiring stamina and courage, and all essentially worthwhile. 'Danni, I'm sorry. I've said before that you could never be selfish in a million years. But let's first see those films.'

Jakko surprised himself with the vehemence of his next outburst. 'One thing I *can* tell you. As long as you want me, I will never leave you. And if the world must end, all I ask is that I can be with *you*.'

* * *

There followed a memorable week as each series of proposals unfolded on the screens. Staff, WPF and Environment Corps trainees alike were at first stunned, then reassured that the human race had at last put together a package of measures worthy in scope and daring of the urgent need. From simple outright final bans on CO_2 emissions and old-type nuclear reactors, to the careful seeding of the atmosphere with volcanic dust when there occurred no 'natural' eruptions to lessen global warming. From the bringing on stream of distillers and fresh water from long lost wadis under the deserts of North Africa: the dream first of Gaddafi, later identified from outer space, to the vast new water grids and pipelines. From new, dry strains of rice; safe, economic use of the world's waste; to changes in Man's diet and improvements in his health with drastic reduction in the Earth's cattle population; in-filling of swamps; all aimed at reduction in methane damage to the ozone layer. Perhaps most stirring of human imagination, the vast multi-purpose projects aimed simultaneously at sustaining life and maintaining the level of the sea: diversion of great rivers, new dams, fresh water reserves and irrigation; continental ring mains to distribute cheap, clean power from fusion plants, augmented from dam-generated, solar, tidal, and wind sources. Above all, a willingness by Man to work together for his own survival and that of other animal and plant species, without which he too must have perished, and the availability not only of know-how and resources but the financial billions freed for creative purpose in a law-abiding world.

By guest night dinner on Saturday, all concerned appreciated that they had shared in a unique experience. It was no surprise when, after grace and the World Government toast, Goodssen rose again at the head of the long dining hall table.

'You will agree that this has been a momentous week, and that the Eminent Persons have done a thorough and imaginative job. I have this evening received from WPF HQ Europe instructions regarding Unit 2001. As you know, trips overseas are included in each course by way of familiarizing new WPF personnel with different parts of the world and providing an opportunity to understand the lifestyles, problems, hopes and fears — and languages — of others. Your tour of the West Indies, which took in also the Amazon rainforests and the Galapagos, was the first such scheduled part of your course. I have to tell you that your second expedition has been cancelled.' At this there were a few groans of disappointment and some laughter as Goodssen cautioned silence.

'However, I have some exciting news for you instead.' At this, muted, good-natured approval. 'HQ is sending you and other personnel to Africa.' Now, all was attention. 'The object is to familarize you with territories in which major WG projects are scheduled and in which there will be a need for a WPF presence. In particular you will visit El Alamein and the Qattara Depression; Cairo; Port Sudan, following the road and rail route to Atbara, thence Khartoum. From there to Tigray, scene of surely the worst misery which ever resulted from climatic conditions (and, of course, from past civil wars); then on to Harare which is, as you know, the next site for the World Government: "the heart of Africa" in the eyes of that lovely old man, Nelson Banana.

'You will leave in two weeks' time and spend three weeks in Zimbabwe. The object is threefold. Kariba and its dam constitute an outstanding model of a man-made fresh water lake and the provision of vital, clean electricity. Secondly, one of the Eminent Persons' immediate projects — and, with the possible exception of Port Sudan/Nile, easily the most extensive — is the essential safeguarding of the Kariba complex in face of the gradually diminishing flow of the Zambezi. Thirdly, and you may think it remarkable that those in high places in the WPF possess souls, you will be taken to Hwange National Park and to Victoria Falls to see examples of unspoiled natural beauty which man must preserve if he is to save himself. Incidentally, you will see for yourselves fish farms and how the elephant, rhino, and crocodile populations have been cared for and preserved. That, ladies and gentlemen, is the content of the signal that I have received from HQ Europe. I wish I was to be one of the party. I doubt if ever a single trip took in so much.'

As applause broke out, Goodssen once more called for silence. 'In the meanwhile (and on your return to College), you will concentrate upon preparation for your various careers as soon as your potential appointments are received. In that connection, all forms stating your preferences are to be handed in without fail by midday tomorrow. Thank you.'

* * *

'Danni, I have a suggestion.' They were once more in Danielle's room. 'Go on, Jakko ...'

' Well, suppose we both became ace VTO and helicopter pilots, we could ask to be posted to the same stations. Surely, that way too, we could make ourselves indispensable to every operation in which we were involved. We'd be escorting site working parties, equipment, machinery, all kinds of materials, emergency spare parts, provisions, vehicles; carrying security personnel, visiting VIPs, casualties ... even perhaps those evacuating wildlife, plants and animals, from potential flood sites, helping the Environment Corps. There is no end to the usefulness. I'm afraid that the security aspect itself will be important for some years. With any luck we could ask to be on the same station or patrolling the same projects.'

'Super! Oh Jakko, and how about flying Mark III *Penelope's* full of WPF personnel, equipment, and stores. I'd love to fly one of those huge things. I believe they are incredibly light to handle. Remember: the very first Mark I prototype was built in Northern Ireland, Pippa Brightwell told us.' Danielle was now bubbling with enthusiasm. 'We could be *heliwizards* as well. I've already done the basic course in *them.*'

'Then you agree to the idea?'

'Of course! How you say it ... fabulous! Let's fill out those forms before we change our minds.'

149

27

Euro College 11 became caught up instantly in a spirit of urgency which pervaded those in authority all over the world. The college telescreens, notice boards, and messenger services were hard put to it to handle the instructions and information with which World Government and Regional agencies and establishments were flooded.

WPF HQ Europe, receiving Unit 2001's career requests overnight, transmitted most of the approvals with equal expedition. Only a few volunteers were diverted from their declared preferences: in every case to join Security Forces, of which there would be a need on many project sites without deflection of regular World peace-keeping troops.

Individual approvals were delivered to all volunteers, while lists were posted on notice boards for general information. Unit 2001 was split into specialized classes. Eight other volunteers besides Jakko Mann and Danielle de Croix had requested and been approved for advanced VTO and helicopter training. New class timetables and information packs on the Africa trip were delivered to all rooms.

Jakko and Danielle were congratulating themselves light-heartedly that early morning square-bashing had been discontinued, leaving only the PT, and were going over their new daily schedule of instruction, when attention was called to the telescreens. It was Goodssen. 'Unit 2001. We have just received confirmation of our recommendations for commissions. Eight members of your Unit have been selected as trainee WPF Officers: Dean-Matthew Barry, Karl Brandenberg, Monika Brandt, Danielle de Croix, Jakko Mann, Chantelle Ouchaner, Jamina Scott and Gustav Svensen. This is sixteen per cent: the highest figure that any Unit here has achieved to date. Details are being posted on the notice boards. Those concerned will be presented with preliminary insignia at your Unit's passing-out parade from College. In the meantime, your newly announced training schedules will not be interrupted. I should point out that there is plenty of time for *any* of you to be selected during your careers. On a separate matter, I would be glad if Monika Brandt and Jakko Mann would please report now to my office ... Monika Brandt and Jakko Mann, please. Thank you.'

Spontaneously, Jakko hugged Danielle as tears, this time of happiness at their future commissions, welled up in her eyes. Then suddenly she pushed him aside. 'That *Monika* again! ... what can it be *this time ... what have been you doing?* ...'

Jakko, innocent, surprised by the vehemence of the question, wrapped his arms round her again, but she fought him off, eyes blazing. 'Danni, what are you *doing*?' Strong, he held her again, tightly this time as she struggled to get free; then — momentarily spent — she kissed him fiercely as the struggle ceased. Just as unpredictably, another change of mood:

'I am much in favour of united Europe, but you belong to *me*!' Simultaneous giggles, tears, then laughter.

Much later, recalling that moment, they realized that it had been one in which their relationship had changed ... further deepened ... become forever an unassailable alliance. Immediately, Jakko admitted, it had been an internal battle that he knew he had to win. Initiated, then taught and physically satisfied by Jamina, he told how in that moment he had suddenly wanted her, Danielle, with a compelling longing. It had been a conflict between, on the one hand, mere desire — understandable in the circumstances and commonplace enough — and, on the other, his deeply-felt admiration for her extraordinary combination of absolute genuineness, innocence, and courage, which he had believed it a unique duty and privilege to respect, to cherish and protect.

But now he pleaded that he must report to Goodssen, kissed Danielle with the tenderness of those swearing unspoken allegiance, and made his way with all speed to the staff block.

Monika Brandt was already waiting. They entered together. The College Principal bade them sit down. 'Congratulations to you both on your potential commissions. I'm afraid that with the intensive training and WG urgency as regards environmental

151

action, it may be some while before you can be spared for your officers' course. In the meanwhile I have a small mission for you. It requires two reliable people, and one must be a woman.

'Jakko, you of course know all about the girl Sylvie Mennin. For Monika's benefit, let me explain that she is a suspect in connection with the Crawley bombing in the spring. Subsequently, in trying to hide in South America she was unfortunate enough to be caught in the plane disaster in which you both did so well in *Andromeda*. Miss Mennin suffered burns in the crash, and has been in hospital in Barbados pending being sent back to the UK for interrogation. Although still under treatment, she is now fit enough to travel, and the authorities — to their credit — want to establish her innocence, if indeed she *is* innocent, as soon as possible to assist her full recovery. I have been asked to arrange an escort. It requires a no-nonsense but at the same time humane attitude . . . which is why I am sending you two to Barbados to collect her. Miss Mennin is to be handcuffed to you, Monika, throughout the journey, except of course when in the washroom, and even then you are to remain with her. If she *did* plant those bombs, she is a potential murderess. You are to take no risks, you understand. There is a WPF Entente IV flying to Barbados tomorrow. Please report to me here at 0900, when I will give you your written orders. I know you will handle this efficiently. Of course you are both of the same seniority, but for the purposes of this mission, Monika, you will be in charge. Thank you. Be here at 0900 tomorrow morning.'

Danielle listened to the news. She didn't say anything immediately, then put her arms round Jakko's neck. '*Mon dieu!* Two of them. It is a conspiracy!'

'You can trust me, Danni,' he said. 'That is a promise.'

152

28

Monika Brandt and Jakko, bags in hand, duly collected their orders, ready to be whisked away in a small WPF helicopter belonging to the College. This would deliver them to the WPF base from which the Ententes flew. Jakko had already said a somewhat emotional goodbye to Danielle as the first of the day's instruction periods would already be under way.

They lifted off strictly on time and swung away westwards. Below, they could see the newly augmented VTO and helicopter class grouped round their instructor and a Dragonfly machine: smallest, reliable, fast maid-of-all-work, of which the WPF employed large numbers all over the world.

Euro College 11, sited as it was in the UK, had borrowed before Goodssen's time, but he had been enthused by the idea, something of the one-time British navy's enthusiasm for competitive drills requiring imagination and initiative. WPF trainees would compete in *ad hoc* teams in such absurd tasks as the dismantling, transporting across imaginary obstacles, reassembling and taking to the air of small VTO aircraft and helicopters as their instructors, stop-watches in hand, shouted encouragement. Although few, there had been some injuries over the years. It was well known that, a hundred years before, a seaman in the Devonport Field Gun's crew, competing in the Royal Tournament, was so hyped up during training that he had inserted his finger to prevent a wheel falling off when someone else had dropped the steel pin, running beside the gun so that his team won by one tenth of a second. That he lost his finger had been a small price to pay.

Likewise, at dead of night fifty years before *that*, the British Mediterranean destroyers at Malta would be ordered to land their searchlights complete with generators and have them burning at 0600 ten miles from the creek where the ships lay. That none of their boats were big enough to carry the equipment was but one of the problems. Similarly, they might be told to strike and land their topmasts or some other seemingly impossible exercise. It was hardly surprising that, when the test came, such ships, even if initially blown in half by a fifteen-inch shell, carried on regardless and fired their torpedoes with the rest of their flotilla.

Danielle's comment to Jakko that she had already done a course in small VTOs and helicopters had been something of an understatement. She had in fact established with a team of trainees from their Unit a new record in fault-detection in craft deliberately put out of action by instructors.

* * *

The WPF Entente IV headed west towards the Caribbean, full of WPF personnel returning from leave or taking up new appointments; diplomatic, regional and national staff; scientists, representatives of companies already researching projects outlined in *the* Report. No time was being lost. It was all 'go'.

Jakko, already affected by having to leave Danielle, had barely talked to Monika before. Tall, blonde, healthy and efficient, she had ushered him into the outside seat. 'Maybe you would like to look out at the sea and sky. I have seen too much of them.' She was taking charge automatically. Then, 'Well Jakko; this is the kid you rescued, isn't it? I do not understand this ''escaping'' to South America if she did not do it. What do you think?' (Shades of Jamina).

The English lad confided to her Sylvie Mennin's final plea when she believed that she was drowning. Monika's reply did not surprise him. 'Yes; of course I too believe in God, but one has to look after one's self. Anyway, we must carry out our orders.' She pulled a pair of handcuffs from her service bag. 'You take the spare key . . . just in case of accidents. I intend to follow our instructions to the letter.'

She changed the subject. 'Tell me about England.'

'Well,' hesitant, 'I come from the West Country. I suppose we are simple people down there . . . farmers . . . nurserymen . . . we used to mine tin, and we do still produce china clay;

154

it's quite an important export. But of course during the past hundred years, since the greenhouse thing really started, we have borne the brunt of the hurricanes that have hit Europe from the south-west. There are virtually no trees at all now in Cornwall, and our river Severn has often burst its banks. The country *is* warmer and wetter, as the scientists predicated nearly a hundred years ago.'

To Jakko's surprise, his companion was genuinely interested. He continued in friendly vein, 'The most important changes by far have been in our farming methods. Towards the end of the nineteen-hundreds, our livestock farming had reached horrific extremes: everything designed to make the maximum amount of money, regardless of the cruelty and suffering. People tell me that we were not worse than anyone else, but I only know about my own country . . . apart of course from our trade in live calves and sheep to the continent, and the grim conditions in the hell ships in which thousands and thousands of Australian sheep used to be exported.' He paused for a moment, but the German girl was listening intently, and he continued.

'In my country, the pigs and veal animals, and of course "battery" chickens and other "intensively stocked" creatures, suffered most. Pregnant sows for instance were often confined in so-called stalls between iron bars, or were actually so restricted that they couldn't take a single step forward or back . . . for fifty weeks of the year, I mean. I have seen old photographs and films. I remember the first time. I had to go out and be sick. They used to de-beak battery hens with a red-hot iron to prevent them maiming each other when they became mentally unstable, hardly being able to move or even stretch their wings. Veal calves were fed a revolting gruel with minimum iron, in order to induce anaemia and produce so-called white meat. And the conditions in our slaughterhouses were terrible. As I say . . . anything for profit. *They even used to mince up animals and poultry that had died and make livestock food from them . . . and then wonder why animals became sick. "Mad cow" disease was rampant: bovine spongiform encefihalopathy!*'

'Oh well *done*, Jakko!' Monika was warming to her new companion because he knew his business.

'The fact is that the whole livestock thing had become "commercial", with creatures treated as so many units in a production process with little thought for morals or their welfare.

It was a far cry from *While shepherds watched their flocks by night* . . .'

'Monika — may I call you Monika? . . .'

'Of course.'

'You may think it sloppy, but my folk and people like them still believed in God and that all living things had a right to consideration while they were alive, and to a dignified, humane death if they must be killed. Mercifully, vegetarianism and fish farming have drastically reduced meat eating.'

'Go on.'

'Well, the important thing is that England pioneered UCFR — "under cover free range" — methods and buildings which are now becoming standard in hurricane areas. We claim the credit for humanity, but as much of southern England, battered and flooded for nearly a century now, became a treeless bog in which neither the growing of crops nor livestock farming outdoors — except ducks! — were possible at all, we invented the vast tough steel-braced hanger-like buildings which are being copied in many parts of the world. Indeed, we export prefabricated versions complete with the electrical plant. They comprise huge single-storey, essentially low-density units housing large numbers of animals and poultry with companionship of their own kind, freedom of movement, *ad lib* food and fresh water in controlled conditions of humidity and temperature, with ample dry bedding (from our new Scottish grain belts) and separate dunging areas where appropriate . . . for pigs, for instance. *They* are so clean when given a chance, and they are highly intelligent.

'Talking of Scottish grain, our northern areas have taken over, now they are warmer, like Canada has replaced the United States Mid-west, although of course on a much smaller scale. And Scotland — like Norway — has become a vast fish producer, but even that has its problems: disease resulting from overcrowding and pollution; weaker strains that have never swum in the wild open sea. But a lot of trouble is being taken to get it right because it's so important.'

Monika Brandt had been all attention. Like all efficient people, she respected others who were knowledgeable in their different fields. 'I am glad that we are chosen to do this little duty together. After university, I became a secretary in our, I mean German, civil service. I achieved rapid promotion and moved to the offices of the Federal — European — capital. So

156

I have been completely immersed in the development of the wider Europe which was triggered in the first place by Gorbachev and the reunification of my country. It has been a fascinating experience, but I am afraid that I was not satisfied with that miracle. I wanted to move even higher . . . on to the *World* plane. So here I am. I am glad for myself, and for you Jakko of course, to be selected already for a commission. I would have been very disappointed had I failed so soon.

'I am interested in what you tell me. Yours was a completely different world from mine. I was spending my life in a high-powered, technology-driven, office atmosphere. Of course it was all part of the fascinating political, financial, industrial development of the eventual ideal world . . . but it was a bit stifling. I wanted to *see* more of that world that we were all working so hard to create. Also I was incensed that anyone should stand in the way of ''One World''. The WPF stands behind the World Constitution and the Supreme Court, behind international law and order . . . and the striving for that ideal. I wanted — at the same time — to see the world and to see that progress towards world order and civilized behaviour *was not interfered with.*'

Jakko sensed in the last remark something of the supreme toughness and arrogance of the people who twice had taken on half the world, and all but won on both occasions. He was a little scared, yet genuinely wanted to be friendly and admiring. To his own surprise, as the Entente IV flew on towards the Caribbean, he asked deliberately the one question which would provide the answer. 'How do you see reunified Germany's role in the world?'

He was not disappointed. 'Of course reunification was completed a long time ago now. But the answer to your question lies in the care with which it was effected.

'There were two essential forces at work. First of all, starting with the rejection at last of Communism in the East because it had failed to deliver, and the pulling-down of the Berlin Wall, there was impatience and a tremendous ''feeling'' about reunification. After all, *we are one people, and we had been artificially divided.* Secondly, and even more importantly, our people were *very much aware of the potential fear of a united Germany* with an eighty million population: by far the largest and potentially dominant state in the new Europe. It would not be an exaggeration to say that the Poles were "terrified of it all happening again". In the Low Countries, even in France, which had together been, with West Germany, the engines of the EEC and the European process, there was genuine anxiety. Our own people had not forgotten the Second World War. There was a strange mixture of pride and horror there. We were (and are) a proud, hard-working, and highly successful nation; but determined this time to play a leading part in the developing and uniting world and its institutions. We had much to offer. But we *understood the fears that existed*, and were determined that — however purposeful and successful we ourselves became, and Jakko, we knew *that* to be inevitable! — those fears should prove unjustified. So it has proved. And all credit to those who helped to forge *united* Europe. *That* was essential, indeed *urgent*, at the time. As to fears that Germany might meanwhile prove a threat, remember too our preoccupation with the huge task of re-building the East.'

She lowered her voice, changing the subject. 'It used to be said that England and Germany could have taken on the world. It is a pity that you renounced the initiative after 1945. Perhaps your country suffered from never having been almost totally destroyed . . . retreating behind the English Channel with terrible old outdated machinery and little of the spirit, "get up and go", I think you call it, which a new start from ruins would have created. England had ruins of course, but not like ours. In brief, we in Germany have tried — and succeeded — to use our national characteristics and our strength for the good of all as well as for ourselves. It all boils down again to that word "Federal". We are content to let history be our judge.'

So ended high in the sky this exchange of views of youth. The sun beamed through the aircraft's windows as Monika returned the handcuffs to her bag.

* * *

Gong. 'We shall be landing shortly at Grantley Adams Airport. Transport to Bridgetown will be waiting. Nice to have had you with us. I hope you have enjoyed your trip.'

29

The sky darkened somewhat as the Entente neared Grantly Adams. The Captain was on the intercom again. 'We will be landing in a few minutes. Do not be alarmed at the reduced sunlight. We have been briefed about an eruption of Soufriere. That is the volcano in St Vincent, a hundred miles due west from here. Soufriere was active twice during the last century. The most recent major eruption was in 1979. It has merely covered a lot of people with dust a couple of times since: sort of friendly, just reminding everyone of its presence! Maybe it will save the boffins a bit of trouble by filtering out some of the radiation.'

Assorted passengers were soon bussing along the coast road to the Barbados capital. Others would be flying on. Monika extracted their written orders from an inner pocket. 'It just says ''Report to the SO WPF Bridgetown.'' He will be Army or Air, I would think.' The bus disgorged its passengers at intervals until the driver turned round with, 'Anyone left *not* for WPF HQ?' and, reassured, set off for that place.

A middle-aged woman colonel rose as they were ushered into her office. She was white with a rather large bosom, hair in a bun and an efficient, precise, but somewhat prissy manner. They shook hands. 'Miss Brandt, you are in charge of this little exercise, are you not?' She bade them both be seated. Turning to Jakko, 'And you rescued the little lady we are talking about.'

'Yes, Ma'am.'

'Well, I find the whole story ridiculous, but orders are orders. *Andromeda*'s captain came in to see me at the time. He is a human being, of course. So is the Admiral in Antigua, but I suppose they couldn't risk making a mistake. The girl is wanted in England for interrogation so that was the end of the discussion.

159

'We have a flight to the UK tomorrow forenoon, so please report here at 0900 to collect Miss Mennin. I have arranged transport to the Airport.' (Rather obviously) 'She will be brought from hospital, where she has been free but under supervision. *We* didn't want to lose her either! She looks a bit of a mess, poor child, but further treatment for her burns is now only a matter of her appearance. So you have the rest of today free — and the evening. We have an excellent WPF club in Bridgetown, and there is a dinner dance tonight if you care to come.

'You have brought handcuffs of course. So, 0900 it is.'

She pressed a button for an orderly to show them to their rooms. They saluted and left.

* * *

A routine WPF minibus delivered Sylvie Mennin's escort back to the city. Monika insisted on seeing everything, buying a map so no time was lost. Tour completed, she pronounced judgement. 'Overpopulated of course, and still oddly British. Nothing but cricket! But they all seem very happy.' Then, 'It's only about eighty kilometres round the island. Why don't we have something to eat and then hire a car?'

Jakko fell in with the suggestion. They were soon on their way clockwise up the coastal road. Monika drove. Intermittent communities, higher ground, tropical flowers, music. To the west, seabirds wheeling over the crystal-clear blue water. Overlooking Archer's Bay they left the car and stood for a while gazing out to sea, but it was just another moment of experience rather than romance. The volcanic dust overhead, thinning now, was drifting away. Monika remarked again upon the happy people crammed into a few square miles, making a living from sugar, tourism, light industry, and the modest WPF presence, a contrast to the pulsating heart of Europe. And yet, she mused aloud, like those in Western Europe, these people too were participants in WISO, each with a direct personal stake in the world's wealth.

'Jakko! You are not listening.'

'I'm sorry!' He returned to earth. 'My thoughts were in Martinique.' Then, '*I* will drive the rest of the way, so you can

160

enjoy the scenery.'

He got a look for that, but they set off. In due course, relaxed by the colour, beauty, intermittent music, fresh sea air, and friendly waves from the inhabitants, they were back in Bridgetown, thence to base to clean up for the evening, and to the club for dinner.

NORTH AMERICAN AND CARIBBEAN FEDERATION
WELCOME TO BARBADOS WORLD PEACE FORCE CLUB

Obviously constructed in the first place as a large uncomplicated, functional building, the entrance was framed with tropical climbers with which clearly much trouble was taken. Monika and Jakko were welcomed by a steward — 'The Colonel told us to expect you' — who showed them through the hall, alive with more colour and club notice boards, to the reception lounge. The place was beautifully furnished, and every inch was spotless. The gentle rhythm of the inevitable steel band could be heard from the restaurant beyond. They signed in, went through to be greeted by the head waiter. Once again, 'We have your table; the Colonel told us to expect you.'

It was early. A few other couples sat, scattered amongst the tables. At the far end, half a dozen cheerful characters with their steel pans soothed those present after a warm day. Flowers again. Flowers everywhere. There was ample time for cool drinks, to look around, to study the menu and the printed welcome.

You may wonder why your scribe bothers you with trivia, but the folded note on each restaurant table spoke volumes for the spirit of local WPF officialdom.

Welcome to Barbados WPF Club. This is a World Peace Force establishment. It belongs to Mankind and you are its part owner. We who manage it do so as trustees on your behalf.

161

Membership

WPF forces of all ranks stationed in North American and Caribbean command are granted automatic membership. Visiting WPF personnel are awarded honorary membership during their stay, upon application to the Secretary.

Civilian membership is welcomed at a modest subscription fixed from time to time.

Dress

Smart casual dress is requested at all times in the reception, lounge, library, restaurant and ballroom areas.

Sports facilities

Details are posted at Reception. Those wishing to play Cricket, Tennis, Water Polo and other team games should in the first instance please contact the appropriate Committee Secretary. The Club has ample facilities for Sailing, Water Ski, diving and undersea study of marine life. There is a large Clay Pigeon Range. In common with all WPF establishments, the causing of distress to other species is discouraged. Shark and other fishing for 'sport' is prohibited from the Club's boats.

This Club is the current holder of the command's Cricket, Water Polo, and Bridge cups.

A word on costs

The Club is expensively furnished and equipped, not from unwarranted expenditure of public money but from the generosity of Units and ships of this WPF command, many service and civilian individuals, and businesses on the island. In this respect WPF Clubs are not unlike World Colleges which have been recipients of much generosity at the hands of their host countries. We ask for your kind co-operation in maintaining the very high standards permitted by all the kindnesses that we receive.

Bar and restaurant prices are as modest as efficient financial management permits. Gratuities are at your discretion, but they are pooled so that all staff may benefit.

BELINDA LOPEZ
Colonel Commanding, Barbados Base

To round off their meal, the two young Europeans treated themselves to the Club's very own special rum banana, prepared at the table with a ritual first cousin to that normally reserved for crêpes suzettes. By now the restaurant was full. It was an international gathering: part service, part civilian, of all ages and colours. By now the pan players had disappeared, their place taken by a small convivial dance band and their female vocalist.

Apart from couples who clearly 'belonged', there seemed little hesitation in asking strangers to dance, and it was not long before Monika became a centre of attention. Jakko had learned something of these matters at Euro College 11, but was still hardly accomplished. In any case he was in the early, most intense throes of love for D de C. He was wondering whether to risk inviting Monika on to the floor and perhaps spoil their relationship, by the success of which he was much encouraged and indeed somewhat relieved, when a tall fair-haired Canadian Lieutenant asked his permission to dance with her. Somewhat embarrassed at being asked for his approval, he accepted with as much matter of fact poise as he could muster.

It was at that moment that he saw out of the corner of his eye the figure of Colonel Lopez bearing down like the proverbial galleon under full sail. 'May I sit down?' she asked. Jakko, jumping up, 'Of course, Ma'am.' Then, taking his courage in both hands, 'Perhaps you would like to dance, although I am afraid I am not an expert.'

163

'Yes, why not! You don't have to, you know. I just make a point of having a word with visitors.' But it was too late for escape. They took to the floor. To Jakko's amazement, the formidable Colonel, light as a feather, guided him with such relaxed skill that for all the world he believed himself in charge. The music stopped and they returned to the table. The Lopez bent over and whispered in his ear, 'It's all part of your training . . . and the gaining of experience! Now go and find yourself a pretty girl. I'll see you in the morning.'

Before Jakko was faced with this small test of his increasing confidence, a pale brown female naval rating of mixed race, with long hair, accosted *him*. She was extremely pretty. Again, surprisingly, a maple leaf on each shoulder. She grasped his hands, pulled him to his feet. 'Hullo, England! How long you here for?'

'Only this evening, I'm afraid.'

'What a shame! You look nice. Come and dance with me.'

They took the floor. 'I am on temporary loan to Barbados. I don't know any of these people. My own base is Halifax, NS. There isn't much of a naval presence here.' After a few moments, 'Can you hold me a little closer.'

Jakko did as he was bidden, and very soon it had the intended effect. 'You are very beautiful, but you are doing things to me. Please be good and stop it. I am surprised that you are allowed to have your hair down like this in uniform.'

'It has to be up on duty of course.'

'Please don't *nestle*, or I'll have to leave you. I have a girl in England. She is French.'

'Yes,' quietly, 'but she isn't *here*, is she! Why don't we go outside. It's a lovely evening.' Jakko, embarrassed on the ballroom floor, agreed readily. She took his hand, leading the way.

It *was* a beautiful evening: the air full of tropical scents; the sound of music fading as they went. A starlit sky. Inevitably Jakko's thoughts strayed to Danielle, the Golden Gates in Port of Spain, as his companion, silent now, led him on into the night.

Presently she stopped. 'I feel lonely here. They do tend to stick together a bit.'

Jakko: 'I wouldn't have thought *you* would have any trouble.'

'That's nice of you.' She turned towards him, took his hands and clasped them behind her back. 'What is your name?'

'Jakko . . . Jakko Mann.'

'I like that.' Then suddenly, 'Was it you I read about in the aeroplane disaster? What are you doing here?'

She was close to him now. 'Two of us have come over to take the girl Sylvie Mennin back to England for interrogation into that bombing in the Spring.'

'Of course we all heard about that . . . and about you.' She stopped talking for a moment. Then, 'You are very good-looking.'

Jakko attempted to head her off with 'This isn't any good, you know. Nothing can come of it.' Then, suddenly it occurred to him that here was an opportunity to make love to an extremely willing, pretty temptress who he would never see again. She was actually asking for it. Doubtless it would surprise her that he was almost certainly more experienced than she: that he could probably teach *her* a great deal; give her much more than she bargained for . . . perhaps teach her a lesson. There was even a suspicion of sadistic *cruelty* in that final thought. Suddenly he felt terribly ashamed. It was all Jamina's fault. The girl was clinging to him now, warm and inviting. 'I have already said that you are very beautiful. I am not as naive as perhaps you think. But — and I'm sure it sounds terribly old-fashioned — I am "not available". If you behave like this, one day somebody will really hurt you . . . could do something terrible. I fear for you. You are a very, very attractive child.' He realized suddenly that use of the word 'child' came from his own increasing maturity and confidence. In an attempt to defuse the situation, 'What is your name?'

'Chantelle.' He was melted anew by that. 'We have a Chantelle in our Unit. I had never heard of one before.'

At this, she reached up and kissed him, tenderly at first . . . gradually with increased intensity until he eased her away gently. 'I want you too . . . Chantelle . . . I cannot bear to push you away. Forgive me, *please*. I would so much like to make love to you, but I have loyalties.'

He was afraid that she might react fiercely, and was intensely relieved that no rough stuff proved to be necessary. Instead, 'Goodbye, Jakko. You are very unusual. I wish you were *my* best friend. I could be *passionately* loyal too.' She kissed him once more, but understanding had been reached, the passion had subsided. 'Oh Jakko, I will remember you. Will you think of me . . . sometimes. Let's carry on with our walk under the stars and then wend our way back to the club.'

* * *

'Well!' said Monika as they said goodnight before heading for their respective rooms at Base. 'She *was* a little darling, wasn't she?'

She gave him the matter-of-fact kiss usual between equals, but it wasn't lost on Jakko that it lingered for the split part of a second.

30

Down to the Club for a swim; pineapple, breakfast, the Base CO's office by 0845.

Promptly at 0900 there was a knock on the CO's door and two WPF orderlies entered, between them Sylvie Mennin.

Jakko rose involuntarily as the three of them stepped forward. One whole side of the girl's face was pink after initial recovery from burns. A few scars revealed more serious damage where, later, plastic surgery would be necessary. The dyed hair had grown sufficiently to reveal its true blonde colour. Her 'good' wrist was handcuffed to one of the two men.

The girl looked first at Colonel Lopez, then suddenly she recognized Jakko and cried out to him, but the two men held her back. Jakko was choked with emotion. It was as well that no comment was called for.

The CO stood up behind her desk. 'Bring a chair; take off those handcuffs and let her sit down.'

'Miss Mennin. You are among friends and, in passing, I am glad that the UK authorities had the compassion and good sense to send over to collect you someone that you already know and trust. Miss Monika Brandt and Mr Jakko Mann will take you back to England this morning. The Captain of *Andromeda* and the Admiral have put in a word for an immediate investigation. You were foolish to flee to South America. That clearly has increased suspicions in the UK. You are young, and we all make mistakes. I like to think that the world is now much more of a humane place than it was.

'When you have recovered from your ordeal, I hope that you will lead a useful life. Perhaps you will consider the WPF or the Environment Corps as a career. I am sure that Mr Mann can advise you. Come and let me shake your good hand. Have courage my dear, and good luck.'

At this, Sylvie wept, then — pulling herself together — she took the Colonel's hand with 'Thank you for looking after me. I *am* innocent. I will not let you down. Perhaps one day I will see you again. Oh ...' remembering ... 'Could you please say thank you for me, again, to everyone in the hospital and to the frigate Captain.'

'Of course.'

Then 'Right. Away you go. There will be a vehicle waiting.'

She shook hands with Monika and Jakko. 'I hope that you enjoyed your evening. You both seem to have made an impression on the locals! Come back and see us some time' ... standard phrase in the Caribbean.

* * *

The trip was uneventful, conversation regarding the previous evening restricted by the Mennin presence. Sylvie, handcuffed and subdued, was mostly silent. The Entente landed and they disembarked last. Jakko promised to attend all parts of the Enquiry for which he could obtain permission. Sylvie was turned over to an escort from the base.

Thence VTO to College 11. Report to Goodssen, 'Mission completed'. Besieged by colleagues: 'All right for some while *we've* all been working!'

* * *

The VTO and helicopter class was working overtime before the Unit's African tour. It was not until shortly before the evening meal that Jakko met Danielle in her room before they changed. They wrapped their arms around each other and held on tightly for all of half a minute before a word was spoken.

Jakko broke the silence. 'It has been a fascinating trip ... and one of mixed emotions. We brought Sylvie Mennin back all right, but I had a terrible experience last night at the Barbados Club.'

'Tell me all about it. How did you get on with dear Monika?'

Jakko explained that Monika was not the problem. She had

168

behaved impeccably . . . and efficiently of course. Absolutely 'officer material'. 'We talked the whole way across the Atlantic . . . about our differing backgrounds, the UK West Country, Germany, Europe . . . Monika's ambitious. She will never be satisfied until she reaches the very top. But she isn't ruthless about it; just determined. I am glad that we did the trip together. I understand and I *respect* her now.'

He told her then about Chantelle. 'Danni, I love you beyond everything, and I tell my thoughts only to you. She *was* being deliberately seductive, and no doubt we would both have enjoyed a loving, all too brief affair. I'm sure it would have been a beautiful experience, as I know that one day ours will be; nothing like those revolting movies of the late nineteen-hundreds where people, even upon first acquaintance, devoured each other for the hell of it in that disgusting fashion. Actually, Chantelle reminded me of *you*.'

'So you think I am seductive!'

'I am serious. I mean, I could be very *loyal* . . . and so could she.'

'You fell for her very much in such little time.'

'Is that surprising if she reminded me of you?'

'But you said ''terrible experience''.'

'I know. I explained that I owed my loyalty to you, and she accepted that. But then came the frightening bit. When I realized that we had agreed, almost with affection, *not* to make love, I suddenly had an extraordinary, unexplained, desire to *hurt* her . . . so she would never forget. Maybe one day she will land herself in trouble and get hurt. Maybe she will deserve it. But why should I feel like that towards someone so young and warm and harmless? *Jamina has done something terrible to me*. It wasn't the real me at all.'

Danielle thought for a moment. Then, 'I do not even need, what is the expression, ''female intuition''. It is all obvious to me. You fell in love completely with your Chantelle . . . and I love you because you resisted the temptation. Then you felt frustrated. Perhaps subconsciously you wanted to *revenge* yourself on women. I do not think you are mentally ill! After Jamina, it is understandable. You must forget that moment.'

She paused. 'Jakko,' even more serious now, 'let me say it for you. We are of different religions, you and I. But we believe in the same God. Besides, I do not believe in Confession: do

169

something you know to be wrong, confess, and do it again. And I am in favour of a sane view on birth control: particularly with the whole world in turmoil about survival, climate, populations, food . . . and everything. Religion to me is a very personal thing: my own relationship with God and with my conscience. I do not need "intermediaries". Jakko, I know we are young and only now starting our careers, but I think we should get married.'

Stunned silence from Jakko. Then somewhat absurdly, 'You forgive me . . . '

'Of course . . . you silly boy! Don't look so surprised. I don't mean *tomorrow*. But if we had an "understanding" . . . no-one else need know, but we would feel safe whenever we were separated.'

Jakko, recovering, 'I thought it was the male who was supposed to do the proposing.'

'I just make sure before the next Chantelle.'

31

The ten members of the reconstituted VTO/helicopter class had already received basic lectures and practical instruction during their general course. Danielle in particular, passionately keen, had obtained approval to fly Dragonflies in her spare time. They were now to endure probably the most intensive further instruction ever meted out to volunteers for anything ... to ensure competence by the end of the next two weeks with, on return from Africa, fine tuning and the maximum of practical experience before EURO 2001 passed out from the College.

Meanwhile the whole Unit was reminded of African requirements and, in particular, of WG concern at the rapid spread of tropical diseases, skin cancer, and ultra-violet eye damage.

The information pack contained a fascinating mix, adding much to the enthusiasm and anticipation with which the young people looked forward to the trip.

OBJECT

Following the REPORT OF THE EMINENT PERSONS and the decisions outlined in the WG film ACTION BY MAN, substantial increases are required in World Peace Force and Environment Corps personnel as work commences on world projects planned as a result of those initiatives. Of the immediate projects, four are in Africa.

Courses at World Colleges are being shortened and will include one only of the usual visits to different Federations. Additionally, all those under training will now be sent on this African tour before passing out from their respective Colleges. The tour is designed to replace the second usual period of travel with its gaining of world-wide experience and knowledge, and to provide a background to postings to African project locations.

ITINERARY

MALTA
BENGHAZI
CAIRO
KHARTOUM
HARARE

I   MALTA

Valletta City. Biblical and historic connections. St Paul's Bay. Cathedral. Opera House. Grand Harbour. The George Cross. World War Two memorabilia.
WPF naval and air bases. Ship repair yard.

II   From BENGHAZI

1. N. African sites of Gaddafi WATER RECOVERY projects from previously lost wadis and under-desert sources.
2. N. African distillers and Sahara irrigation.
3. Afrika Corps memorabilia.

III   CAIRO

Current Regional Capital (by rotation) of FEDERATION OF ARAB MIDDLE EAST. REGIONAL WPF OPERATIONAL HQ.
The largest city in Africa. Centre of Egyptian life for more than a thousand years.
Once described as 'The metropolis of the universe, the garden of the world, the nest of the human species, the gateway to Islam, the throne of royalty ... a city embellished with castles and palaces and adorned with monasteries of dervishes and city colleges lit by the moons

172

and stars of erudition.' (Ibn Khaldun. Fourteenth century historian)

Ancient City. Cairo Museum. Modern City. Gizeh: Pyramids and Sphinx.

Underground water pumping and land drainage. Relationship of proposed Qattara, Port Sudan, and Amfile Bay sea intakes to the saving of the City and Nile Delta from the sea.

IV From CAIRO

1. Visit to SINAI CITY, thriving Capital of new Palestine. Extreme example of achievement by World aid and goodwill and the exertions of a people.
2. EL ALAMEIN
   Second World War memorabilia. Base for QATTARA DEPRESSION project. EL ALAMEIN/QATTARA projects pipeline route.
3. NILE VALLEY and ASWAN
   5,000 years of history. Irrigation. Hydro/electric power. Egypt is 'the gift of the Nile.' (Herodotus)

V From KHARTOUM

PORT SUDAN/ATBARA projected pipeline route.

VI HARARE

Former Capital (by rotation) of PAN AFRICAN FEDERATION.
WORLD FEDERAL CAPITAL designate (by rotation) **2085.**
Tour of City. Government Buildings. University. Zimbabwe WISO centre. Agricultural Research Establishment. Botanical Gardens. Electricity Supply Authority.

VII From HARARE

1. Prehistoric sites and early Man.
2. Grain, cotton, citrus fruit, horticultural and exotic

produce, new strains. Forestry. Agriculture.
3. BEIRA/MUTARE projected pipeline route and branches to MUNYATI and SABI rivers.
4. KARIBA lake and Dam.
5. HWANGE, VICTORIA FALLS, OKAVANGO
Unashamed inclusion by WPF HQ of a diversion amidst the natural world, and the heritage that it is an important part of our purpose to protect.
Hwange National Park. Victoria Falls. Chobe River. Okavango Delta.
6. KALAHARI DESERT
A diversion based upon the possibility (noted but not included in ACTION BY MAN) of pumping the sea into this, the largest continuous stretch of sand in the world, in the event that intended measures prove inadequate to prevent catastrophic flooding of the world's land mass.

VIII ADMINISTRATION

As mentioned above, WPF and Environment Corps Units at present under training in all Federations (and Units that follow, for the foreseeable future) will be sent on this tour. Dates will be staggered to facilitate transport and administration at the various locations.

One-day Joint Assemblies

The opportunity will be taken to organize at the Harare Conference complex a series of one-day Joint Assemblies with distinguished guest speakers of world stature and Evenings, for *two* Units (2 x 50 = 100 participants) on each occasion, from different Federations. The first of these will be held on Unit EURO 2001's last day in Zimbabwe before their return to the UK, and will be attended also by Unit AME 106 (50 trainees from WPF, FEDERATION OF ARAB MIDDLE EAST) on their first day in Zimbabwe.

A concert will be given after the joint dinner on each occasion by the University of Zimbabwe Orchestra, which has deservedly won worldwide acclaim.

The cost of these important one-day joint functions is

being met by Industrial and other organizations and Trusts
— to whom the World Government is greatly indebted —
and not from WG public funds.

The WG is also much indebted to the City of Harare,
to Zimbabwe University, and to the Agricultural Research
Establishment in that city.

Tour Groups

While on tour, each Unit of fifty, accompanied by one Staff
member, will be divided into three groups of seventeen for
convenience of administration and transport.

EURO 2001 will be accompanied by Captain Pippa
Brightwell from College. The three groups will be led by
Monika Brandt, Gustav Svensen, and Jakko Mann.

BRUSH UP YOUR ARABIC!

* * *

The final two weeks passed quickly before the Unit was due to
leave for Africa. Study and more study. Training and more
training. Assembly of kit and tropical necessities. The
VTO/helicopter volunteers requested — and obtained —
approval to put in an additional two hours daily between tea
and supper: 12 x 2 = 24 valuable extra hours of flying.

The concert due to be given on the final Saturday guest night
before departure for Malta on the first leg of the trip, involved
the London Schools Symphony Orchestra. WPF HQ Europe
— unaware, perhaps surprisingly, of the extraordinary history
of the Orchestra — raised with Goodssen the possible
cancellation of the concert. It was in fact hardly their concern;
they were doubtless anxious merely that the Unit should not
start half asleep on the exercise with which so much trouble had
been taken. Goodssen, however, had heard the Orchestra in
concert in Norway and travelled as often as possible to London
when it was performing in the capital. There was no question
but that the fixture must remain. He believed — somewhat
passionately for so orthodox and textbook an officer — that
music, being a language that knew no frontiers, could play an

important part in the creation of international goodwill.

The anxieties of HQ Europe did however prove justified to some small extent. Appreciable, if in the final analysis responsible, quantities of liquor were consumed in the Defenders Bar. Jakko Mann (who now had three), Monika Brandt, and one other of their number had received from HQ the tiny not-over-conspicuous rosettes worn on the left breast to indicate their new Commendations: further excuse to add to the carnival atmosphere and 'just one more before dinner' as these were spotted by their colleagues.

The seventy young (very in some cases) members of the Orchestra were to be entertained in the Dining Hall *after* the concert. Thus they were not present to hear the story of the LSSO as related in the Dining Hall by Goodssen after the toasts.

'I am able to enthuse unashamedly about our guests tonight, as I am myself not British,' he began. 'But I have heard the London Schools Symphony Orchestra on a number of occasions, both here and in Scandinavia.

'The Orchestra was formed one hundred and thirty-three years ago — in 1951 — and was supported enthusiastically by the then London County Council. From 1967, I believe, membership was restricted to full-time students under the Inner London Education Authority, which continued when the elected Greater London Council — successor to the LCC — was abolished. Subsequent abolition of the ILEA put in some doubt survival of the enthusiasm and "equal opportunities for all" policy which had been essential features of the project.

'By then the LSSO had performed under many leading conductors, before Royalty, and to unstinted acclaim in almost every country of what was then Western Europe, and from coast to coast in the United States. The spirit lived on until London once more had its own co-ordinating body, able to foster what had become one of Britain's success stories of the century.

'Why am I so emphatic? There are two aspects on which I would like to comment. First, the international "mix" which constitutes London's children who are, after all, its adults of tomorrow. I understand that there have been as many as fifty nationalities represented in a single East End school, working and playing together. Secondly, the ambassadorial role played by these young people during the past hundred years when many of the adult population, football and other hooligans, have often set a less worthy example. The valuable publicity has been most favourably commented upon by the British "diplomatic".

'The youngsters who are our guests tonight have inherited, and they continue, an enviable reputation. We who are essentially international in *our* outlook are extremely glad to have them with us.' These remarks were well received, but there was more to come.

The silver model carriage with its decanters was making a second journey along the table towards Danielle and Jakko with reinforcements of old port and cognac, when a member of the Orchestra entered the room and made his way to where Goodssen was sitting. It had clearly been pre-arranged. The evening's President called for silence and introduced the lad.

'Mr Goodssen, Sir; Ladies and Gentlemen,' he began. 'Perhaps I have spent too much time making music because languages are not my strong point. However, I believe that, while those present come from all over Europe, the courses here are conducted in English. I am glad to say that the London Schools Symphony Orchestra has already toured France and Italy this year, and we had among us experts who were able to say nice things in their own tongue about our hosts. May I say on this occasion that it is a privilege to be here with you who try to make it One World. In our small way, we too try to do that.

'I am happy to tell you that, in secret discussions with your Principal, Mr Goodssen, it was decided that we should play for you this evening Mandela Moses' *'The Saving of the Elephants.'* At this, the youngster's remarks were all but halted by the spontaneous murmur of delighted approval, but he continued, 'This seems appropriate in any case, as you are all so soon to visit Africa.

'Thank you for your hospitality. I hope that you will enjoy your evening, and that we will have deserved your kindness.'

Jakko turned to Danni. 'I think that was jolly good for a kid. I'm sure they deserve their reputation.' She was slightly misty-eyed at being reminded of the elephants.

The gun carriage had reached them. 'I know what *you* will have,' he whispered. 'But you'll have to help yourself. It is against tradition for me to do it for you.'

32

World Government authorities knew what they were doing in the training of their forces: belief in physical excellence; the challenges and pride in their achievement; knowledge that the world's peace and progress lay largely in their hands, that they were its toughest yet its most caring elite; competent, hard-headed, practical, yet artistic and appreciative. Volunteers like twenty-year-old Jakko Mann and Danielle de Croix, still unbelievably (just) in her teens, who could paralyse in a split second with a stop gun, shoot to kill in one, or land a large VTO aircraft on a five World cents piece, were equally moved by a starving child or an injustice.

That final Saturday provided a fitting climax to the toughest period of their careers. Arrival of the Commendations, announcement of the record number of recommendations for Commissions, the guest night atmosphere, and Mandela Moses' music played by seventy inspired London children of mixed races, put the seal on the first part of their training. The *Chorus of the Hebrew Slaves* which, as usual, brought the evening to a tumultuous conclusion, was sung with surely as much passion as it had ever roused.

Sunday was given to final preparations for the African tour. Monday dawned brightly as if the duty Angel was commending Man's whole-hearted attention at last to the saving of the world. Promptly at 0900, five small VTOs full of youth and baggage took off in the morning sun for the nearby WPF base.

This time it was a Penelope III: part seats, part cargo, that headed for the Mediterranean. Less snow each year on the Alps now, in Europe's warmer climate ... Sardinia ... the blue Sicilian Channel and Cape Bon. They passed down the west side of Malta, losing height, then turned back to the north west towards Luqa, used by larger WPF aircraft by mutual agreement with the civil power.

It had rained. Thus the island, always fascinating with its very own but often somewhat pale, washed-out beauty, welcomed the new arrivals with a blend of fresh green, mellow sandstone, and the blue water of its historic harbours. As they came in low over Marsaxlokk Bay, Danielle, who was glued to the window of the aircraft, cried out, 'Oh, look! There's a frigate at anchor.' She turned to Jakko. 'I know you are right, but part of my heart is with the world's sea forces. Look how beautiful she is . . . paler grey than the ships in the West Indies.' But now they were over the leading edge of the SE/NW runway; in a few moments the big aircraft had made a copybook landing, and the Unit was bussing to the WPF complex in the old St Angelo fortress buildings overlooking the north-east corner of Grand Harbour.

After a quick meal, the rest of the day was their own: to explore the island and its amazing history from the shipwreck of St Paul in AD 60, its many rulers, to the award by Britain's King George VI of the George Cross, highest civilian award for gallantry, during World War Two, and its development since as a highly successful European tourist attraction and WPF base.

Some idea may be gained of the diversity, from the universal respect for the Blessed Virgin, whose likeness, after two thousand years, still gazed down upon the passengers in every public bus; bars around Grand Harbour and Sliema Creek, still named after British warships; and Europe's newest WISO centre — last word in sophisticated wizardry — in Floriana, overlooking the historic harbour.

Malta is particularly well-blessed with saints and with church bells. This enables the population to make whoopee in a series of carnivals spread over six months of the year. Unit EURO 2001 had arrived on the opening night of these festivities, in which an immense fireworks display was to take place from craft both moored and under way, and from the shore.

Naturally perhaps, Monika, Gustav, Jakko and Danielle had become increasingly friendly, particularly since the two latter had reached their 'understanding'. They now hailed a passing *dghajsa* and crossed the harbour to explore the capital on foot, taking in the Grand Master's Palace and St John's Cathedral, then gazing over the harbour from the Upper Barracca. From this vantage point, from ancient fortifications, and the mole, the people of Malta, nearly a hundred and fifty years before, had cheered and cheered again returning warships, sometimes grievously damaged by the German 'first eleven' flying from Sicily, and — with tears of emotion — merchantmen laden with desperately needed food, fuel, or ammunition, survivors of convoys which had fought their long way from Alexandria, as they steamed slowly, on fire, awash and sinking, into Grand Harbour.

Tearing themselves away, the young people hired a car and, piling in, set off on a full circuit of the island: Sliema, St Julians, to the site of St Paul's landfall, Mellieha, and down the winding road to sandy Mellieha Bay for a swim. On again then to Marfa Ridge, with Gozo across the blue water to the north. Here they sat for a while in the sun, drying their hair until Monika suggested that they press on to Ghajn Tuffieha where, the tour guide said, there was a once-British, now WPF shooting range. They asked for and obtained approval to fire a few rounds (a 'possible', of course, by Danielle), then — Jakko now driving — to Mosta, to see the church and its world-famous dome.

The light began to fade as they climbed back into the car and set out once more for Valletta, via the medieval walled city of Mdina, ancient capital built on a high plateau. Here they stopped, absorbing the fantastic views, the Mediterranean evening gradually fading; all four, for all their tough training, much moved by the experience.

As they drove into Valletta and returned the car, Monika took charge as usual, generously this time. 'I am taking you all to dinner. No argument. I reckon we have time before the fireworks.'

By now, the church bells were ringing in a hundred towers in honour of the saint in question; people thronging the streets. Soon the whole capital would be *en fête*.

This was Malta with its history, its success, its zero unemployment; enthusiastic part of Europe; important contributor to the WPF process; participation in WISO by its whole population. This was Malta, happy at the beginning of a new carnival season.

There are many locations on this planet which might have been designed with firework displays in mind, but none to surpass Grand Harbour. It was a sensation that night with, throughout, wildly enthusiastic audience participation. When it was all over, Danielle turned to her companions. 'I am sure Goodssen knew about this. I bet he fixed it with HQ that we should arrive today.'

* * *

The following morning was serious and instructive, with an official tour of the WPF naval base and dockyard, then a bright interlude at midday when the Unit was received aboard the Frigate *Jupiter*.

But first they were shown a permanent memorial set up beside the refurbished old No. 4 Dock.

From this dock on 8 April 1942 sailed the severely damaged British Cruiser *PENELOPE* to take her chance and 'fight it out in the open sea'.

It is recorded that during the first week of April the Luftwaffe made 5,715 sorties, dropping 6,730 tons of bombs on Grand Harbour, the Dockyard, and Air Strips. An estimated 2,000 sorties by 1,000 aircraft were directed against *PENELOPE* in twelve days.

The dock was without power, the cruiser being hauled out of dock by seamen, soldiers, survivors from sunken ships, dockyard workers, and civilians: climax to a feat of courage that may never be surpassed.

On 9 April it was reported that 'grey dust hangs in clouds over Valletta, covering like a shroud the City's gaping wounds . . . Searches are being made for victims among the shattered homes, palaces, and offices. But Valletta is still alive and its inhabitants still haunt its bomb torn streets, silent and grim, determined that their City shall rise again'.

On 15 April 1942 King George VI made the following announcement: 'To honour her brave people I award the George Cross to the island Fortress of Malta, to bear witness to a heroism and devotion that will long be famous in history'.

This Memorial was erected by the Government of Malta upon the Island becoming formally a part of the EUROPEAN FEDERATION and offering its services to the WORLD FEDERAL GOVERNMENT that there shall be no more war upon the Earth.

The party read the memorial's wording, in small groups in turn: Monika, Jakko and Danielle together. As they stood aside to make way for the next few colleagues, Monika commented, 'Sometimes I think people forget what the WPF is all about. I'm glad that the Government here has erected this reminder.'

And so to the bustling repair yard: a far cry from the old yards of the past. Here, the world's most up-to-date facilities and an enthusiastic workforce guaranteed valuable World currency to add to income from tourism, the boatyards, light industry, and as much exotic horticulture as the island's size allowed.

The Unit minibussed to Paola at the inshore end of the harbour to inspect the yard and slips where tugs and other small vessels were built, and thence round to Marsamxett Harbour, the marina, and the thriving boatyards building small pleasure craft, dinghies, and yachts, before returning to *Jupiter* at midday.

Interestingly, the frigate's upperworks were silvery-grey, the hull dark. (Could it have been a legacy from *Penelope* of so long ago?). *Jupiter* lay alongside a jetty, spotless of course. Danielle's emotions were once again mixed as they stepped off the brow on to her quarterdeck. This time the brass plate announced

WPF EUROPE
3rd MEDITERRANEAN FAST FRIGATE
SQUADRON

JUPITER	31
MARS	32
MERCURY	33
NEPTUNE	34

PLUTO	35
SATURN	36
TITAN	37
VENUS	38

The ship had prepared a welcome. Her awnings were spread; officers on hand, properly dressed; likewise representatives of the government. Refreshments and music. They had taken the visit seriously.

WPF shoulder flashes were mixed: Italy, France, Malta, England ... and, amongst those shore-based, two officers 'on exchange loan' from ARAB MIDDLE EAST.

There were two short speeches: the Captain and a member of the Malta legislature. The former, 'Just to welcome you to *Jupiter*. We of the World Peace Force have enormous pride in what we do ... and, as you can see, in the Mediterranean Command we are very "international". In my time the WPF did not organize these trips for trainees. They are an excellent idea. We are of course very worried about our friends in Egypt ... and for the whole world with the twin threats of drought and flooding. Our role is likely to be one of bringing aid to our fellow men and assisting the civil authorities if disaster strikes. I can think of no career likely to be more rewarding. Welcome! Crew members will be glad to show you the ship. She was well-built on the Clyde. Thank you.'

The Malta government spokesman took over. 'We have a long history here and have learned — and indeed suffered much — in this vital strategic location in the Mediterranean. Our central position now provides an essential base for the forces of good order and goodwill. You carry with you the friendly wishes of these islands and our people, and best wishes for the success of your careers.'

Off duty, that afternoon was spent swimming in the sun; the evening, dining in Valletta. The following day would see the Unit in Africa. By nightfall, Cairo ... the desert and the stars.

183

33

While members of the Unit had been absorbing Malta's past and present — and for a few it had been their first (and happy) experience abroad — several tons of stores had been landed at Luqa from the big Penelope III. Ongoing freight for Egypt had been loaded.

Meanwhile at St Angelo the Unit had been briefed in detail about North Africa. Three small hand STOP guns had been issued: one each to the leaders of the small groups into which the Unit had been divided. In the ordered state of the world, this had seemed to those concerned an unnecessary precaution, but they had no option but to comply. The guns were small, not provocative, and of course they could not kill.

They took off very early for the short hop to Benghazi. It would be a long day. The aircraft was to wait and then fly them on to Cairo in the evening whence it, the aircraft, would continue the next day with a relief crew.

At Benghazi Airport buses were already waiting with a WPF scout car as escort, to take them down the coast road beside the Gulf of Sirte. From Al Burayqah airfield they would fly inland in a much smaller but fast plane 350 miles over the desert to Sarir and one of the fresh water projects resulting from Gaddafi's intuition a hundred years before.

The buses stopped fifty miles on, beside the remains of an old tank, doubtless forced off the road during the final push by the Eighth Army. Little remained. It was a sad reminder of a different age.

Jakko Mann's group was in the leading bus, following the scout car. A gentle breeze off the sea carried inland the dust thrown up by its tyres. They could see the road in front and, in the distance, the coast turning south-westwards along the bottom of the Gulf.

Danielle de Croix sat beside Jakko, scanning the desert and the road alternately with her binoculars. Presently she stopped her 'sweep' and concentrated on a spot some way ahead. 'What is it, Danni?' Danielle screwed up her eyes and removed her sunglasses for a moment. 'Some sort of commotion. The sand is being stirred up.'

It was not long before the scout car stopped, and then the buses following. An enormous wagon, piled high with bales, lay askew across the roadway. The nearside rear wheel had fallen apart, the axle digging into the surface of the road. Ahead, an emaciated horse was being bludgeoned repeatedly by a tall Arab with a heavy bar. As the blows rained down on its head and neck, the animal, its legs barely on the ground and unable to get a proper grip, managed to drag the embedded axle a few inches at a time.

Danielle was first out of the bus, closely followed by Jakko and the others of their group, but Jakko pushed her aside, drawing the STOP gun and bellowing at the fellow to desist.

'DON'T SHOOT!' It was Danielle. 'DON'T SHOOT!' It was a 'staff course', as distinct from an emotional reaction. But by now the man had both hands in the air, unaware that the weapon was not lethal. Danielle: 'I'm sorry, Jakko. But that could lead to all kinds of trouble, and he might die of shock. Then where would we be?'

The crew of the scout car had gathered round. One of their number brandished a repeater handgun. Behind them now, the rest of the Unit.

'KEEP HIM COVERED, BUT DON'T SHOOT! This time it was Captain Brightwell, who had made her way to the front from the third bus.

Jakko handed his STOP gun to a colleague. He and Danielle stepped forward to inspect the horse. The head, neck and foreleg had been lacerated by the sheer force of the blows. The left eye dangled from its socket. Danielle turned away for a moment; then, with a visible act of willpower, she resumed her examination. She and Jakko ventured round to the offside. The jawbone looked to be fractured; the eye pulped. She turned at once to Pippa Brightwell. 'I am a country girl, Ma'am. This animal must be put out of its misery at once. We will all support you, if ever any questions should be asked.'

The Captain turned to the armed member of the scout car crew. 'Aim for the head. Fire the whole magazine. Every round you have.'

Most of the onlookers turned away. There was a burst of fire and the animal slowly collapsed, suspended in grotesque fashion by the wagon's shafts.

'Thank you,' Pippa Brightwell said. She turned to the assembled members of the Unit. 'I want to make one comment. In this day and age, I do not want to hear any condemnation on account of race. Unfortunately there is cruelty *all over* the world still. Remember the animals in the laboratories in Europe, America, and the Far East; the duck "hunters" and rodeos in the United States; and the Australian sheep. I am truly ashamed for the human race today, but, sadly, that is nothing new.'

The WPF soldier with the now empty gun asked, 'Do we take this man with us, Ma'am?'

Captain Brightwell's eyes blazed. It was a side of her character that her protégés had not seen before. 'Certainly not! It's only fifty miles to Benghazi. Let the unspeakable *bastard* walk.'

She turned to the others. 'This trip is designed to broaden your outlook and teach you about life. Well ... that process has begun this morning.'

* * *

The convoy, scout car leading, pressed on to make up for lost time. It was now a good, metalled road. Initially, and not surprisingly, there was an unnatural hush. It was becoming very hot.

At Al Burayqah their aeroplane and a new WPF guide were waiting to take them southwards across Cyrenaica. They were soon airborne, and the guide called for everyone's attention.

'Welcome to the Sahara. We understand that you are the first of a number of Units under training who will be making this trip to see for themselves, on the ground, some of the problems that Man now faces if he is to survive. As of course you all know, the Earth is becoming steadily warmer and wetter at high latitudes. Meanwhile the drought areas are spreading outwards, north and south from the Equator. Water is both the key and the problem. *Salt* water is rising, and threatens to flood huge

186

areas in which millions live. The supply of natural *fresh* water in a total of some seventy degrees of latitude centred upon the Equator is steadily diminishing. The flow of a number of the Earth's most important rivers is substantially less than it was a hundred years ago, including the Colorado, Mississippi, Niger, Congo, Nile, Zambezi, Tigris and Euphrates, to name only a few. (In passing, the scientists cannot agree upon the headwaters of the Nile, but you will hear more on that problem when you reach Egypt.)

'There are three main sources of fresh water. First, rain: natural or man-induced; taken direct from rivers, used for irrigation, or stored in natural or man-made reserves, lakes, reservoirs and so on. Secondly, distillation of fresh water from the sea. You will over-fly a number of such plants on your way to Cairo this evening. Thirdly, location and recovery of subterranean (sometimes referred to as "lost") sources and reserves. It is with *these* that we are concerned today. Scientists more than a hundred years ago located several, not just one, huge water reserves trapped under the Sahara sands. It is believed that a great fertile belt extended across Cyrenaica, watered by rivers carrying to the Mediterranean the rains from the mountains in what is now the south-eastern corner of Algeria, and Tibesti in north Chad. Remains of hippo, elephant and buffalo support that view. When we land, you will see a large relief map of the area. You will agree that north-east flowing rivers would have been a "natural" from Fezzan and Sarir.

'It is to the credit of Colonel Gaddafi — not always popular in his time, one understands — that he first had the vision of *the Great Man-made River*: the pipelines since laid right across Libya.'

He produced a bundle of small maps which were quickly distributed. 'If you will look three hundred and twenty miles due south of Benghazi, you will see the one-time confluence of no less than four former rivers, and further south — lying in a south-west/north-east direction — the old route taken by waters from the south and west. We will land at the northerly of those two locations, where new boring and the siting of pumps are underway. We thought that would be of more interest than simply looking at existing pipelines just stretching away into the distance ... that is where they have not been already buried by the "unrelenting desert"! And we will show you some of the irrigation already operational.'

Their instructor resumed his seat next to Captain Brightwell. A steward produced cool drinks, and chatter was resumed.

* * *

The promised 'relief map' turned out to be a fantastic *model*, military sand-table fashion: a vast coloured work of art at table height, floodlit, with viewing points, each equipped with microphones for recording, and internal telephones. It portrayed the slice of North Africa that lies between 20°N and the Mediterranean, from 5° to 30° East.

Ingeniously, where sub-Sahara water reserves had been identified, the 'desert' had been cut away to expose the water, covered with a pale yellow gauze material so that one seemed to be viewing the desert, yet seeing the treasured water underneath. The south-eastern Algerian high ground and the Tibesti hills gradually gave way to the lowlands once watered by the tributaries of at least one great river of the past, flowing north-eastwards towards Egypt and the sea. One could almost *see* the hippos of five thousand or more years ago bathing in the shallows, the bigger animals drinking. Already to the north and east in upper Cyrenaica, huge areas of irrigated crops evidenced the earliest water reclamation, while pipelines disappeared to the eastward in the direction of the distant Nile.

The trainees were awed by the imagination which had conceived the whole Libyian project; impressed equally by the problems and sheer determination behind its implementation. But the *pièce de resistance* was to come. 'The World Government, in conjuction with the FEDERATION OF ARAB MIDDLE EAST, has announced *today*(!) that Libya *is* to be connected to the Nile. You will of course know about the Port Sudan/Nile project . . . and I believe you fly the pipeline route to Atbara during your tour. The object of that project is to protect, *forever, and whether or not the scientists are correct*, the Nile flow, irrigation, and dam power: all of which are vital to Egypt with its teeming population. Like the Port Sudan/Nile project — *this too is to be reversible*! The whole Libyan network will be connected to the Nile upstream from Cairo and the Delta.'

The schedule was tight. 'We have a snack meal ready for you.

In the heat here, and as in any case it has all to be brought down from the coast, I hope you will forgive that. But it will keep you alive! Afterwards, we will have a look at a big borehole, and then we fly you — over the irrigation area — direct back to Benghazi, where the big aircraft will take you on to Cairo.'

* * *

It was still daylight as the Penelope III took off from Benghazi and headed east over the North African battlefields of World War Two. Nearly a hundred and fifty years ago now. The names still retained their magic amongst those whose ancestors had fought their way with Rommel along that coastal strip, retreated, and advanced again in an attempt to take Egypt or — from the UK, New Zealand, and Australia — fought and died in the prevention or, later, advanced to the west for the last time.

It had been first an emotional, then inspiring, but hot and tiring day. Nonetheless, with cool air and cold drinks, young spirits revived and as they flew, lowish for a big plane, over Derna and Tobruq, Monika Brandt and compatriot Karl made their way between the seats to suggest a little nostalgia. It *had* to be, once more *Lilli Marlene*. And so, as they crossed the Gulf of Salum heading for Siddi Barrani, the German and British nationals led the song that will be sung for ever . . .

* * *

It was all but dark as they landed at Cairo West Airport. Buses to WPF base. A hot meal and a night's sleep in eager anticipation of the wonders of the morrow.

It was as well, Jakko reflected as he lay awake until overcome with tiredness, that *he* had not been issued with that repeater handgun. Precipitate action might have done no good to his career.

189

34

Cairo. After early breakfast at WPF Cairo (West), where the Unit would be based during their Egyptian stay, they assembled for an introduction to Cairo and the Nile by a female air force Captain of WPF Arab Middle East. She was exquisitely proportioned, and her facial make-up derived direct from the ancients, with heavy accentuation of perfect almond eyes. There was an audible intake of breath. The Captain was perhaps accustomed to good-natured approval, for she smiled with 'Now boys, be good!' There was to follow — in perfect English — a condensed but wide-ranging review of Egypt's achievements in general and now formidable problems, and those of Cairo in particular.

'Welcome to Cairo,' the beautiful creature began. 'Cairo and the Nile are beset by conflicts and contradictions, but Egypt's role for good in the world was never more important than during the most recent hundred years. This is the largest city in Africa. Egypt, as part of the African continent and at the same time essentially of the Arab world, has played an important part in creating the friendly, co-operative spirit which now exists between the two. Simultaneously, this country has exercised — at times to its own cost — a moderating and co-operative role in a part of the world subject for generations to division, passion, extremism and strife. I think it may be fairly said that Egyptian influence has been exemplary, indeed vital, and it has not always been easy. Importantly, we now have not only a WPF base here, but one of its permanent Operational HQs.

'But let me deal first with the physical aspect. To start with, it is this city's good fortune, yet *mis*fortune, to contain within comparatively small areas monuments both Islamic and Pharaonic. While there is no question of "competition", *all*

Cairo's medieval buildings, which include some of the world's most notable have, until recently, been threatened by neglect, overcrowding in the rest of the city, and by rising ground water and sewage; and help from the outside world has tended to favour the Pharaonic.

'The water and drainage problems are themselves complicated and contradictory. Cairo, the Nile valley and Delta depend for fresh water, irrigation, and electric power, upon maintenance of the Nile flow. Simultaneously, much of the Delta, the areas round Alexandria and Port Said, up river, and of course in the west, are below sea level. The city faced actual decay from rising groundwater and poor drainage. The Nile flow had to be, and still must be, maintained. The Mediterranean had to be, and still must be, kept out. What we have to preserve is priceless and irreplaceable. I refer not only to the past but to our ongoing survival, prosperity and influence.

'Our problems have been compounded by inability of climatologists to agree upon the likely future of north-eastern Africa. Predictions relating to the Earth's warming and its effects are generally being proved remarkably accurate, but opinions continue to differ regarding the upper Nile.

'We have never forgotten the near-panic a hundred or so years ago. In 1987 and 1988, it was feared that the turbines of the Aswan High Dam might actually have to be shut down because of the reduced flow into Lake Nasser from the south. At that time, a quarter of the country's power was provided by Aswan. On those occasions the rains came in time, but a big power station building programme was nonetheless put in hand.

'Meanwhile, during the past fifty years or more, immense and costly work has been continuous: to improve the infrastructure, contain the river, and keep out the sea, with emphasis upon new buildings *and* ancient monuments. As regards power, there is now the world project to feed the upper Nile from the Red Sea. Any risk to the Nile flow is unacceptable.

'In passing, Egypt is "expert" at re-siting important structures., We have had a good deal of practice! You will see the temples of Abu Simbel, for example, which were moved block by block. (They would have been drowned by Lake Nasser when we built the High Dam.) More recently, we have moved and rebuilt a number of important medieval structures in Cairo itself.

'The turning point — physically *and* politically — was the return to Cairo in 1990 of the Arab League secretariat. The League was of course a collection of delegates: not an elected government, and we are all federalists now, but it was in effect the forerunner of the FEDERATION OF ARAB MIDDLE EAST. The Arab League secretariat had been moved from Cairo following our peace treaty with Israel. Its return in 1990 was greeted emotionally in our country, and put fresh heart into all our undertakings, beginning with a mammoth clean-up of Cairo itself and the sincere endeavours of our then President to further the interests of peace in the region during the Iraqi crisis.

'A few words on Sinai. Our so-called moderating influence reached its triumph in the creation of New Palestine, which has been so overwhelmingly successful, *and* which quite possibly saved the world from further war. Deservedly, the whole project has been of immense value to Egypt, to our Federation, and to the world. New Palestine in Sinai *is* a separate state. It sends its own representatives to our Regional Federal Government. But its *sympathies* and prosperity are so enmeshed with Egypt that the boundary is no more than a technicality. At that time — I am still referring to the later years of the last century — there was in our part of the world a much increased desire for mutual understanding and co-operation. It was in 1990, for instance, that serious discussion began on the link between Saudi Arabia and Egypt across the southern end of the Gulf of Aqaba by way of Tiran island. That led to construction of the fantastic causeway that joins us together via Sinai today. Saudi Arabia had, only a few years before, in 1986, financed the causeway linking their country with Bahrain. Then there was our co-operation with Libya to the west, regarding fresh water and power. The Kuwait crisis hit Egypt hard: the cost of it all; reduced Canal revenues; collapse of tourism; loss of the income sent home by our countrymen who fled the disputed area; huge numbers to care for and re-settle. But in the long term we were determined to lead co-operative progress in the region.

'The purpose of your stopover in Egypt is concerned in the main with measures to be taken to implement the Report ACTION BY MAN. That, in our context, means preservation of the Nile flow and stabilization of sea levels, rather than contemplation of past glories, tourist attractions, prosperous economies, and the goodwill within our Federation. Before setting off on your project studies, we will show you the WPF HQ complex. God forbid that it will ever be operational, but, like similar establishments in other parts of the world, it is meticulously maintained and rehearsed, ready for immediate use.

'Later this morning we fly you to El Alamein, just 140 miles, and from there the sixty mile route to be followed by the water pumped out of the Mediterranean into the Qattara Depression. This is the simplest of the "big four" immediate projects and will, it is hoped, save Alexandria from flooding until other measures are completed.

'I need hardly remind you, since you all come from Europe, of the World War Two significance of El Alamein. The narrow strip between the Depression and the sea, a mere forty miles, was the only and the last natural defensive position before Cairo and the Delta. It was the scene of one of the decisive land battles of history.

'This afternoon, on our return flight, we take you on a short detour over Alexandria and Aboukir, where the English Admiral Nelson destroyed the French fleet on 1 August, 1798. On that occasion, of course, it was Napoleon, not Hitler, who had his eye upon Egypt! Naturally, we are interested in these battles of long ago. I find reassuring the *humanity* evident during the fierce sea battles of those days between European powers. It is well-known that when the French Admiral Brueys' huge flagship *L'Orient* caught fire during the Battle of the Nile and was likely to blow up, Admiral Nelson, himself wounded in the head, came on deck and ordered every available boat to be sent to save her crew. When finally the French flagship blew up with an explosion seen and heard *ten miles away* at Rashid — you call it Rosetta — English sailors, horror-struck, dragged as many survivors from the sea as they could grasp. (It was the same with German sailors from the *Bismarck* in 1941.) It is interesting that the French (then Rear) Admiral Villeneuve escaped in *Le Guillaume Tell*, one of the only two surviving French ships of the line, to lead — in the *Bucentaure* — the combined French and Spanish fleet seven years later at Trafalgar.

'So, today it is a mixture of locations for urgent action to save the Nile Delta and of eighteenth/twentieth century European history. Tomorrow will be spent in Cairo, ancient and modern; the day following, we fly you to New Palestine — 200 miles

— and return in time for you to have an evening on your own in Cairo. Thereafter we helihop up the Nile before you leave us to fly to Port Sudan and up the pipeline route to Atbara . . . and thence south.

'I expect you were warned about the heat, ultra-violet, food, stomach upsets, and so on. Please play safe, avoid sudden changes in diet to which you are not accustomed. You *are* on duty, and we cannot have stragglers left behind when you move on. Protect your eyes.

'Please be ready in half an hour.'

* * *

Though young and fit, and resulting as much from the heat as from the non-stop itinerary, the young people were glad of that 'evening on your own in Cairo'. Bewildered by the city's glittering choice, they headed in taxis, relaxed and in small groups, for the Cairo Golden Gates, following their happy experience in that company's establishments in the West Indies and earlier that day in Sinai.

Monika, now escorted by Karl, Danielle and Jakko wandered first through the reception areas of another of the world's great hotels. Marble staircases; murals of the desert; twinkling stars invisibly suspended, of varying brightness, visible overhead between the palm trees stirring in a gentle breeze. Skilful use of vast mirrors so that, beyond, the desert stretched away: seemingly infinite, timeless; at once romantic, beckoning, yet unknown and a little frightening, under the night sky.

Scattered groups with cool drinks, visitors from every corner of the Earth in formal, national, or casual attire, evidenced Cairo's pre-eminence, where seemingly there met every religion, nationality, and culture. Regional capital, at the junction of three great Federal groups: EUROPE, PAN AFRICA and ARAB MIDDLE EAST.

None of the young volunteers spoke for some time until Danielle, the least inhibited, flung her arms wide with 'How beautiful it is . . and to think that we are here just as part of our *training*!' and then, 'I feel that I owe the world so much already.' At that, Jakko took her hand as they entered one of the hotel's great bars, with, 'We couldn't do more, darling, than

194

we are doing.'

They settled at a marble table with deliberately conventional drinks; physically weary for all their fitness, glad to sit down; waving to a group of their contemporaries; then bubbling with conversation after three days packed with five thousand years of history, strange beauty and achievement. 'There cannot be another city like it.' It was Monika. 'Such a fabulous mixture. One could spend a lifetime and not see it all. The old buildings and mosques, that *museum* and the *bazaar* . . . I suppose it isn't very romantic, but those new sewers were fantastic. I'm so glad that we were shown *them*! It's all so important to this marvellous city.'

Danielle: 'Tutankhamun's *shaving things*! . . . '

Monika continued, 'And Mena House, the Pyramids and Sphinx . . . and what about *today*!'

Karl: 'I have good pictures of you girls on camels.'

Danielle's comment might have been expected. 'I'm not sure about camels. They don't look very happy creatures, do they? There is a sort of "resigned" look about them . . . is that the right word? . . . but, at the same time they have preserved their dignity and "independence".'

Monika's comments were more basic. '*I'm* not very happy with the Egyptian obsession with *death* . . . in the past, I mean; and I cannot think that the masses had much of a life. The priests seem to have kept everything mysterious in order to protect their own position. And how were the Pyramids and these other massive structure built? Didn't that man say that there were *two million* blocks of sandstone in the Great Pyramid? I suppose they built ramps and hauled the blocks up one at a time . . . a fantastic achievement of course and I am glad that we have seen it all. Like Danni said, other people *pay* for trips like this.'

Jakko had not contributed much to the conversation. Now he came out with, 'Something worries me about that fantastic parliament complex in Sinai this morning. You do realize, all of you, that those beautiful trees which were landscaped in hundreds round the buildings were *Cercis Siliquastrum* . . . Judas trees.'

Monika: 'So?'

'Well, I don't pretend to be very worldly wise, but I do remember "He came unto his own and his own received him not." Those trees are called Judas trees because Judas Iscariot is supposed to have hanged himself from one in a fit of remorse after betraying the Son of God. Perhaps I am seeing too much in surrounding with those trees the New Palestine centre of Government. It could be interpreted as provocative.'

Monika: 'Jakko! I'm surprised at you. Really I am! You are such a kind person. How can you have thoughts like that?'

Danielle supported her. 'Quite right, Monika. I don't know what Jakko is thinking of! To be serious, I'm sure it wasn't deliberate. We have those trees in France too. It used to be said in Europe that their boles were always twisted because they are so unhappy at being associated with the betrayal. But surely they wouldn't have planted them to upset the Israelis. Not these days. Thank God people just don't think like that any more. Anyway, I think Egypt is fantastic.'

Monika: 'Come on; if you've all finished your drinks, let's go in for dinner. We shouldn't be too late. It is a long day tomorrow.'

35

Everyone was up very early for their day along the Nile. The WPF authorities at Cairo (West) had organized that the party fly past the Pyramids at sunrise — an experience not to be forgotten — on their way south.

They flew then, fast and direct, to Aswan.

The Egyptian WPF Captain accompanied the leading group. 'This is business with pleasure,' she said as the party gathered round, shielding their eyes. 'Practical measures to preserve modern Egypt, and visits to some of our most remarkable legacies from the past.

'People began to settle in the Nile valley about ten thousand years ago. They relied for water and irrigation on annual flooding which lasted for about four months, from July to October. The British Dam was built at the end of the nineteenth century and opened in 1902, to create a reservoir so that the people did not have to rely on the ''inundation'', but fifty years later President Nasser announced plans for a new dam. The result is before you.' She remained silent for a few moments while the young people took in the sheer size of the achievement. 'It took ten years to build and was opened on 15 January, 1971. It is 3,600 metres long and 110 metres high. The hydro-electric turbines can produce two million kilowatts. That is a lot of electricity! As you see, a huge lake was created (and named after President Nasser) as the water built up behind the dam. It is nearly *200 miles* upstream to Wadi Halfa! Meanwhile, the road and rail route which you can see over there skirts Lake Nasser, and at Wadi Halfa (which is just in Sudan) it joins the route to Atbara and the sea. The Aswan — Wadi Halfa stretch of railway and truck road were only completed early in the present century.'

She waited to give her audience time to look around them. A gentle breeze relieved the heat. Then, 'You are of course going on to Zimbabwe before you leave for Europe. The Kariba Dam and Lake were created on the same principle: a man-made fresh water lake building up behind a dam built to provide electricity; and in our case, vital irrigation as well. While there was some doubt in the past regarding the Nile headwaters until we decided that the risk of drought was unacceptable, there has been *no* doubt about the need to feed the Zambezi. The Zambezi flow is now substantially less than it was fifty years ago. Hence the breathtaking project on *their* agenda.'

The Captain drew attention to where temples once stood on Philae. 'I'm afraid that your time does not allow for detailed examination of the temples which were moved . . .' There were some disbelieving gasps. 'I *mean* actually moved. When the Old Dam was completed in 1902, the island of Philae was sometimes under water, and the New High Dam would have meant that it was submerged permanently. The temples were taken to pieces and rebuilt on the island of Agilkia.' Then she added, 'Don't despair. Please return to your aircraft, because we *do* show you Abu Simbel which is even more remarkable.'

It was but a short hop and, before they entered, the Captain told them how — to save them from the water when the New High Dam was built — the temples had been taken apart, block by block, and reassembled; a feat almost beyond imagination, when the size and weight of the pieces is considered. Four huge seated figures of Rameses II, each *sixty-five feet high*, dominated the facade of the temple, of which eight colossal statues constitute the pillars.

The original temples had been sited so that — twice a year — the rays at sunrise shone through the first hall into the second. Here they lit up four statues on the far, inside, wall. This feature had been reproduced precisely during the rebuilding. A second, smaller temple, also built originally by Rameses II, was dedicated to his wife Nefertari. Here there are six statues: four of the king himself and two of the Queen, again all faithfully re-sited. All this the group witnessed, marvelling, as had millions of tourists, at the magnificence and sheer physical size of these monuments to a tremendous, powerful, age.

The party returned to Aswan, thence via Luxor back to Cairo. It was over the evening meal, in the ballroom of the Golden

Gates Hotel, that Jakko turned to his three companions in somewhat serious vein. 'I don't discuss this very much, but we all know each other pretty well now ... I found today a bit disturbing.'

'Go on, Jakko.' That encouragement from Danielle.

'Well, a long time ago one of my family married a girl whose mother believed strongly in reincarnation. I don't mean one of those pseudo-spooky people. By all accounts she was particularly well-educated, completely sane and rational, and very gifted as well. Among other things, she drew and painted and made things with her hands. Anyway, it was you, Monika, wasn't it, who commented yesterday or the day before on the obsession with *death* in ancient Egypt. Well, this relation of mine had lived on Atlantis — the continent that submerged — then in ancient Egypt, Greece, Rome, France during the Revolution, and in England. She may be on this Earth again now, for all I know.'

At this point a waiter arrived with coffee and, simultaneously, the band struck up some gentle, incredibly old-fashioned dance music. But Jakko's listeners were now absorbed. 'Well,' he went on, 'what really made it all make sense to me was that she started to write six autobiographies.'

Monika: 'How do you mean *six* autobiographies?'

'Well, she wrote each one as a novel, but they were actually her own stories. The first covered her life on Atlantis. She was there when the continent submerged following a vast volcanic upheaval. She described in detail how the buildings crumbled ... how she escaped with a few others in a boat, and how eventually they reached Egypt. There *are* sites in the Aegean; I have looked at detailed maps; where there are obvious remains of volcanos. Look at Thira — Santorini — for instance. It would make sense that enormous waves were created and that boats could have made their way or been driven south and washed up on the Egyptian coast.

'The second book told of her life here. She was a priestess in one of the temples. What really scares me rigid is *how good a person she was, yet how much she had to suffer*. I simply haven't studied enough to know whether life in ancient Egypt was extremely tough, or whether it is a question of very high standards being required by God.' Not surprisingly, his companions were silenced for a moment.

199

'The third novel was devoted to her life in Greece but, after that, she died before completing the series. I'm sure that was a terrible tragedy . . . a great loss to the world. A convincing and logical factor is that on the flyleaf of each book appears *a list of characters who reappear in succeeding lives* — or do *not* reappear in one, but perhaps *do* overlap with their former contemporaries in the next. That all seems to me to make sense.'

'Has Egypt done something to upset you?' It was Monika again. Karl and Danielle were silent.

'I can't put my finger on it. Oh, I'm sorry. Perhaps you do not understand the expression.'

Danielle reached across the table. 'Perhaps, Jakko, you have been here before!'

Karl, not very convinced, 'Perhaps we all have.'

Danielle was serious. '*I* think this is very important . . . but how do we *know*? The world has progressed a long way . . . not only in science and technology . . . and of course financially . . . it has been doing those things for hundreds of years; but, this century, in the *humanities* and *caring* . . . look at WISO. And what are we doing here in Cairo anyway?' She answered her own question: 'Learning how to be members of a force for good which *exists* only to help the whole world. What more are we supposed to do?'

Jakko was concerned, oblivious for the moment to the other two. 'Don't be like that, Danni. I wish I hadn't mentioned it. Come and dance and talk about something else.'

'OK.' She had recovered. 'But first, can we change the subject? Before we leave Egypt I want to visit the Brooke Hospital for animals. It's only a few minutes in a taxi from the centre of things. That was one of their ambulances at Aswan. In any case, it is world-famous and,' turning to Jakko, 'it was started by an *English* lady, Dorothy Brooke, in 1934 — that's exactly a hundred and fifty years ago — after a long campaign to rescue old English war-horses that had fallen on hard times. Now, I believe they have clinics and mobile first aid facilities all over this part of the world.'

Monika, ever efficient, 'We leave in the morning. I cannot see when we have time.'

Jakko, concerned now, 'Is this place open at night? We could get a taxi before we go back to Cairo (West).' He beckoned to a passing waiter, who needed no encouragement to elaborate

200

upon his affirmative reply.

'My father has horse. They look after him *very good*. They are there all day and all night. Never close.' He made off, suitably rewarded.

'Very good!' Danielle repeated. 'Come on, Jakko. Let's dance the night away ... and then go to the hospital.'

Dinner was over. The great hotel's guests relaxed with liqueurs, more coffee and mixed scents as the last word in air-conditioning wrestled with camels and cigars, horses and high fashion, the night air and the Nile. The inevitable *gully-gully* man had long since retired. It was time for romance under the stars.

Jakko, quietly as they danced together, 'Danni, do you remember Port of Spain?'

* * *

The taxi disgorged them at the Hospital.

Danielle looked at her watch. It was 0100. She led the way. The four of them entered. They were met by a large, shiny, new notice.

BROOKE HOSPITAL FOR ANIMALS CAIRO
1934-2084
150 YEARS OF SERVICE

---

and a small, very old notice.

OPEN ALL HOURS
at night, please ring for attention
Many Thanks

من فضلـــــك ... .

إضــــرب الجرس ... للتنــبيــه ...

شــكرا جـزيلا

201

Danni rang, and there appeared an Egyptian veterinary nurse. 'Can I help you?'

'We are WPF trainees visiting your fantastic country. We couldn't leave without seeing this famous hospital. Please may we come in? It is our only opportunity.'

The girl spoke good English. 'Of course, but there is only a small staff at night: the duty vet, two syces — the word comes from the Arabic *sassa*: to treat kindly — the duty ambulance driver and two nurses.' She motioned to them to follow. 'If you will come in to Reception, I will tell you a little about the Hospital; then I will show you round.'

She began, 'It all started in 1934.' She rummaged in a desk drawer. 'This is what Mrs Brooke herself wrote after the Hospital was opened: "*Our Hospital stands to the memory of the twenty-two thousand of our* (she meant British) *army horses who served in the Middle East in the Great War, to those who were killed in battle and to those, far less fortunate, who died in bitter servitude in Egypt, and to those found and ransomed who ended their days in peace and comfort in the stables that have now been converted into the Hospital that stands to their memory*".'

Her listeners were moved by this. The girl continued, 'This is the main hospital. We also have clinics in Alexandria and Mansura looking after animals in the Delta, and at tourist centres on the Nile: Luxor, Edfu, and Aswan. Although the helicopters are now almost as numerous as the flies, there are still many carriage horses. And of course there are the agricultural animals and markets. During the last hundred years, the original clinics have all been rebuilt, together with shelters from the heat and fresh water drinking facilities. The whole situation has completely changed since the middle part of the last century. There has always been friendship and co-operation from the Egyptian authorities, but now the owners of animals welcome the facilities that we provide, and — for the most part — bring in their own animals when they are sick or injured, and they gather round our mobile units out in the country.

'We also have hospitals in India, Pakistan and Jordan, as well as in the suburbs of Sinai City (New Palestine) and on the coastal strip. All hospitals and clinics have mobile facilities and ambulances attached.'

The visitors were as much impressed by the girl's self-assurance as by the huge scope of the work. She paused. 'Before

202

we walk round, perhaps I should explain the policy behind our operations.'

'First of all, animals are brought in voluntarily by the owners, or at their request. All treatment and feeding is free. In many cases the animal is essential to the owner's livelihood. Our ambulances are sent any distance, and they are all fitted with tail lifts so that injured animals do not have to be manhandled up a ramp or suffer unnecessary stress. No animal is ever discharged from hospital until it is fit for work, and it is impressed on owners to bring in their animal at the first sign of injury or illness, although the wisdom of this is now widely appreciated.

'Mares brought in for foaling are given special care, and we keep them for four weeks after the birth. All patients are re-shod free, and badly fitting harness is attended to.

'Finally — and I am afraid this aspect upsets some of our visitors — we do not let hopelessly lame, injured, worn-out, or very old animals go back to work. The hospital buys the animal — which gives the owner a little, often much needed, money — and the animal is humanely destroyed. Those that are not in any pain are given a few days of good food, care and comfort before they are put down. You will see one or two of these in a few minutes.'

There was silence from her listeners.

'A hundred years ago, already some 25,000 animals were being treated every year. Now, it is four times that number, but our increased facilities are mostly responsible, not an increase in ill-usage. Much the reverse, I think. We have achieved big improvement, friendship and trust . . . Since you are members of the WPF, I am glad to say that much international goodwill comes into *our* work as well. We often have visits from veterinary authorities from other countries.'

At this point Jakko asked whether, before they left, they could become regular subscribers. 'It wouldn't be terribly much . . . we are all still under training . . . but I'm sure we would all like to do *something*.'

'That is very kind of you. It would be so much appreciated. I can give you the papers before you leave; then you can discuss it first with your colleagues. *Thank* you.'

She led the way into the hospital, continuing her commentary. 'We have forty loose-boxes altogether here, an operating theatre and two large Kraals for convalescents, a farrier's shop and of course stores for medicines and feed. The whole place is fly-proofed and — as you will see — meticulously kept.'

They were permitted a quick look at the operating theatre and the impressive reserves of medicines and animal foods; then they progressed quietly down the row of dimly-lit loose-boxes. All was peace, a haven of caring. The animals were silent, mostly sleeping. No-one spoke.

Presently their guide stopped and motioned to them for complete hush. Then she whispered, 'there is a baby donkey in the next box. His mother died when he was three days old. He is being bottle-fed. He will be asleep now.'

They tiptoed to the half door, to be greeted by a scene straight from Bethlehem. The tiny animal of total innocence lay sleeping beneath the still-empty manger in the semi-darkness, beside him a young veterinary nurse seated amidst the straw bedding, lovingly watching for the slightest movement by her charge.

The girl looked up as they peered into the loose-box. It was as if she half expected the Virgin Mary to arrive at any moment, but alas — although surely no place on Earth was more qualified — that night it was not to be.

Her Egyptian colleague broke the silence with the merest whisper. 'This is Collette . . .' then, to the nurse, 'We have some late night visitors; they are leaving Cairo in the morning.' It was at that moment that Danielle spotted the French tricolour on the shoulders of the girl's Environment Corps uniform. Excitedly, but under her breath (and surprisingly in *English*), 'Collette! You are from France!'

'*à jamais*!'

They embraced over the door.

36

A few members of the Unit were conscious, the rest — including the Brooke Hospital four — still asleep, when the telescreen in their temporary quarters sprang to life. It was the Egyptian WPF Captain, bright, already on duty, beautiful reminder as always of the pharaonic past.

'Attention Unit EURO 2001! Attention Unit 2001! I have to call you early. We have received orders during the night that your itinerary has been amended.

'I need not remind you that feeding the population in much of Ethiopia, particularly in Eritrea, Tigray, and North Wello, has been the subject of world concern for a century. The problem has now reached its gravest proportions ever, due to the prolonged, total drought of recent times. Six million people now face starvation.

'The Khartoum leg of your trip has been cancelled. As I understand it, you were to have flown the route from the coast to Atbara. You will now proceed from Cairo direct to Asmara to assist in relief work.

'Breakfast will be at 0730. You will receive further briefing at 0900 and take off at 1000. The following will please report to my office at 0700: Dean-Matthew Barry, Monika Brandt, Karl Brandenberg, Danielle de Croix, Jakko Mann, Chantelle Ouchaner, Jamina Scott, and Gustav Svensen. Thank you.'

The eight named duly reported to find Pippa Brightwell already in the Egyptian Captain's office. She fell them in and reported to the latter that all were present and correct. 'At ease! I do not need to spell out the food problem in the area we are talking about, but at last there is a new element in the aid. I refer of course to the WG's imaginative plan outlined in ACTION BY MAN, whereby distilled water from the Red Sea

205

will create a vast reservoir and one of the most ambitious irrigation projects in the world. That is a welcome departure from the past, when — however well-intentioned — many millions of money were necessarily devoted, time after time, to keeping some of the people alive for a few weeks. An Aid organization executive will elaborate a little at 0900 when the whole of your Unit is assembled.

'Meanwhile I have I think unprecedented, and I am sure exciting news for those of you here now. Such is the call upon WG personnel: both WPF and Environment Corps, besides the Food Organization and others, that each of you is to be granted, as of today, Acting Commissions.' Restrained excitement. 'Further, we are informed that there are three exceptional trainee VTO/helicopter pilots amongst you who have not yet formally been awarded their wings. I refer to Miss Danielle de Croix, Miss Chantelle Ouchaner, and Mr Jakko Mann. You three are to be awarded your wings this morning. The eight of you are to report here at 0845 before the nine o'clock group briefing. The Colonel commanding Cairo (West) base will present you with your insignia.

'After breakfast, I advise you to get your bags packed. There will be little time after the briefing. Thank you.'

0845; Colonel Hassan. 'This is an unexpected pleasure for me . . . and a unique occasion, as far as I am aware. We have received very good reports of you all from Euro College 11, and on behalf of WPF Europe I am delighted to present you with your insignia.'

Captain Brightwell called each name, and they stepped forward in turn. The Colonel again, 'I think that, given *acting* rank in this way, you have perhaps more responsibility than usual. I am sure that you will be worthy of the confidence that WPF is placing in each of you.' To the three pilots: 'I am a flyer myself. Remember that the lives of others are in your hands. Be brave, but do not become over-excited. Always take care, and abide by what you have been taught by your instructors. In time, you will react correctly by instinct.

'I hope that you have all enjoyed your brief stay in Egypt, and that you will come back one day when you are on leave and have more leisure time. Live up to your calling in the WPF. It is One World now; we are a proud part of it.' The last comment, however sincere, seemed to be standard procedure.

* * *

0900. The Egyptian Captain introduced an executive of the World Aid Organization.

'I am glad to have this opportunity to give you the background to this alteration to your plans,' he began. 'I fear that there is little glamour attached to the decision. Put bluntly, the availability of fifty young, fit, and dedicated WPF recruits when we have some *six million* people starving, a thousand lorries to man, and many thousands of tons of food to be distributed, was a chance too good to miss. There is another factor: more important than it may appear at first sight. You young people — as a matter of WPF routine — have been immunized against everything possible; you have the right clothing with you; and the best of protection from ultra-violet. Other help is on the way, but you can help to save a lot of lives in the meantime. I am sure you will be glad of the challenge and the opportunity.'

The speaker signalled to two colleagues who darkened the room and activated a projector.

'There is the Horn of Africa.' He indicated in turn the starvation area, Amfile Bay, Lake Asale, and the potential irrigation areas from the vast proposed man-made supply; then, turning to the immediate, Massawa and Port Assab (entry ports for aid shipped in bulk); the roads through Asmara and Dese and the now extended airfields capable of landing large aircraft: a major factor in campaign plans.

Then some horrific shots of the starving, dead children, and scenes such as those which had become familiar on screens all over the world.

Light restored, the speaker continued, changing the subject. 'I take it that the three qualified pilots can handle most small aircraft . . . we can always let them have a few dry runs! . . . and that all the girls can drive trucks. I would like to know how many girls are medically or first aid qualified.

'Finally, will the men organize themselves into three teams: X, Y and Z, to do the humping in rotation. It is tough work at any time . . . particularly in the heat. We are talking about 13° to 15° North.'

He turned to Pippa Brightwell. 'Captain, may I suggest that you take charge of Team X, say, with Mr Barry; Miss Brandt and Mr Brandenberg take charge of Team Y: and Miss Scott and Mr Svensen, Team Z. The remaining girls, truck drivers, to be split between the teams. Thank you. I hand you back to the WPF.'

* * *

WPF Cairo (West) to Asmara is 1,765 kilometres as the crow flies (which it doesn't), which route — since it is well clear to the eastward of the Nile valley — was that followed by relief aircraft flying by way of Egypt. The authorities, accustomed to last-minute changes of plan, makeshift arrangements, and making the best use of every inch, packed the Unit into two big cargo planes scheduled to leave that morning.

Colonel Hassan and the Egyptian Captain saw them off, but not before the latter had impressed them all with last-minute thoughtfulness. 'After the first twelve hundred and fifty or so kilometres, you will cross the Port Sudan — Atbara road, rail, and now potential fresh water pipeline route. Khartoum has of course been deleted from your itinerary,but I have asked the captains of both aircraft to lose height so that you can see the sort of terrain involved in the Red Sea/Nile project. You will arrive Asmara in early afternoon. By this evening you will have been absorbed into the current relief operation. Let us hope that, in its present form, it will be the last. Good luck in Ethiopia .. and in your careers.' She stood waving, shielding Nefertari eyes with her other hand as the big planes taxied away.

They flew well above 'local' traffic, but low enough to catch a farewell glimpse of the pyramids at Giza, boats in the lower Nile, and light aircraft and helicopters already busy with tourists; then swung away towards the Red Sea in the distance, thence south-east to take part in their first assignment.

Members of the Unit settled on the cargo floor, others on sacks of aid stamped with the name of the donor country and the WG logo. The big cargo plane had few windows, and as they steadied on their course to the purposeful noise of its great engines, small groups engaged in conversation while others settled down to sleep off the nightlife of the Egyptian capital.

Danielle's eyes strayed for the umpteenth time to the little silver bars on Jakko's uniform indicating a Junior Lieutenant in the service of mankind, thence again to the wings and insignia of a VTO-cum-helicopter specialist. Instinctively but unostentatiously, she felt for the similar additions to her own uniform to make sure they were in place. 'You notice that the Aid character didn't include us in the humping parties. That means we will be flying.'

'I guess so.'

'He didn't say anything about aircraft types . . . you don't suppose they'll just tell us to fly something we've never seen before.'

'Of course not; that would be crazy.'

'I know, but this is going to be the real world . . . like *six million people* with no food. How, in this day and age (isn't that the English expression), could the world *let* it happen *AGAIN?*'

Jakko was slightly apprehensive. 'Danni, don't get so wound up. It's a miracle . . . what *has* been achieved.

'After millions of years, we now have an elected World Government, a Rule of Law, and a Peace Force to see that international law is adhered to. And look at the unbelievable amounts saved on armaments now used for social services and things. But the WG can't "deliver" everything overnight. Remember Gorbachev. He triggered the biggest revolution ever, and was expected instantly to fill the shops from Leningrad (as the city was then called) to Vladivostok. And — since we'll soon be in Zimbabwe — we have been reminded about *their* problem: a high birthrate and a fantastic educational programme after Independence, and then hundreds of university graduates with no suitable jobs. Danni darling, these things take time to adjust.'

'Maybe, but your trouble, Jakko, is that you always see the good in everybody. You need me to keep you in the real world.'

'I thought I'd *got* you!'

'You *have*, but that doesn't explain why six million people are starving *again*.'

Jakko, perhaps surprisingly insistent, 'Of course there is no end of ammunition for anyone wanting to say what a mess the world is in. Suppose we wrote a book enthusing about how far the human race *has* got by 2084 and someone read it a long time in the future, or if someone was able to read it *before* 2084, it would be easy enough for them to say "Yes, but they were still in an unholy half-baked mess." A gift to the reviewers! OK. I accept that, but I would call ours "The Age of Readjustment". For the first time, Man has made a real effort to deal with *fundamentals*, like *saving the Earth itself; sharing its wealth amongst all its inhabitants*; in recognition of *the rights of all living things* ... a complete revolution after the twentieth century. Anyway, you are not going to get away with that remark about always seeing the good. *You* are the most caring person in the world.'

'Is this a very private discussion, or may I join in?' It was Chantelle Ouchaner, one of the eight Junior Lieutenants (acting) and the third VTO/helicopter specialist.

Danielle, 'Of course.'

Jakko manhandled a large aid bag down for the girl to sit on. Her deep chocolate-coloured skin showed up to particular advantage not only faultless teeth but her commission and her pilot's wings. 'I guess mutual congratulations are in order ... Isn't it exciting? I expect we will be flying by this evening. I hope they will be aircraft that we know.'

Jakko disclosed that Danielle had asked the same question, adding, 'If they are something that we haven't met, I'm sure we will be given proper briefing. I hope the three of us can stay together. I reckon we are the lucky ones. All the others will be loading lorries all day ... apart from the girl drivers.'

Chantelle was warm and friendly. She looked up under long eyelashes as she sat perched on the bag of grain listening to Jakko's reassurance. Inevitably he was reminded for a moment of another Chantelle, half the world away, but it was Danielle who produced the compliments. 'You are a very lovely girl, you know. What is your ancestry?'

'I am afraid that I am a strange mixture ... Zimbabwe and West Indies ... and of course I am *English*!' She indicated the St George's crosses on her uniform.

Danielle, 'Well, it produced a very beautiful result. Did you ever think of modelling?'

'Oh, thank you,' slightly embarrassed. 'No. I felt that I was privileged to be born into a happy family, with a vote in my adopted country and enough to eat. And I love music and was able to learn. I did one overseas tour with the London Schools Symphony Orchestra. It was wonderful. Seventy of us, all under eighteen, and we were received with such *friendship* everywhere ...'

'That was what put internationalism into my mind. One day, much later, I saw a WPF ad in the newspaper ... and, well, here I am in an aeroplane heading for Ethiopia!'

Jakko hadn't missed the reference to Zimbabwe. He asked Chantelle if she knew the country. 'Oh, yes! It is fantastic. I was born in London, but I have been out several times to stay with relatives.' She needed no encouragement. 'Zimbabwe has always been a leader after 1980. Now of course they have a member of the World Executive and the WG moves to Harare next year. But it is the actual country itself that is so marvellous. To begin with, Africa is *vast*, and to me is the beginning of the world . . . eruptions millions of years ago . . . huge rocks hurled enormous distances . . . still lying where they fell . . . the colossal *power* of it all . . . primitive Man . . . wonderful cave paintings four thousand years old, still to be seen, in some cases action studies which surely have never been bettered . . . and five different climates which allow a unique variety of crops. And the sheer beauty of the country and the wildlife! I am so glad that we are spending some time there. It will be like a lovely free holiday for me.'

It was somewhat uncomfortable perched on a sack. She stretched her long legs and continued as the big aeroplane droned on. 'Of course, being in the Southern hemisphere, Zimbabwe's seasons are the opposite of ours. Their spring is September, and their summer is during our European winter; May is roughly their autumn, with winter during our summer. The rainy season starts "officially" in October. I can't make up my mind which is the most beautiful time of the year, any more than I can at home.' By home, she meant England.

'I often wonder whether autumn isn't the most beautiful of English seasons. The fresh greens and blossom give spring its own inspiration, but a beech wood in autumn as the sun filters through the golden leaves after a shower can be *so* beautiful. The squirrels are busy collecting nuts then, and the summer birds are assembling for their flight together to warmer climates for the winter. *And they all know the way.* But now we have messed up the whole world, and they are becoming confused.' There was a suspicion of tears in the dark eyes.

The other two let her continue, aware for the first time in their hectic schedule of the gentle nature of their colleague. 'We should have arrived in Zimbabwe in their autumn, but now I guess it will be winter. During Zimbi's winter, the countryside turns to gold. The long grass and shrubs out in the bush are dry and parched. Animals gather round the waterholes. The maize stands waiting to be harvested. Tobacco, still an important crop, has already been gathered in. The cotton, much of it grown in the Sabi valley, and highly rated in world markets, is ready to be picked. Trees are still in leaf; indeed most of the deciduous species shed their leaves for a short time only before spring. The appearance of the countryside varies with location and rainfall, but in general it is by now tawny and golden. In Zimbabwe it gets dark suddenly, somewhat dramatically; in Autumn and Winter between five thirty and six pm. There is no twilight. It becomes colder, and at night the temperature can still fall even to zero during June and July. But during the day the sun beams down, and there are many who believe their winter to be the most beautiful time of the year. The domestic gardens are also then at their colourful best. To me, the climatic threat to *Zimbabwe* is the most awful thing for which Man has ever been responsible.'

37

The two aircraft touched down in quick succession at Asmara. Working Party X, the pilots, nurses, and food aid were to be retained there. The aircraft, refuelled, would press on with the rest of the Unit to the big base at Massawa to the north.

Even as the party disembarked and hurried down the ramps, brush vehicles were already vacuuming sand and dust from the runway. Fuel was on its way. The young people piled into a waiting bus which set off at high speed to cover the short distance. They were ushered into a holding area. Within a minute, yet another WPF Colonel — a tough-looking character, if ever there was one — hurried to greet them, followed by two junior officers. Captain Brightwell saluted and reported, 'Unit 2001 personnel, Sir.'

'Thank you, Captain. Welcome to Asmara. Please sit down.' He gave them a quick look-over. 'This is my idea. So you know who to thank! I doubt if you will regret it.' He looked along the rows again, clearly not expecting any comment.

'We live in a hopeful age. Man is taking the initiative and doing what needs to be done instead of endlessly finding excuses for inaction and setting up more bloody committees. I dare say some of the World Government's other plans are just as far-sighted: the Zambezi and Nile projects in particular; new reservoirs in North America; river diversions; keeping out the sea; and so on; but our job here is unique. Millions of lives are being saved — hopefully in one of the last ever relief operations of its kind — and the WG is getting stuck into the creative job: preventing these poor buggers and the *women* and *kids* here ever starving again in the first place (sic).

'A little about the geography, the job we are doing, and the team here.' There was a much-fingered map of the Horn of

213

Africa on the wall. 'Here,' pointing, 'are the two points of entry (Massawa and Port Assab) for bulk aid by sea and by big freighter aircraft . . . the Penelopes and so on. Airports at both ports, and here too, have been extended but the idea is, as far as possible, to *retain established distribution routes*, perfected — if that is the word! — during a century or more: roads through Eritrea; southwards from Massawa through Tigray and northern Wello to Dese; and south-westwards from Port Assab. A lot of effort and Aid money have gone into these roads. They are pretty good now. We are talking about often rough, parched, rocky country, and very mixed altitudes. There are recognized points from which food is distributed. Everyone knows how it works. Even during the old civil war, government, ''rebel'', and voluntary personnel all eventually worked together or — more precisely — allowed each other to play their part in the areas under their control. It is a sad distinction, but Ethiopia knows the starvation ''routine'' better than most.

'The terrain is not conducive to the siting of airfields of any size to short-circuit the long, dusty roads, although — in passing — the national airline had long been run effectively and at a profit. Today is an exception. The food that came in with you this afternoon will be distributed from here . . . leaving truck convoys from the north to pass through uninterrupted. We do this each month to save time, sixty-five kilometres, and lorry space.

'A major effort has however gone into creation of small strips and VTO/helicopter pads. These act as distribution points for villages far from main truck roads. Some of them are at high altitudes or sited in valleys with high ground on two or even three sides. This calls for pilot skill. The Dragonfly helicopter is too small. It carries a very limited load. There are a few of them here. The VTO Kingfisher has proved an excellent compromise: not too big, but carrying a significant weight for supplying scattered villages.

'As regards aid itself, the WAO distributes a month's supply at a time: grain (which the people grind themselves), vegetable oil, and a high protein mix. With these, the people make their *injera*, a basic dough. They supplement this with meat and vegetables if available. In the past the grain came from North America, some from Australia, and maize from African countries to the south which had a surplus. Now, with the US

Mid-west mostly barren, Russian Central Asia is the world's biggest producer. Some comes from Canada, the West's new bread-basket. Zimbabwe, exporter of surplus maize for a century now, in spite of its own population growth, continues to help.

'You will expect me to say something about the Amfile Bay/Lake Asale project. The main operational base will be at Massawa. Already the organization is taking shape, surveys are under way, international consortia being formed to handle distilling, pumping, and subsequent irrigation. There will be a bewildering array of planners, scientists, engineers, contractors, and administrative personnel. Helicopters will swarm over the area. Later, the heavy stuff will arrive by sea. Meanwhile the airports will work round the clock. There will be people of every nationality under the sun, and — even in these enlightened times — doubtless a few villains who pilfer or direct money or material to their own use. The WPF will keep order and "police" the project with its usual mixture of firmness, goodwill, and public respect.'

The Colonel spotted a mosquito menacing one of his staff officers. Wham! 'Sorry, Fido!' Then to the Unit, 'I call him Fido because he carries everything around and never forgets anything . . . about the only good thing to come out of this bloody drought is a lack of these pests in the area. But — wait for it! — when we've flooded the place: that'll be *another* problem for the boffins!'

The tone changed, serious again. 'The World Aid Organization, to its credit, has paid increasing attention to getting the population *involved*, not only in humping sacks but in water provision, land reclamation, tree planting, crops, and the whole business of making their own country viable: a very different scenario from one in which people simply watch each other die while waiting for aid to be delivered. The WG has already flooded the country with publicity about Lake Asale and future irrigation. There is enthusiasm here. There will be local employment, with World Government pay and enlightened conditions for the workforce. Above all, a whole generation in yet another country will experience at first hand enthusiastic co-operation in a *creative* undertaking by experts and volunteers from all over the world.

'The WG has organized manpower reinforcements to get the country over what we all hope is the last "hump", but they

215

don't arrive for another three weeks. That is why I requested that your Unit be diverted to help the Aid boys to tide over the gap: to get an extra month's supply into people's hands; particularly in outlying, smaller communities.' He turned to his staff officers and Captain Brightwell. 'Carry on, please.' Everyone stood up smartly. It was that kind of situation.

* * *

Captain 'Fido' took charge. 'I am Salvatore. I come from Napoli ... Naples. Do not pay too much attention to the Colonel's little jokes. He is tough, but a "good fellow". He gets things done, but he looks after everyone. We are all very happy. It is a small world. One hundred and fifty years ago, one of my family sprayed mustard gas on the people here ... he was one of Mussolini's pilots ... so I owe them all that I can do for them.' Then, returning to the job in hand and consulting his notes, 'Party Y and Party Z are to have something to eat now. There is an orderly to show you to the canteen. You take off for Massawa as soon as the aircraft have been cleared and refuelled.' He turned to Pippa Brightwell. 'Captain, will you please take your party ... Party X ... back to the aircraft now, to help our people to unload the cargo. The bus is waiting. The nurses and the three pilots please remain.' The atmosphere was now more relaxed. Monika and Karl, Jamina and Gustav, detached themselves from the rest of their group to bid a temporary goodbye to their fellow acting officers.

Monika: 'Well ... this is it ... for the time being.' She kissed affectionately Danielle and Chantelle, then hesitated before embracing Jakko. 'Take care, Jakko ... till we meet again in Harare.' Karl shook hands with them in turn. Then it was Jamina. She too hesitated after embracing the two girls.

'*Au revoir*, Jakko.' Then, in little more than a whisper, 'I'm sorry we drifted apart, but I am glad at your success. Look after yourself.' She squeezed his hand quietly. Jakko flushed momentarily, stirred anew by the contact and by torrid memories. He managed only 'You, too' as she turned and Gustav led her away.

Danielle had registered the 'moment'. 'Jakko, what was she saying?'

'Just wishing us well; that's all. Please let's leave it like that.'
He was rescued by a call from the second staff officer:

'Now, please may I have the three pilots.'

They gathered round. 'I take it that you have experience of
Kingfisher VTOs.' The two girls looked to Jakko to reply.

'We've had instruction on them of course, and we have all
clocked up respectable hours, but none of us has experience in
the field. If the urgency allows, I think we should have a couple
of days' refresher before going operational.'

The staff officer agreed. 'That is a responsible suggestion.
Please report to the VTO hanger at 0900 tomorrow. I will have
an aircraft set aside for you.' He added, 'Perhaps you will not
be offended if I come with you in the afternoon.'

They spent the next two days together in the Kingfisher,
taking it in turns to circle Asmara airport between other aircraft
movements, and carrying out approaches and landings from
every direction. 'It comes back very quickly,' Jakko commented
as they broke for a quick evening meal before four hours' practice
in the dark. The following morning, a half load was placed in
the VTO, topped up to operational maximum in the afternoon.
Obligingly, a stiff breeze blew up before dark, affording further
experience with the laden craft. They reported at midnight that
they were confident to begin deliveries, to be assured that
experienced locals would crew on every trip to identify landmarks
and liaise with the villagers in their own language while en route
and when they had touched down.

* * *

Pippa Brightwell and Team X had meanwhile entered with
enthusiasm into the spirit of the operation, loading in turn trucks
destined to top up supplies in outlying villages that could be
reached by road, and Asmara's three additional Kingfishers,
so that the aircraft could effect deliveries alternately in pairs.

And so, on the third morning, two laden VTOs took off for
a village in northern Eritrea. They flew south-eastward in
convoy, Danielle piloting the leading plane, accompanied by
Jakko and a local navigator-cum-interpreter, Chantelle following
with native crew. It was a beautiful day for any mission;
particularly for the young people on their first, perhaps life-

217

saving assignment. The overnight wind had dropped. It was very hot, with just a fresh breeze off the sea. Away to the left the sun glinted on the water of the Massawa Channel, while below and to their right the light shone on the scrub-covered east faces of high ground inland and the occasional tree, an acacia or red-leaved fig perhaps, cast a small shadow on the rocks.

Once clear of base, Chantelle pulled ahead, and for a while the two Kingfishers flew side by side so that pilots and crew could wave to each other. Then she dropped back to comply with regulations.

Their destination was a strip sixty-five kilometres from Asmara, nestling in a valley leading eastwards in the direction of the sea, with high ground on each side. There was ample room for two VTO aircraft, although they were called in singly.

Danielle had made a copybook landing, taking care to leave plenty of room for the second plane, when suddenly Chantelle's voice came over the intercom . . . 'This is Chantelle . .. Able Zero Two. I have engine trouble. Over.'

'Danni, *TAKE OFF AGAIN AND GET OUT OF IT . . . QUICKLY . . . steer for the sea . . . '* Jakko's reaction had been instantaneous. Then, 'CHANTELLE . . . ' there was no time for call signs . . . 'we are clearing the strip. It is all yours. *COME IN QUICKLY WHILE YOU STILL HAVE POWER . . .*'

To their Ethiopian colleague, 'Do they have firefighting equipment at these places?' It seemed a vain hope, but he added hurriedly, 'Please warn them on the ground . . . as quickly as you can . . . '

Meanwhile Chantelle Ouchaner and her crew were in real trouble. The restricted space ruled out anything but a near-vertical touchdown for which engine thrust was essential, and their engine had failed. The girl came on the air again even as the ground rose to smash the laden Kingfisher to pieces; cool, collected, almost matter-of-fact. 'My engine has now failed completely. We are falling.' Then finally, '*Please* God . . . ' There was a sickening crunch, a cloud of dust, a sudden burst of flame, then an unnerving scream as the aircraft's auto crash homing signal was activated.

Danielle was already heading back. Jakko: '*Keep to windward. Quickly, we must try to get them out . . . Oh, poor Chantelle . . . It couldn't be her fault. We must find the red box,*' and then, 'Oh, that *bloody* noise. It's marvellous if someone comes down

218

in the wild, but not now ...'

They scrambled out as Danielle cut their engine and made for the burning wreck. The locals had already reached the spot, mostly watching helplessly, but two of their number with foam were winning the battle to subdue the flames. 'Foam *here*! ... fantastic!' It was Danielle. 'Come on!' But Jakko held her back. And then the flames were doused. Jakko called for silence.

'Chantelle, can you hear me? For a brief moment there was no reply, and then there was a cry from one of her crew members. Your scribe has no inkling of the translation, but Allah surely was involved. *There is no God but God.* It was sufficient to electrify the onlookers. Feverishly they smothered the wreckage with pieces of their clothing, blankets, and materials to prevent a further conflagration, and very soon Jakko and two of their number had effected an entry. Then, one by one, the members of the crew and finally their brave pilot were handed down carefully to the waiting crowd.

Their kinsmen laid out the crew. Jakko and Danielle knelt beside Chantelle. She opened her eyes for a few moments: still beautiful, then pleading, then resigned. Then faintly 'We were completely crushed on impact ... I am afraid it is all over.'

Danielle was in tears. To Jakko in a whisper, 'She must have internal injuries.' She was silent as Chantelle once more opened her eyes, but it was obvious that she was failing fast.

'Goodbye, Jakko and Danni ... may I call you Danni ... I have been so happy knowing you.'

Then, faintly, her last hope which was to become a WPF, and later a world, legend: '*I do hope that the grain is OK*', and her brave, gentle spirit fled.

38

'Able Zero One to Asmara.' Acting Lieutenant Jakko Mann took charge. He reported loss of the Kingfisher, Lieutenant Ouchaner and local crew . . . finally, 'Part of aid grain intact. Intend return Asmara forthwith with bodies. Have recovered "Red Box" undamaged. Strip operational for single aircraft. Have placed local guard on crashed VTO. Over . . .'

* * *

The world's media lost no opportunity to boost the image of the WPF. That night tributes were paid in many languages to Chantelle Ouchaner and her local crew. Typically, EURONEWS: 'This evening we report yet again an example of devotion to their fellow human beings by members of the WPF . . . on this occasion, those working with relief teams in Ethiopia. Early today a Kingfisher VTO aircraft piloted by Lieutenant Chantelle Ouchaner, aged twenty, with a local crew, crashed south-east of Asmara while delivering food aid to a village unapproachable by road. The aircraft's "Red Box" confirms engine failure which rendered the pilot helpless in the confined space of the airstrip. Lieutenant Ouchaner, of mixed Caribbean and Zimbabwe parentage, a British member of an all-European Unit, is reported to have been of outstanding ability, recently awarded her commission, and an example of good citizenship which we would all do well to follow. Her last words to a colleague were to express the hope that the grain that she was carrying had survived the crash . . .'

39

Jakko and Danielle saw Chantelle into a northbound freighter aircraft . . . in a plain, makeshift box — labelled. Jakko, as they stood watching and the plane was lost to sight, 'She was very special.' Spontaneous, innocent, the ultimate tribute. Nor would the media better it.

They phoned Crawley for the address. Each wrote to the parents.

Thereafter, with local crews, they flew the remaining Asmara Kingfishers to distribute food to scattered, least accessible, starving communities. The base, smarting from the loss of their aircraft and a pilot diverted from the WPF course, now serviced the sand, dust-covered VTOs in rotation with increased thoroughness. Party X in the heat loaded the aid for both air and road distribution. After two more weeks, all had acquired, before their careers proper had even begun, the WPF's essential blend of toughness and compassion; they were sun-scorched, seasoned and exhausted. The expected additional Aid manpower had arrived at Massawa. Their colleagues rejoined them from that place. It was time to press on to Zimbabwe. When therefore a cargo plane arrived from Harare with maize, the Asmara Colonel expressed no-nonsense appreciation and bundled them aboard for its return to the Zimbabwe capital.

Distances in Africa being always vast, the flight to Harare was some 3,800 kilometres: five hours or so in the heavy cargo airplane. They would cross the Equator about two and a quarter hours out from Asmara. For all their new experience, they were still young. Suitable provision had been made. The small hours saw Captain Brightwell attired as a bearded King Neptune, trident in hand, making a short speech of welcome to the newcomers to his domain, even if arriving by air (traditionally

221

.not always approved). Booze consumed, certificates signed
Neptunus Rex were handed out. It was time for song, small talk,
and sleep, before dawn and first sight of the Zambezi.

* * *

Harare boasted one of the world's finest airports and indeed
two of its longest runways and, while the WPF had its own
extensive airfield (the largest in Africa), big civilian aircraft used
the civil complex. Thus members of Unit 2001, met by WPF
personnel, bussed through the early morning freshness of the
Zimbabwe capital on their way to base.

Like all visitors, they were immediately impressed by the
generous lay-out and wide city streets, even in 2084 seemingly
designed to cope far into the future. The city was immaculately
kept. Disclosure by their guides that the spaciousness derived
as much from one-time need to turn an ox-drawn wagon as from
inspired city planning did nothing to lessen admiration.

Autumn/early winter deprived the party of the sight of
Harare's street trees in flower, as Chantelle had warned: the
jacarandas — imported originally from South America — and
the indigenous flamboyants. Nonetheless, both these and most
deciduous tree species were still in leaf — many shed their leaves
only for a brief period before spring; and the newly-stocked city
flower stalls, varied green and meticulous hedges in the suburbs
added to the atmosphere of an outstandingly beautiful, well-
ordered metropolis. Even the threatening notices about guard
dogs and security patrols had long since vanished from the gates
of private houses in this law-abiding place.

The WPF base out in the country was equally impressive.
The Unit unloaded their belongings, were given a quick meal
and brief stand-easy, then mustered for introduction to
Zimbabwe.

The Duty Officer: 'Welcome to Harare. We have been briefed
about your trip, and how it has been overtaken by events.
Inclusion of Zimbabwe is intended not only to acquaint you with
a capital city in southern Africa, our way of life, progress and
ambitions; and to show you locations involved with the immense
Zambezi project in ACTION BY MAN; but unashamedly to
let you experience the beauty of the natural world and its

222

inhabitants: to see part of what is left of that world that Man is at last committed to preserve. We make no apology for admiring the WPF for this aspect of its training.

'Unfortunately you are behind schedule and we are under pressure to return you to Europe. Your stay is cut to two and a half weeks. There is no time to take you to Botswana and the Okavango Delta; the combined conference between Regional Groups is cancelled; the ARAB MIDDLE EAST unit has already left. But we will use every minute to show you what we can.

'Logically, you should first see Kariba, Victoria Falls, the reduced Zambezi flow; the drying Sabi valley; and then what is to be done: the routes of the fresh water pipelines to feed the Sanyati and Sabi rivers. But that would involve crossing the whole country twice. You will fly *down* the pipeline route to Beira; back to Mutare; thence by road down the Sabi valley to Birchenough Bridge, then Great Zimbabwe, Masvingo, Harare, Kariba, Victoria Falls. The last two days will be spent amongst the wildlife in Hwange National Park. Sounds like a travel ad, but it is a trip that you will not forget.'

The duty officer's mood changed. 'All ranks here parade at 0930 before commencing their day's assignments. The base Commandant expects you to take part. The PAN AFRICA personnel are tough and smart. We expect visiting units to be the same.'

As soon as they were on their own, Captain Brightwell exhorted them to shift into their clean uniform and be ready in good time. 'Same formation as College . . . with the officers in front. Keep those arms up . . . plenty of swank! Remember: about the only thing Britain did to help the ''frontline states'' was to train the troops guarding the Beira Corridor! . . . and, before that, they had fought for and won independence. They have much to be proud of.'

It was a blunt return to service life. The sun was up, pleasantly warm; tough, business-like, mostly Zimbabwe personnel, immaculate with their country's flashes on their shoulders (a few from Zambia, Botswana, and South Africa). A sizeable contingent of Air Arm. The band loud and enthusiastic.

As the Unit later headed for Beira, Jakko well summed up their morning. 'If I was a villain, I wouldn't like to meet those boys on a dark night! It's good to see such excellent fellows on the side of world order and peace.'

* * *

Beira docks; cranes, dredgers at work, black balls and red flags, railways, shunting wagons, aircraft, lorry convoys, dust.

Mountains, hillsides, valleys. The Eastern Highlands covered with timber in every stage of growth up to maturity; much of it cared for, thinned, and brashed in a country that had long been a friend of the environment.

Five climates. Apples, avocados, bananas, custard apples, grapes, strawberries, oranges and lemons, passion fruit. Cotton, tobacco, tea, coffee, sugar cane. Potatoes. Maize. Wheat in the lowveld. Commercial cut flowers: roses, proteas. Freshwater fish. Clean, fresh wines. A wealth of sources of nectar for the bees, smaller, inexplicably, than their European cousins; coming in heavily-laden, to land with an audible 'plop', smothered with pollen. Long-established knowledgeable Botanical and Agricultural Research Establishments. Fifty per cent of the population still on the land. But less water and more anxiety now.

The countryside parched; vast rock formations; great boulders worn smooth over the millennia, balanced like huge figure-of-eight bread rolls, the soil long since washed away. Dried-up water courses; trees and scrub clinging to life, warned surely (how else) to fruit to the last to ensure survival of their species. Animals at the waterholes, taking their turn.

Pylons ... pylons ... overhead cables, telephone wires; more pylons and cables, stretching away into the distant haze; a country of clean air and even cleaner power.

The Odzi and Sabi already crying out for rain. Armed guard still on Birchenough Bridge (to keep off a climatic nightmare?). The river Save running slowly beneath, the mud showing.

Time to pick the cotton, harvest the maize ... maize everywhere, but not so tall now, not so full. Time to take yet another anxious look at the sources of national power ... a country long determined to supply electricity to every industry, enterprise, and home, producing *no* CO_2 in the process.

The unit had now reached Masvingo on their clockwise route, to pass on their way north the spot where a thoughtful Creator

224

had anticipated the surveyors by placing the Sabi and Munyati headwaters in close proximity. Thence Harare and north-westwards to the Zambezi and wildlife finale to their tour.

As they made their way to yet another aircraft, Jakko turned to Danielle. 'I understand now how Nelson Banana II felt when introducing the film series . . . and I can't help thinking of Chantelle and how she loved this country.'

* * *

Once again, they were divided into handy minibus size groups, each with a guide: this time junior female WPF officers, to whom it was a welcome break from base routine and a chance to extol the wonders of their country. They touched down at Kariba and minibussed to Observation Point to view the dam. Their guide was flirting a little with Jakko who was in charge of the first group, Danielle asking questions to divert her attention. 'Yes. It was built by the Italians. The temporary structure shielding the main dam during construction was carried away, and some of their men were lost . . . the church of Santa Barbara up there was built in their memory . . .'

The girl gave them all the statistics: the dam wall, 579 metres long . . . 128 metres high . . . 'The generators supply clean power to Zambia as well as Zimbabwe. We used to export electricity to South Africa . . .' In reply to a question, 'No; not any more.' Their guide, serious now, 'You see why we have to ensure that adequate flow reaches the dam . . . and other hydro-electric sites. After 1980, the country was *built* on education and electricity . . . and of course irrigation.'

They made way for the next party, then viewing the lake, shielding their eyes. 'The water built up behind the dam to make the world's biggest man-made lake: two hundred and fifty miles long and twenty-five miles wide in places. You can see a few trees alive in the shallows. Animals come in increasing numbers now to drink.' She pointed to a single giraffe and a small group of elephants on the far shore . . . and hippos bathing. Then she led them to the Memorial to Operation Noah, in which nearly 5,000 animals were rescued as the water rose.

Danielle, reading aloud: 'Lion 10 . . . elephant 23 . . . rhinoceros 44 . . .'; their guide, 'Not so many now.'

Danielle continuing, 'Zebra 46 . . . wart hog 585 . . . fantastic! . . . baboon 268 . . . and . . . and . . . all these other lovely people.' She was enthralled. 'It is super that they cared so much.' It was about as far as one could get from common currencies or votes cast for the WCA.

On next day to Victoria Falls: awe-inspiring, timeless, romantic even to the young. They viewed the statue of Dr Livingstone on their way. Their guide enthused. 'The Zambezi rises in Zambia. The river is 2,650 kilometres long, discharging into the Indian Ocean. There is evidence that it once flowed southwards to join the Limpopo. Major upheavals divided the river; the Limpopo continued to flow into the Indian Ocean; to the north the water found its way eastwards to form the present Zambezi. At all events, the river's course has changed over the years.' She pointed to the Falls. 'Geologists reckon that the water in the Devil's gorge is gradually taking more of the water.

'A hundred years ago, nearly twelve million cubic feet of water flowed over the falls every minute during months of maximum flow. Now, it is significantly less . . . that's why we are here, of course! My own regret is that the new water is not to be introduced here but at Kariba. That,' smiling at Jakko, 'is of course a ridiculous comment; it would require a further 600 kilometres of piping, more back-up pumps, and more delay, and of course it *is* the electricity that matters. Meanwhile,' mixing her units, 'these falls are 150 million years old, more than a mile wide, half as much again as Niagara, with *twice* the drop! Rain forest conditions here in the warm spray encourage unusual plants, as you will see.' She remained silent for several minutes to allow her listeners to take in the vastness of the spectacle.

That evening as the light began to fade, the Unit found themselves afloat above the falls in the direction of Kalunda island. Here, even a century before, the Zimbabwe bank of the Zambezi had formed part of a reserve and retained its natural vegetation. Now, great palms of varying height stood where, long ago, elephants had deposited the seed as they passed by, their fronded tops scarcely moving in the pastel silence. It was a moment to be equalled only as they entered Hwange National Park the next day.

Having deposited overnight belongings for the last time, at

226

Hwange's small WPF complex, they set off on safari in the Park: 5,637 square miles in extent and one of the largest and best-managed of the world's elephant sanctuaries. More than a hundred animal species and four hundred species of bird had for generations learned to trust Man, and lived a natural life far from so-called civilization, rubbish, and pollution. As the young people passed in the safari vehicles, groups of animals looked up with idle curiosity or continued grazing unafraid: buffalo, wildebeest, water buck, zebra: the young still without their stripes; giraffe; the smaller buck: numerous impala and nervous little duiker; wart hogs, tails enchantingly aloft; guineafowl running across the tracks in front of the vehicles . . . even rhino, numbers increasing, minding their own business.

In late afternoon, sun low, the party arrived at a man-made waterhole, where they climbed in silence to a large viewing platform. Here one of the guides explained their country's policy on ivory and conservation — about the only issue upon which Zimbabwe and South Africa had long been in agreement. If left to their own devices, the elephants would multiply until, leaving devastation in the limited areas of suitable terrain left in a shrinking, drying world, they died from starvation and were lost for ever. Alternatively, these most wise, gentle, and caring of God's creatures would suffer wounding, mutilation, and death at the uncaring hands of poachers until they were extinct. Government policy, it was explained, had for a hundred years avoided the hysteria of supposed good intent, being aimed instead at the safety and well-being of a substantial but sustainable elephant population; careful monitoring of their numbers; maintenance of herds compatible with the resources; limited necessary culling of the old or injured by humane, experienced experts; and rigorous extermination, no less, of the poachers.

It was a sane, practical, and humane policy, of which abundant proof was shortly to be seen.

With silent measured tread, elephants began to appear out of the bush as they made their way towards the water. On the platform no-one spoke as more and more elephants joined the early arrivals refreshing themselves at the end of a long day. Some rolled in the water, others showered themselves or gently nudged their small offspring into the pool; the whole picture one of civilized behaviour, dignity, and caring on the part of some two hundred elephants of all ages in this place alone.

The following day, after a dawn safari in known lion territory, during which a young female of the species, if not her lazy husband, endeared herself to all, the Unit was flown back to Harare, now under College pressure to put them on a night flight to the UK.

All were relaxed as cruising height was reached and the aircraft headed north. Danielle, flicking through a small diary, had just announced, 'I make this our *forty-ninth* flight since we left England!'

Jakko, more serious, meditatively, 'I will never forget the elephants at that water hole. *They can teach us so much*. If only for their sake, the world *has* to be saved.'

40

EURO COLLEGE 11. Dawn. Telescreens: 'Unit 2001, please deposit your baggage, then assemble in Central Hall. Please assemble in Central Hall. Thank you.'

Goodssen addressed them. Formal but friendly.

'Welcome back! Reports from Africa have, without exception, been favourable. This reflects well upon all of you and College.

'It was not intended that you be diverted to assist with famine relief, but you would not have wished it otherwise. You have seen something of the world as it exists. We all profit from experience.

'We were saddened by the loss of Lieutenant Ouchaner. But regret is mitigated by pride in the example that she set. Her last words will be remembered. There will be a short Memorial Service at the weekend. All friends will be welcome.

'Meanwhile, your trip and now remaining training have been shortened so that you may become fully operational as soon as possible. You will resume specialized instruction this afternoon for three weeks only. Your final Saturday Guest Night dinner and concert will be attended by General Commanding WPF Bases, Europe, who will take the salute at your Passing-Out Parade on the Sunday morning. Traditionally the parade is followed by a farewell service and reception, at both of which it is hoped as many as possible of your families and friends will be able to be present.

'A revised action pack is being delivered to your rooms. You are free till noon.

'Thank you for your attendance.'

* * *

The first two weeks — all too short — were devoted to instruction related to each volunteer's chosen career; the third to a final mini staff course for the whole Unit, upon world and regional relationships and attitudes and the making of decisions. Jakko, Danielle and the other Air Arm volunteers were in their element: hurrying to hangar or workshop after morning PT, food, and exhaustive medical examinations, perfecting their skills in the air and related engineering knowledge; putting in maximum overtime allowed. After a compulsory break, they flew again each night.

Meanwhile on the first Sunday, off-duty staff and the whole Unit crowded into the worship room, to support Chantelle's unusual mix of West Indies and Zimbabwe parents and relations as they wept silently beside Goodssen and his wife in the front row. Jakko, once too shy even to accost a stranger at a country market, had asked if he might read the lesson. Goodssen announced that a special posthumous Commendation had been awarded by WPF Europe. Ma Ouchaner, although New Zealand was surely one country not concerned in her own ancestry, had asked if the service might close with the singing of the *Maori Farewell*.

This proved a moving end to the little ceremony amidst West Indies flowers as Chantelle's colleagues, shoulder flashes from all over a continent, said farewell together.

> Now is the hour
> When we must say goodbye;
> Soon you'll be sailing far across the sea.
> While you're away,
> Chantelle, remember me.
> When you return you'll find me waiting
> here.

* * *

A good deal of wine, fine old tawny and liqueurs were consumed on the final Saturday night as the General, on Goodssen's right at the head of the table, surveyed the latest sample of the world's youth about to pass formally into its service. For all the racket, or because of it, he seemed well pleased with the spirit evident. Presently there occurred one of those moments of hush amidst hubbub which sometimes occur on such occasions when by sheer chance, everyone happens to stop talking at the same time and something a bit special is called for to rekindle the bonhomie.

Danielle, sitting next to Jakko, was urging him to say something momentous when, further up the table, Monika Brandt rose amidst applause from Central Europe and, from somewhere, *Underneath the lamplight!*

But Monika was serious. 'Mr President. This may be the last opportunity . . .'

'Shame' . . . laughter, etc . . .

'This may be the last opportunity . . . to say, on behalf of all of us, how much we appreciate the friendship and guidance we have received during our course from you, Mr Goodssen, Sir, and all the staff. Of course Norway took a bit of time before joining the rest of us in a United Europe . . ' At this there was a chorus of 'Ooooh' and 'Careful' lest, unwittingly, she was about to put an undiplomatic foot in it, but she continued ' . . . but it was our gain when the whole of Scandinavia made the big decision . . .' Noisy approval. 'They are lovely people and, anyway, who can blame them for their past traditions of neutrality. In thanking Mr Goodssen and Captain Brightwell . . .', applause for Pippa . . . , 'I know that I express the feelings of all of us. On a further serious note, we Europeans are now heavily outnumbered in the World Assembly, and in other things, but we have our experience, our tolerance, and much else to offer to the world. It is largely due to Mr Goodssen and everyone here in College that we have become one happy family during our training . . . and really now we need to look at each other's shoulder flashes to see who we are! I have not said that very well, but we have a strong European feeling *as well as* love of our own countries. The College, in preparing us to serve the people of the world, has made us proud to do that as European members of the WPF. We will not let you, or Europe, down. How is *that* for my English! I ask my colleagues to be upstanding and to drink the health of Mr Goodssen and all the staff of Euro College 11.'

Neither Hebrew Slaves nor Italians ever sang Verdi's *Chorus* with more feeling than that final Guest Night audience, as — accompanied by the visiting General, Staff, and civilian guests

231

— members of the Unit rose from their concert seats in Central Hall for the last time.

* * *

And so to the next morning, Sunday, which should have seen the routine formal launching of forty-eight young members of the World Peace Force into their happy and purposeful life of service to mankind.

Indeed the sun shone down upon the beflagged parade ground as if to give its blessing. Unit 2001 was drawn up before the saluting base, where stood the General, College Principal, and Duty Officer; beside them Captain Brightwell, who had guided the Unit through their course.

To one side, the College staff were gathered; on the other, civilian relatives and friends from all over Europe. Prominent among the latter, sun glinting on their chains of office, the Mayors of the London Borough of Tower Hamlets and its French twinned municipality were surrounded by a contingent of the good people of the British capital's East End, who had come to support Ma Ouchaner. Inevitably, a number of national groups had formed with much shaking of hands, the Mann and De Croix families soon immersed in their best franglais in the farming problems of Normandy and now treeless Cornwall.

Among the elected representatives in the World Assembly, Senate, Regional Federations, and those working in their many agencies, a spirit of One World had long been the norm. But WPF end-of-course celebrations had acquired a tradition of their own, as relatives and friends from many countries gathered together to witness their own and other young people embark on a career of service to mankind. These were people unaccustomed to such functions, and there was no little emotion.

First, those upon whom acting commissions had been bestowed were called up in turn, amidst applause, to receive permanent insignia at the General's hands; likewise three further members of the Unit who had been promoted since. Qualified pilots received their 'permanent' wings; academic and other prizes were presented. Ma Ouchaner received her daughter's Commendation. In all, no less than twelve European countries shared in these distinctions.

The inspection followed. The General returned to the saluting base, and Monika Brandt moved the Unit to the far side of the parade ground.

'UNIT 2001 WILL MARCH PAST!'

The band, which had played light music during the inspection, now struck up with gusto. The Unit were off, wheeling, then advancing faultlessly in line as they neared the saluting base. Monika: 'Eyes *right*.' The General stood at the salute. His eyes followed the Unit for a few moments, then he turned to Goodssen.

'Up to your usual standard!'

At this point, Captain Brightwell — privy to their plans — stepped forward to inform the Principal that the Unit had rehearsed a surprise finale.

During the preceding afternoon, frenzied activity had engulfed the College back regions, as all available equipment was commandeered for the demonstration. Now, within minutes of the Unit's disappearance, a convoy of open and covered trucks, normally used for training purposes but suitably buffed-up, appeared at the far end of the parade ground, preceded and escorted by scout cars. Banners proclaimed: WG PEACEKEEPING FORCE ... DISASTER AID ... PROJECT SECURITY ... PIPELINE PATROL ... FOOD CONVOY ESCORT ... AIR/SEA RESCUE ... GRAIN FROM SCOTTISH FARMS ... SUPPORT FOR INTERNATIONAL LAW ... WPF; FRIEND OF THE PEOPLES OF THE WORLD ... while, above, Danielle de Croix led a formation of five helicopters sporting: BEIRA PIPELINE PATROL ... ASWAN SECURITY ... HURRICANE RELIEF .. . WG EXPRESS MAIL ... EUROPE COURIERS ...

As this unique assortment of purposeful bonhomie neared the saluting base, two VTOs and a huge Penelope IV cargo aircraft, borrowed secretly with two regular pilots from a WPF base, passed overhead with a masterpiece of timing as members of the Unit sat smartly at attention in their vehicles.

When all had left the arena, Danielle circled the parade ground, hovered briefly before the assembled company, then dipped her helicopter in salute.

The General turned to Pippa Brightwell. 'Well done, Captain! They have developed a fine spirit. That was a splendid mix of meaningful commentary and fun.'

* * *

The girls of Unit 2001 had decorated the College worship room for the goodbye service. It was *very* beautiful, with flowers flown in by quite a few parents and well-wishers on the Continent. This, following hard upon such purposeful ability, struck a more than usually effective note with the visitors, who now crammed into the limited space until the aisles were full.

The service was so contrived that everyone present, regardless of their own precise denomination, might ask for a blessing on Man's good intent; those present were much moved by the simple sincerity of the request. It ended, once more, with the World's anthem.

So, finally, those who had passed out from College and whose day it was, the inspecting General, College staff, friends and proud relatives from all over Europe, gathered in Central Hall for the farewell reception; while outside the sun beamed down on southern England, the Channel and beyond.

It was, with every justification, a happy occasion and one of no little European pride and satisfaction. Moreover, this was one of the rare College functions upon which, in the interests of Regional Federal goodwill, expense was never spared. The tables in the great hall were laden with good things, the chatter soon loud, friendly and good-intentioned, if in mixed languages; the liquid refreshment chosen carefully to reflect every taste.

* * *

The happy party was well under way when the main College telescreen sprang to life, calling urgently for everyone's attention, and there was — suddenly — silence. It was the Duty Officer.

'I have to announce that a very severe volcanic upheaval — I understand by far the most devastating such disaster in recorded history — has, within the last hour, destroyed much of Japan. It is feared that many millions of people have already perished. It will soon be nightfall there, which will make forecasting and reporting difficult. A World Government

234

announcement is to be made in a few minutes. This will be relayed on the College screens. Thank you.'

Of the world's peoples, the Europeans, to their credit, were perhaps the least hysterical, and — apart from a few stifled gasps of incredulity and initial horror — quiet persisted in the College Central Hall. Some of those present put down their glasses in a subconscious gesture; a few helped themselves to a large refill. Many of the guests stopped in the act of putting small eatables into their mouths, reacting instinctively against continuation of a party while millions of fellow human beings would doubtless find themselves alone, bewildered, perhaps trapped, seriously injured, or dying, as night fell.

They were not left long in doubt. The big screen lit up, and there was absolute quiet. 'This is George Washington Grant. It is my sad duty as a member of, and on behalf of, your World Executive Board, to inform you all that at 1123 GMT today there occurred in Japan what is unquestionably the most severe natural disaster since records began, and indeed perhaps in the history of the world. Scientific details, which I am not qualified to give to you, will be reported immediately following this bulletin, but I want to tell you in human terms what has occurred.

'Japan, being nine hours ahead of GMT, will soon be in darkness, but we already know that an immense upheaval — the epicentre was almost exactly midway between Tokyo and Osaka — has left the mainland island of Honshu with, as it were, its back broken. Imagine, if you will, an immense, beautiful vessel seriously holed amidships so that the centre section has subsided deep into the water; the bow and stern raised in grotesque fashion. That, as I understand it, is the state of thriving, beautiful Honshu.

'You do not need me to tell you that, including as it does, Tokyo, Yokohama, Nagoya, Osaka, Kyoto and a host of other heavily-populated areas, this is perhaps the worst possible location in the whole world for a disaster of this magnitude. The population of Tokyo alone is of the order of thirty-five millions, and that city is the site of the world's biggest WISO centre but not, mercifully, at present, of the GFE Regional Government. We do not yet have an idea of the number of casualties, but fifty millions is not an impossible figure, and the disruption is incalculable.'

235

By this time, some of those in Central Hall, in shock, had gathered in little groups for mutual comfort. Some were already in tears of sympathy and horror. Overall, dignified silence greeted the news, which seemed too big for comprehension.

George Washington Grant was continuing, 'You will forgive me if, before I continue with such general information as is available, I repeat various instructions which those not tuned in to their respective channels may have missed.

'Attention, Citizens of the GFE, NORTH AMERICAN, and Russian Federations. *Please immediately tune to your Federal Telescreens for information and instructions.* Immense waves are certain to be created by the upheaval, and these may cause destruction and loss of life equal to or even greater than that caused by the initial shock.

'PEOPLE OF SHANGHAI. Only immense efforts have hitherto kept out the sea as its level has risen in recent years, due to climatic change. Your defences are now certain to be breached. Twenty million people are at risk. *Tune immediately to GFE Federal Telescreens and keep them on. Hurry.* Listen for instructions and keep calm. I say again: *Tune immediately to GFE Telescreens.*

'The same applies to other centres of population bordering the Sea of Japan, from Vladivostock down the Korean coast, the coasts of the Yellow and East China Seas, Taiwan, and Hong Kong, the Mariana and Marshall Islands. *Tune to GFE Federal Telescreens and keep them on.*

'Turning now to the Pacific, the North American Federal Government has already issued warnings to communities on the Pacific coast including Vancouver, San Francisco, and Los Angeles, where it is still night and millions will be sleeping. Wake up your neighbours. I say again, *Wake up your neighbours. Tune to your Federal Telescreens and keep them on.*

'Here is a direct message for SHIPS AT SEA. It is recommended that all ships in the North Pacific and in waters bordering Japan should turn immediately towards position 36°N 138°E, batten down, and steam slowly in the direction of expected waves. Ships in exposed harbours or anchorages should proceed to sea immediately and follow the previous instructions. To remain in harbour is to risk damage or destruction against jetties, or being driven ashore. Ships now approaching exposed anchorages and ports are urged to turn to seaward and follow these instructions. These suggestions are immediate interim measures. Your usual Met Offices and bulletins will advise you of developments, once conditions can be assessed.

'AIRCRAFT. All aircraft in the air with Japanese destinations are being diverted as their fuel permits. Federal aviation authorities are already holding all civilian flights in the area until further notice.

'The WPF . . . ' At this, hush was complete

'1. All operational WPF naval units, worldwide, prepare for sea immediately and await instructions.

'2. Ships at sea or in exposed anchorages in the Pacific and disaster areas, turn towards 36°N 138°E and await instructions.

'3. All leave is cancelled. All personnel report to your units as soon as possible. As soon as the requirements can be assessed, teams will be flown to the disaster area to assist in life-saving, evacuation, provision of temporary accommodation, food, water, medical supplies, and general assistance in restoring order, and in support of the civil power.

'4. All WPF aircraft being serviced should be returned urgently to operational state.

'In my capacity as a Member of the World Executive which is, collectively, C-in-C of the World Peace Force, I have no doubt that this will be your finest hour, which will be ever remembered.

'ACTION BY MAN PROJECTS. The Japanese disaster does not lessen the need to press ahead with projects already scheduled: to save the world as to its climate, fresh water, food, and peoples. Work will continue uninterrupted at every site.

'It may well be that vast quantities of volcanic dust will be spread over the Earth and — perhaps for a year or more — reduce significantly global warming. I cannot bring myself to rejoice at this ''good'' news, even in the climatic context. If we are to be blessed with a short respite, let us make the most of it, as a small tribute to those who have perished in the creation of our opportunity.

'Finally, before I urge you all to tune to your Regional authorities, a brief word on behalf of the World Government and, I am sure, on behalf of all the peoples of the world, to the people of Japan. Nothing I can say now will suffice to express the depth of our sympathy and horror at this uniquely terrible moment in the history of our planet.

'It may well be that communities all over the world will soon

237

be privileged to receive into their midst some of those from a different country who have lost their all.

'Even in this grim hour, let me tell you a short fairy story. There was about a hundred years ago a once-great power with a remaining thriving, bustling democratic colony threatened with absorption by a then dark totalitarian oppressor. Its highly successful, freedom-loving people requested an assurance that, if the worst came to the worst, they had the right to flee to the parent country whose passports they held. The reply: a small number only would be accepted, based upon how much money they possessed. Of course, that *is* only a fairy story.

'We know from past experience of superb Japanese technology, enthusiasm, enlightened work practices, care of and interest in the wellbeing of the individual, love of life, beauty, art, and much besides.

'If the Japanese people are spread over the earth as a result of this disaster, it will be a privilege and our gain to welcome them where ever they decide to settle. If there was to be any priority — which emphatically will not be the case — it would be in favour of those who have lost their all, except the right to live and to make their way anew in a free world. In this moment, let us do our utmost to be worthy of them.

'Now, let us save ourselves. Every man to his task. May Almighty God care for us all.'

POSTSCRIPT

Students of Nineteen Eighty-Four may be interested in a strange coincidence. In 2084, a character called O'Brien gave himself up, admitting to the Crawley bombing. Of diminished responsibility, he was detained — albeit with kindness — at His Majesty's pleasure (for members of Federations retain their Heads of State).

Sylvie Mennin trained as a nurse and later joined the WPF, thus combining two of the world's most noble professions.

Even when subsequently commissioned, she still used a stethoscope labelled simply 'SYLVIE'. Perhaps she had come upon an old copy of this book with the Author's Acknowledgement to MANDY and her colleagues.

Further information on the current debate (1992) regarding Universal Share Ownership may be obtained:

In the UK, from:

WIDER SHARE OWNERSHIP COUNCIL
Juxon House
94 St Paul's Churchyard
London
EC4M 8EH

Telephone: 071 248 9155

In the USA, from:

COUNCIL ON INTERNATIONAL AND PUBLIC AFFAIRS INC
777 United Nations Plaza
New York 10017
USA

Telephone: 212 972 9877

BROOKE HOSPITAL FOR ANIMALS
British Columbia House
1-3 Regent Street
London
SW1Y 4PA

would welcome your support

Telephone: 071 930 0210
Fax: 071 930 2386